OCCUPATIONAL THERAPY

Hillhaven

Hillhaven

Mary Wolfe Thompson

decorations by Allan Thomas

LONGMANS, GREEN and COMPANY
NEW YORK • TORONTO • LONDON • 1949

LONGMANS, GREEN AND CO., INC.
55 FIFTH AVENUE, NEW YORK 3

LONGMANS, GREEN AND CO. LTD.
6 & 7 CLIFFORD STREET, LONDON W1

LONGMANS, GREEN AND CO.
215 VICTORIA STREET, TORONTO 1

HILLHAVEN

PUBLISHED SIMULTANEOUSLY IN THE DOMINION OF CANADA
BY LONGMANS, GREEN AND CO., TORONTO

First Edition March 1949
Reprinted August 1949

To

DENA CORSON

my understanding friend

Printed in the United States of America
Montauk Book Mfg. Co. · N. Y.

FOREWORD

To All Trudys:

It thrills me to the core every time I think of the fine profession, Occupational Therapy, with which this book is concerned, and of the possibility that because I have written the book one of you may choose this splendid career as your own.

O.T., as it is often spoken of, is one of the relatively new professions. It was born of the needs of World War I, and has made tremendous forward strides during and since World War II. The good it does is endless. Not only civilians but numberless disabled veterans are being restored to active lives, or are at least being helped, by O.T. treatments. Because of the great numbers who need O.T., newcomers to its ranks are more than welcome. O.T. covers a vast field, so vast I could not compass it in one book. Of its five main lines of work I chose the orthopedic, which, it seemed to me, lent itself most readily and with most interest to fiction.

It was Charlotte Clark, a Captain's wife, and herself active in volunteer O.T. work, who suggested the subject to me. I shall always be grateful to her, not only because I have *Hillhaven* as a result, but because the research involved in writing it gave me an insight into the profession I admire.

I am indebted to many people for help with *Hillhaven*; to Dr. S. P. Bartley of Brooklyn, N. Y., and to Dr. and Mrs. Wayne W. Hall of Ridgewood, N.J., for information on anatomy and surgery; to Chester F. Bray of Newark, N. J., about accident insurance.

As to the O.T. information, I am grateful to a whole list of therapists for their patience with and understanding of the thousands of questions which I asked; to Miss Viola W. Svensson, Director of O.T. at the New York State Rehabilitation Hospital at Haverstraw, to Miss Edith H. Brokaw, instructor in O.T. at the College of Physicians and Surgeons, Columbia University, to Miss Doris E. Nichols, Director of O.T. at the Hospital for Special Surgery in New York, and to her assistants, Miss Jeanne Lavendar and Miss Virginia Nowicki. At Bellevue Hospital I owe many thanks to Miss Helen C. Mathias, Supervisor of O.T., and to her assistants, Miss Olive A. Woodman and Miss E. Adele Palmer. I am much in debt to Mrs. William R. Brandt, Director of O.T. at the New York Orthopedic Hospital, and to her assistant, Miss Carol F. Smith. I am also indebted to the Hospital for Joint Diseases, New York, for information I received there.

Mrs. Helena L. Ratzka and Miss Frances Sekol of Goodwill Industries, Inc., New York, generously took time to give me an idea of the fine work that organization is doing.

Last, and far from least, I am happy to say that Miss Mary E. Merritt, O.T.R., Director of the Occupational Therapy Division of the City of New York's Department of Hospitals, and Miss Wilma L. West, O.T.R., Executive Secretary of the American Occupational Therapy Association, have given *Hillhaven* their approval. And now, if you Trudys approve it?

MARY WOLFE THOMPSON

Hillhaven

CHAPTER 1

TWENTY minutes to nine. So said the clock in the main corridor of Hillhaven Hospital, and Trudy Wescott quickened her already brisk steps. She wanted to be early, not late, on this her first morning on her first job. Such a grand job, such a grand profession, she thought with a little thrill and envied no one, not the crisply uniformed nurses, not even the doctor or two, who stood in the waiting elevator.

"Occupational Therapy, please," Trudy said in a voice both proud and shy, and the operator nodded.

"Eighth floor."

The elevator took a leisurely course upward, dropping its passengers at stop after stop. When it reached the eighth floor, evidently the top of the building, Trudy was the only one left.

"You the new O.T.?" the operator asked, using the initials as almost everyone did in speaking of the profession. As he turned to clear his indicator of signals, she saw that a stiffened leg made him move clumsily. He was crippled.

Why, of course. Trudy felt no surprise. In fact, it seemed quite in place in an orthopedic hospital, a hospital for the crippled. Perhaps the man had originally been a patient here. He

1

had been operated on or treated, given O.T. to restore strength and motion to his muscles. When he had shown as much improvement as could be expected, the hospital had offered him work which fitted his limited activity.

"Yes, I'm the new O.T." She answered his question.

"Well, the shop's down there." The operator jerked his head toward one end of the glassed-in corridor into which the November sun was pouring almost as brightly as if it were summer. "They've none of 'em come yet, and the door's locked. But they'll be along," he added with a smile as he closed his elevator door and disappeared.

Left alone in this strange place, Trudy was grateful for his friendliness. In spite of herself, her twenty-one years and the confidence which knowing that she was a graduate occupational therapist should have given her, she was tense and unsure. It was her besetting sin, she knew, this lack of self-confidence, but for the moment she could neither reason nor argue herself out of it.

It will be just like your clinical training, she said to herself severely, but another self shouted, It won't! It's much more serious. A student can make a mistake or two, but not an O.T. Never. And you're doing it for money. You must give the hospital its money's worth. Can you?

The word money turned Trudy's thoughts toward home. Money always had to be given careful consideration there. Trudy's father worked in a factory in her home town, Knolton The factory did not give him regular employment, however, and he added to his earnings by farming the small property on which they lived. A very moderate income re-

sulted, and when Trudy first spoke of a degree in Occupational Therapy it had seemed out of the question. Trudy had
had to admit that it was a long course, two years of regular
college; then three years of special training.

Mr. and Mrs. Wescott had sighed. "Well, you can try for
it," they had said, "We'll help you all we can."

Between them they had achieved it. Trudy had worked
summers and taken paying jobs at college. Mrs. Wescott had
made jams and pickles and sold them. Mr. Wescott had risen
with the sun and planted extra crops. Even Trudy's little
sister, Susan, nine years old now, but only four when Trudy
started college, had sold an occasional wilted and extremely
short-stemmed bunch of flowers to a passer-by.

They've all done so much for me, Trudy said to herself. I
must succeed.

And why shouldn't you? said the common sense which in
the end always asserted itself in her.

Very well. Then the first step was to look around and find
where the staff kept its coats so she need not bother anybody.

Quickly, Trudy located a dressing room marked O. T. at
a turn in the corridor. She took off the street clothes which
she had worn to the hospital because it was not professional
etiquette to appear on the street in uniform. Opening her
small overnight case, she lifted out a fresh white one and
slipped it on; then viewed herself in a nearby mirror.

She decided that her appearance was as good as she could
make it. Hair neat, she ran her hand over the warm brownness
which contrasted so nicely with her dark-blue eyes. Face
clean, or was it, in all the city smudges? Yes, it was, and the

uniform was spotless. Insignia in place. Trudy touched the emblems of which she was so proud, the staff and twining serpents of the medical profession, bordered by the words, Occupational Therapy.

She smiled as she thought what Chet Fielding would have said if he had seen that motion.

"At it again!" he would have teased. "Never saw anybody carry the torch so much for her profession!"

You don't say! Trudy was framing an especially apt reply when a cordial voice broke in on her thoughts and she turned to face a girl of about her own age.

"Hello. You're our Trudy Westcott, I believe. We were told to expect a new O.T. this morning, and your insignia say you're it. Aren't you smart to find your way in here and be all ready. You're the early bird. But never mind," the girl rattled on, laughingly, "I did the same thing when I came here three months ago. Let me put your things in my locker for the time being and, by the way, I'm Meta Tripp. Remember the Meta even though the minute we poke our noses out into the professional air of this hospital we'll both have to be 'Miss.'

"I hate formality, but I suppose it has to be that way," Meta added.

"I'm glad to know you." Trudy realized that her own words were formal, but she couldn't help it. She liked this direct and unaffected girl, but the tension of beginning the new job kept her from speaking naturally. "I'll be glad when this first plunge is over," she confessed.

"Everyone is. He or she—it's mostly she in this profession

—may not admit it, but it's so." Meta turned to powder her nose, and Trudy thought suddenly that she was so homely she was distinguished looking. She had deep-set twinkling eyes, a long droll upper lip and a wide mouth which curved continually in a smile. "Well, come along." Meta clicked her locker closed. "Somebody ought to have opened the workshop by now. You never can tell who'll be first—Miss Swift or Miss Compton."

Meta led the way along the corridor. The workshop door was open and they stepped inside, but no one seemed to be about.

"There are Miss Swift's things." Meta motioned to where a coat and scarf lay over a chair. "She must have gone back for something."

Trudy looked eagerly about the room. It was large and long, and had three outside walls banked with tall windows which gave excellent light. The windows on the right side faced a court. However, since Hillhaven, as its name indicated, was built on a considerable rise of ground above the river on which Sayre City was located, the windows on the workshop's opposite wall gave a wide view. In the foreground was the blue ribbon of the river itself. Beyond it, the hills of its far shore stretched in November browns and russets to the horizon.

Oh, that'll help, Trudy thought as she caught this glimpse of distance. She was country bred, and always felt a little choked between city walls.

"We have just about everything in the way of equipment." Meta brought Trudy's attention back to the room. She saw that this was so. A row of foot looms ran down the center of the floor. At the far end were tables with hand looms and space for all sorts of work. Near Trudy was a carpenter's bench complete with tools. Beyond it stood a bicycle saw and a sewing machine. The room's one inside wall was lined with cupboards in which, Trudy knew from her clinical training, materials for the various crafts were kept. A sink and a crock of modeling clay stood in one corner. Everything was very neat. In fact, Trudy saw as she looked a second time, the looms and chairs down the center of the room toed a line in the tiled floor.

"That's Miss Compton, our assistant director." Meta noticed her glance and laughed. "Miss Swift, our head, likes things nice, but she doesn't care as much as that."

"No, I wouldn't think she would." Trudy remembered the interview at school at which Miss Swift had engaged her. She had received the impression that Miss Swift was extremely capable, yet kind and not at all the stickler. "You like Miss Swift, don't you?" she asked.

"I adore her." Meta had opened several cupboards and lifted out a big market basket, painted red and lined with gay chintz. Now she was getting out wools and a small circular frame for hand weaving. "I'm on ward work," she explained.

"Oh, yes." Trudy knew that the basket was for carrying materials, and that Meta was preparing work which had been planned with the ward patients on the previous day. "Can't I help you until the others come?" she asked.

"Yes, if you will. It will be a big lift if you'll warp this frame. There's the dearest girl, Louise Bingham, high-school age, down in Three C. She's a scoliosis; you know, spinal curvature, caused by polio in her case. She'll have to be here most of a year. Of course she isn't always cheerful, but she has what it takes. She's responsive and perks up the minute you speak to her. I think if we can get her interested in this weaving, it will help her pass the time. Of course, this won't have any curative effect on her. It's just—"

"A case of diversional therapy," Trudy put in as she took the frame and began to crisscross the warp on it like a spider-web.

"Exactly. Oh, good morning, Miss Swift." Meta turned with genuine pleasure. "Here's our new O. T., right on time and already at work."

Trudy rose to her feet at once as both courtesy and hospital etiquette required. Before her stood the tall slender woman whose pleasant face she remembered from the interview at which she had been engaged.

"Good for our new O.T." Trudy heard again her clear yet low voice. "Glad to have you here, Miss Wescott. We need you badly. What with the flood of polios from the epidemic last summer we're short handed. Come into my office." Miss Swift motioned toward a door at the right of the entrance to the shop. "I'll orient you a little."

Again, as was hospital etiquette, Trudy was careful that Miss Swift should precede her into the small square room. One side of it was taken up by a huge desk piled with case cards, samples of craft materials and folios of photographs which Trudy knew were visual records of cases. There was a swivel chair, a chair for guests and, against the opposite wall, a cabinet with books and samples of patients' work.

"Sit down, Miss Wescott." Miss Swift seated herself first.

As Trudy took the guest chair, she was conscious that her director was studying her much as she had at their initial interview. The scrutiny was so kind, however, that it did not trouble her.

"You're from the country, I remember," Miss Swift said after a moment. "Have you a comfortable living place in town?"

"I think so. I have a room at an address the Y gave me."

Miss Swift nodded. "Good. And now as to your work here. Part of your clinical training was in an orthopedic hospital so you understand the routine. Every hospital has a few quirks of its own, and I have a few of my own." Miss Swift laughed. "But you'll soon get onto them. I find it works best for a new therapist to be in the shop at first, so you'll be here two weeks. After that you'll accompany Miss Tripp for two weeks on the wards. Then you'll alternate three months' shop work with three months' ward as everybody does except Miss Compton and me.

"Now"—Miss Swift fingered a papier maché pear, very evidently the handiwork of a child, which lay on her desk— "there are two general points I'd like to emphasize. The first is my pet idea, my fundamental principle. It can't be carried out in every case, but I always want to try it. It's this. In all the work you plan for a patient keep in mind your ultimate end, his return to the active world. If his handicap is not too severe to prevent his taking a job when he's discharged from the hospital, shape his interests toward some definite vocation, something in which skill will count more than physical strength, for he may never have that again. If he cannot hope to take a job, at least train him in some skill that he can carry on at home. For instance, a man can do leather work, a woman or girl can do finger weaving right in his or her own, so to speak, back yard."

"Yes, Miss Swift."

"The second point is that we O.T.'s wish everyone in this hospital, staff and patients, to feel that we are friendly. Make your patients feel you want to help them, that no trouble is too great to take for them. Make the staff feel you are cooperative. Nursing care comes first, of course, but make the nurses feel you are glad to make way for them. Even a scrub woman will be grateful if you step aside until her newly mopped floor is dry. It's this sort of thing that makes a department successful, and it's especially important to us because, as you know, in some quarters we O.T.'s have not been taken too seriously and our work has been looked on as play.

"And now I'll take you around the building." Miss Swift had half risen when her telephone rang. "Yes," she said into the receiver, "oh, yes, I'll see him right away." She turned to Trudy. "Seems to me I spend my life changing my plans. One of the doctors is coming up, so I can't take you now. Suppose you go out into the shop, introduce yourself to Miss Compton and see what she has for you to do. Either she or I will take you 'round later in the day."

Miss Swift's friendly nod was a dismissal and Trudy turned through the door into the workshop. While she and the director had talked, it had filled with patients. A young man in pyjamas and bathrobe, which meant that he was an in-patient, a present inmate of the hospital, stood at the work-bench sandpapering a toy giraffe. A woman in street clothes, which proclaimed her an out-patient, a patient who had been discharged and now returned only for treatments, was strapped into place at the bicycle saw, turning its foot pedals so slowly that Trudy's trained eye told her she had a considerable disability. A young girl with a stiffened arm was working at a loom, while a little boy with crooked fingers, eyes bulging with intentness, plaited a Boy Scout whistle cord from red and blue plastic strips. At the work tables two men in wheel chairs were engrossed in wood carving and leather tooling.

There was no sign of Meta. She must have taken her basket and gone on her tour of the wards; but a red-haired girl in uniform and insignia was lifting a chair frame from the top of a cupboard. She was undoubtedly Trudy's fellow therapist. Two slightly younger girls in the colored uniforms of students were gluing a box together, and they with Miss Compton, Trudy knew, completed the staff.

Now, where was Miss Compton?

At the far end of the room a woman with an authoritative air knelt beside a little girl who rode a rocking horse. She must be Miss Compton and Trudy watched a moment before approaching her. In front of the horse stood an inclined board, built especially for the purpose. Every time the rockers tipped forward Miss Compton pressed the outer edge of the child's bare left foot firmly against it.

Oh, yes. Trudy understood the exercise at once. The child was undoubtedly a polio case. She was walking on the inner edge of her foot because the disease had destroyed its balance by weakening the muscles on that side. This exercise would, as all O.T. exercises did by one method or another, stretch the muscles, strengthen them and increase their endurance. By her repetition of the exercise, too, Miss Compton was accomplishing something else fully as important. She was re-creating a pathway in the little girl's mind, an image of the correct pattern for walking.

"Away we go! Away we go!" Miss Compton chanted with each swing of the rocking horse, and at the sight of the little girl's happy face Trudy thrilled as she had in the elevator. Miss Compton would repeat this motion of the rocking horse a hundred times, five hundred times, a thousand times; and one day this little girl would walk like other little girls again, no limp, no hitch, free as a bird, to run, to dance. Occupational Therapy would have played its part in making her normal once more.

And I'll have had a share in it. Trudy was so absorbed in watching Miss Compton's skill, a skill she herself hoped to attain as she advanced in experience, that she jumped when Miss Compton's voice reached her.

"Miss Wescott? You're Miss Wescott, I believe. I'm glad to meet you."

When Miss Compton looked up, Trudy saw that she was far younger than she had thought at first glance. Possibly she was only two or three years older than Trudy herself. Although her manner with the child had been charming, she seemed a little severe when, after introducing the little patient, she spoke directly to Trudy.

"You may continue this exercise if you will. Vary it by having Janice step sideways up the incline, pressing the foot squarely at each step. She should go on for about ten minutes longer."

"Very well." Trudy put her arm about Janice's soft body. To keep the child from feeling shy she started a conversation at once. "I have a little sister at home. Her name is Susan, but I think she is a bit older than you. She's nine."

"I'm six and a quarter," Janice said proudly, and Trudy saw that she need not have worried about shyness.

"Would you like to change and make believe you're climbing a hill?" she asked after a few swings. "Maybe your horse is tired and that would give him a rest."

"Yes, I'd like that." Janice climbed the inclined board with enthusiasm, and Trudy, her hand maintaining the balance of the foot, thought that she felt the faintest of movements in the affected muscles.

She had made a note of the time on the big clock over the office door when Miss Compton asked her to work with Janice. At the end of the specified ten minutes she stopped, and even as she did so found Miss Compton at her shoulder.

"That completes Janice's work for today," Miss Compton said. "Will you call her mother? She's the woman you see waiting in the corridor." Miss Compton nodded toward the open door. "When you come back I'll have other work for you."

Trudy was gone only a moment and on her return found Miss Compton at the carpenter bench with a sheet of plywood stretched before her. "There's a little boy coming in after school—children like Janice and out-patients do not usually come in the mornings, but Miss Swift is very lenient and allows them to under special circumstances. This boy has had a fractured elbow and cannot extend it fully. We are trying to restore complete motion and, as you know, sawing is one of the best exercises for that. He selected this pattern for a birdhouse when he was here last Tuesday. Please map out the sections on the plywood, being as economical of the wood as you can."

"Yes, Miss Compton." Trudy took a ruler and pencil from the bench drawer and went to work. The sections were not complicated, in fact they were well gauged to the sawing ability of a small boy, but placing them economically on the wood presented a nice problem. She was interrupted several times, to adjust the warp of a loom, to prepare some paint for a woman who was finishing a plastic-covered box, to accompany a patient to the elevator, and once by Miss Swift who asked in her kindly way how she was getting along. The work on the plywood progressed slowly and Trudy was surprised to find as she finished that the hands of the clock stood at noon. Meta came to her at once.

"Lunch time. Come along. We all go together and close the shop while we're gone."

Miss Swift and Miss Compton did not join the staff after all. "Entertaining somebody," Meta explained. As they waited for the elevator she introduced the third therapist and the two students.

"Miss Blaine," she said, and the red-haired girl smiled sweetly.

Oh, Trudy thought, she's going to be nice.

One of the students impressed her favorably, too, but it seemed to her that the other student's personality was not suited to the profession. Her voice was high and she showed an assurance that was faintly annoying. "I told that patient a dozen times she wasn't making the movement right." The student referred to someone she had been working with that morning. "And finally I got the idea through her head."

The therapists ate in the hospital's large dining room, but had a table to themselves. All about them at the other tables were the white uniforms and caps of nurses. At the far end of the room sat a group of resident doctors, also in white.

"They're here training to be orthopedic surgeons," Meta explained. "They have to have two years of general practice before they come, so they're a little older than we are and most of them are married."

"*One* isn't," Miss Blaine put in with a significant glance at Meta. "Ask Miss Tripp about Dr. Bradford."

"Dr. Bradford?" Meta laughed and turned to Trudy. "Coincidence. You wouldn't believe it if it was in a book, but Samuel G. Bradford, M.D., is from my own home town. I've known him since we both hung over the back fences. If you see him speak to me you'll know it's for the sake of auld lang syne."

"I was glad to have a chance to make that little speech," Meta said to Trudy as the two girls, finding themselves early and the shop still locked, paused to enjoy the sun in the corridor.

Trudy was conscious that Meta studied her for a moment. Apparently she came to a favorable conclusion, for she said, "You're my sort, so I'll tell you. I do have a date with Sam Bradford now and then. That's permissible, my people know and everything, but it's not etiquette to have it known about the hospital. I suppose Miss Blaine must have seen us somewhere. If she'd been really nice she'd have kept it under her hat, except to kid me a little on the side if she wanted to. However, she didn't, so I hope what I said will scotch any gossip that might start.

"Sam and I have a hard time around the hospital, observ ing the correct procedure," Meta added. "We're supposed to meet like two wooden Indians. 'Good afternoon, Miss Tripp.' 'Good afternoon, Doctor.' " Meta gave such a perfect imita- tion of hospital decorum that Trudy laughed. "Instead we feel like saying, "Hello, Sam!' 'Hello—' " Meta cut herself short, for Miss Compton was unlocking the workshop door. "Come along. School begins promptly at one."

Trudy followed Meta through the door, much amused at her new friend's candor. And how glad she was to make this friend. She had hoped there would be someone of her own age on the staff who would prove to be companionable, and here, on her very first day, was Meta. Perhaps later on when they were really well acquainted, and Chet Fielding came to town, they could arrange a foursome, she and Chet, Meta and Dr. Bradford.

That would be fun, Trudy thought as Meta disappeared with her basket to the wards, and she herself settled down to what seemed a long hard afternoon. The shop was busier than in the morning, and the work, familiar, yet unfamiliar because the place, the staff and the patients were all new to her, tired her more than she would have believed possible. The little boy came and sawed with zest at his birdhouse — "Elbow movement, not shoulder movement, Miss Wescott." Miss Compton's glasses gleamed rather sharply — and after him a succession of patients came under Trudy's hands. Always Miss Compton's eye was on her.

Well, that was natural and right, Trudy thought. She was new, and Miss Compton had to be sure she understood her work and was doing it properly.

On the other hand, Miss Swift did not seem to watch her at all. Late in the afternoon, as Trudy was replacing the brace on a girl's weakened arm, she paused beside her.

"I'm sorry," she apologized, "that neither Miss Compton nor I could take you around the hospital today. But we'll manage it tomorrow. All right?" she questioned with her friendly smile.

"Oh, yes." Eager as she had been about everything pertaining to her job that morning, Trudy wouldn't have given a nickel to see the hospital now. To see it would have meant effort, effort to register departments and personnel in her mind, effort to walk the long corridors.

It wasn't that she loved her profession less, Trudy thought as she plodded toward the dressing room at five. It was that at the moment she was compelled to love her aching feet more.

CHAPTER II

"AND NOW, Miss Westcott, quick, before anything comes up to stop us, let's get this tour of the hospital off our minds."

"Yes, Miss Swift." Trudy, already a little more at home on this, her second morning at Hillhaven, stood aside so that her director might precede her through the workshop door.

"Lovely day, isn't it?" As they walked along the corridor Miss Swift waved her hand toward its windows. Trudy glimpsed the view which she liked so well, the river, deep blue this morning under the touch of a boisterous autumn wind, and the open country beyond it.

"Is your home over there?" Miss Swift followed the direction of Trudy's eyes.

"No, it's just the other way." In her mind Trudy saw it for a moment, the little old farmhouse two miles outside busy manufacturing Knolton. Her father drove back and forth to work in a light truck which he also used on the farm. Sometimes when the weather was bad he complained about the trip; sometimes Trudy's mother complained that the house had no central heating or full modern conveniences; sometimes Susan wailed that she had no nearby playmates; but just the same the whole family stuck to the little place like leeches. They loved it dearly and, for her part, Trudy hoped they would never live anywhere else.

"Here's the elevator." Miss Swift interrupted her thoughts. "I think we'll start with the first floor. That seems logical and I believe you'll remember it best that way."

Trudy was already familiar with the main entrance, its benches for clinical patients, its row of desks and the little shop where you could buy anything from a tooth brush to ice cream. Miss Swift led her directly to an office marked SUPERINTENDENT and tapped softly at the open door.

"Good morning, Mr. Markham."

Trudy saw the man's grave responsible face lighten as he comprehended who knocked. Oh, to have a personality like Miss Swift's, she thought, even as Miss Swift introduced her.

"I'd like you to meet Miss Wescott. She's joining our staff and going to be one of your big family."

"I'm glad to meet you, Miss Wescott." Trudy realized that Mr. Markham's rapid scrutiny fixed her indelibly on his mind.

No one knew better than Miss Swift how busy the superintendent was. "We'll see that Miss Wescott fills out the usual papers with your secretary," she said and turned with a nod. "Now the superintendent of nurses." She tapped at an adjoining office.

Here, Trudy faced an older woman, starched and stiff. Miss Swift introduced her as Miss Primrose, and as they turned away, Trudy could not help smiling at the incongruity of the name.

"Yes, I know." Miss Swift caught the smile. "But if anyone in this world was ever fair and square, it's she. It's a grand feeling to know that if and when you have to go to her she'll help you out of your difficulty. There's a person I admire," Miss Swift said as they passed the cashier's department. Through the grill Trudy glimpsed a sturdy-armed young man.

"Walking on crutches has done that—developed the upper arms. He's been on crutches for years. Always will be. An accident when he was quite young, I understand," Miss Swift said in a low voice. "He never misses a day's work. When some of our patients, not half as handicapped, start whimpering, I always feel like saying, 'Go down and take a look at Mr. Bell; then see if you have anything to cry about.' Good morning, Mr. Bell."

The man looked up, nodded and smiled, and again Trudy felt about her that warm aura of friendliness.

"I suppose Mr. Bell's another patient the hospital has given a job," Trudy commented as, after a pause to meet the director of Social Service, they returned to the elevator.

"Yes, he was a patient. Second floor, please." Miss Swift directed.

Trudy followed Miss Swift into another of the hospital's gray-green corridors. At one end was a door marked PHYSICAL THERAPY. Trudy knew well what its work comprised, for a survey of P.T. had been part of her professional training.

"Oh, here's our sister therapy," she said.

"Yes," Miss Swift nodded. "Sometimes I think we're more than sisters. It's often hard to say where P.T. ends and O.T. begins. Isn't that true, Miss Jenkins?" she said to a therapist who was guiding a small boy through an exercise in muscle re-education.

"Nothing truer," Miss Jenkins asserted, slipping the boy skillfully into his wheel chair. "I think it's an excellent thing, the two therapies being spoken of under one heading, physical medicine, these days."

While Miss Jenkins and Miss Swift talked for a moment, Trudy looked about the room, at the machines for electrotherapy, for sun and lamp treatments; the tables for massage, and the hot-pack machine which for all the world resembled a modern electric washer.

"Well, good-bye for this time." Miss Swift closed the conversation. She led the way to an adjoining room whose door was marked REHABILITATION. "Hello, Miss Devon."

"Hello." Miss Devon barely turned her head, for the room hummed with activity. It was equipped somewhat like a gymnasium. Heavy padded mats covered areas of the floor, and parallel bars stood near the entrance. At the opposite end of the room was a facsimile of a flight of stairs, of a bus step, of a street curb. There was a walkway the exact length of a street crossing. It was equipped with red and green traffic light, and on it, as on the other apparatus, a patient was practicing.

"Good for you!" Miss Swift called as the patient managed to negotiate the walkway before the lights changed. "Now you can get around the city by yourself."

The patient nodded, his face alight.

"Oh, oh!" Trudy exclaimed as a patient nearer by collapsed on one of the mats.

"He was supposed to do that." Miss Devon laughed. "We're teaching him to fall without hurting himself. Here's a difficult case," she added, nodding toward a patient on crutches. "What's the best crutch gait for this man? Crutches alternating, or both swung together? We'll work it out, never fear," she said without waiting for an answer.

In one corner of the room a woman, fully clothed, was practicing sliding from a wheel chair into an empty bathtub. Trudy's eyes turned from her to a table at which patients with disabled hands were practicing on squares of cloth fitted with buttons and buttonholes, on a great wooden shoe with holes for laces, and on a dummy which had a necktie dangling about it.

At another table a woman, under a therapist's supervision, learned to lift a stiff arm and comb her hair, while next to her another patient practiced lifting a telephone receiver.

" 'Physical demands of daily routine,' " Miss Swift quoted the name that had been given these exercises. Her lovely smile came to her face. "I am always moved by this work, as much as by our own. In fact in some institutions we do Rehabilitation ourselves." She looked at her watch and gave an exclamation. "We must keep moving. Good-bye, Miss Devon." She buzzed Trudy around a corner. "We'll just give a glance at the school and the library; then I think that's all that's important today except the wards."

Trudy was beginning to feel a little confused from seeing so many departments and people. She managed to grasp the fact that the library, like all libraries, was a pleasant place; that the schoolroom had adjustable seats for the crippled children and the teachers were specially trained. The long sun-filled wards with their rows of beds rather blurred together. Afterward she remembered faces that smiled at Miss Swift, faces that showed apathy and indifference, faces that were turned away. In one of the wards Meta Tripp was stooped over a young girl in a great cast which enveloped even her head. This was undoubtedly Louise Bingham, of whom she had spoken.

"Hello, Miss Tripp, and hello, Louise. How are you?" Miss Swift paused for a pleasant word; then took Trudy to meet the head nurse in charge of the ward.

"Miss Connor, I'd like you to meet Miss Wescott, who is joining our staff. You are so nice to us all"—Miss Swift's smile won an answering smile from the somewhat stern face before them—"I know that if she needs help she can come to you."

"Surely, Miss Swift." Miss Connor gave a glance through the plate-glass window in front of her desk to be sure that her ward was running properly; then added, "I'll be glad to do anything I can for Miss Wescott." She, too, scrutinized Trudy for a moment, and Trudy knew that, as with the superintendent, she was fixed in Miss Connor's mind.

When the tour was ended, and they had visited the eight wards, Trudy was not so sure, however, that all the heads were entities to her. They seemed to have telescoped into one highly efficient, white-uniformed figure. She only hoped she could straighten them out, identify them later when she had to.

"We didn't go into the X-ray department or the record room, but I'm sure you can find them when you need to. And I haven't shown you any private rooms. We don't go to them except on request. There are two operating rooms on the fifth and seventh floors, but they are entirely outside our province. You didn't see the hot and cold pools"—Miss Swift glanced at her watch—"but we simply can't do it now. A lot of our patients receive treatment in them, and it's wonderful how some of them improve. Some patients can walk in water who can't take a step on the ground. Well, here we are." The elevator left them at the eighth floor. "Tired?" she asked as they walked along the corridor to the shop.

"Not really. Just sort of buzzy," Trudy confessed.

"And fuzzy as to the layout of everything I've shown you." Miss Swift laughed. "I was, too, when I first came here. And it was so terribly important to me, since I was to be the director. I didn't dare get lost."

Miss Swift hurried into the workshop and was immediately engulfed in a wave of administrative matters which had arisen while she was gone. Two parents waited to see her, and Miss Compton said that Miss Temple of Social Service would like her to phone. Also, should Mrs. Polk work on the foot loom with or without her brace?

Trudy was grateful for a moment's rest before Miss Compton outlined her next work for her. She got a drink of water, smoothed her hair; then found Miss Compton at her elbow. She set Trudy to work on a series of tasks similar to those of the previous day, attaching light springs to the beater of a loom—adding resistance, the O.T.'s called it—so that a girl with weak shoulders would have to make a greater exertion to operate the beater and thus strengthen her muscles more; punching the holes for the lacing in a leather cigarette case which one of the men was making. Wherever there was a bottleneck Miss Compton placed Trudy to ease it.

At two o'clock there was a change, however. Miss Swift came from her office with a patient's blue prescription card in her hand.

"Miss Wescott, here's the card of a polio case that is coming up to the shop for the first time tomorrow. It's a very heavy day for us all. We're booked up with our regular patients, so I'm going to ask you to make a preliminary survey of what this patient can do, and what she'd like to do. It's a Mrs. Lansing. She probably won't stay more than half an hour, for she'll tire quickly with the unaccustomed exertion."

"Yes, Miss Swift." Trudy nodded and felt a rush of pleasant anticipation. It would be nice to be doing something so entirely different, and with a patient new to the workshop. Perhaps if she did very well with her, the new patient might become her special charge. She knew, however, that a patient was never trusted without supervision to a beginner like herself.

"Now, the first thing to do"—perhaps Miss Swift sensed her enthusiasm, for she smiled—"is to read this card; then go down to the record room, get the case history and the muscle chart and make a careful study of them. Take notes to keep everything straight; then decide what work you think the patient might take up. Tomorrow morning you'll suggest these projects to her, and unless we see a very definite need of some certain one because it affords the exercise she should have, she will decide which of them she will do. Keep in mind your ultimate end"—Miss Swift smiled again—"strength for the weakened muscles and, if possible, some new skill your patient may take home."

Trudy took the card to one of the work tables and sat down. She had purchased a notebook for just such purposes. Now she flipped it open even as she began to read the card.

HILLHAVEN HOSPITAL was printed at the top, and under it, OCCUPATIONAL THERAPY. In-patient. History Number C28-246. Mrs. Robert Lansing, housewife, 22 years old. Referred from Ward 4A. Purpose of O.T.: functional. Directions or Precautions, Promote flexion and extension of shoulder and elbow, strengthen finger flexion and opposition—oh, yes, that meant the ability of the thumb to meet and exert pressure against the fingers. At the bottom of the sheet was a signature, *Donald Kerr, M.D.*

Twenty-two. Only one year older than I am, Trudy thought as she took the elevator to the record room. I wonder what she's like.

She drew several Mrs. Lansings in her mind, a pleasant responsive one, a peppery one, a withdrawn and indifferent one. On Mrs. Lansing's personality depended her approach to her, and here Trudy faced one of the most difficult points in Occupational Therapy, the first contact with a patient. On it might depend ultimate success or failure with the case.

You must be tactful. You must be friendly. Trudy reviewed her student training. You must make your patient like you and want to work with you. Trudy remembered how carefully she and her classmates had been supervised in their student days, also how they had vied with each other to make successful contacts with patients.

Somehow, perhaps because so far everything had seemed to go very well at Hillhaven, the pleasant image of Mrs. Lansing won over the others. Trudy pictured her as tall, possibly not very good looking, but charming, which was better. Judging by her card she was not much handicapped unless there were other disabilities—and of course there might be— so serious that there was nothing to be done for them and consequently they were not mentioned on the prescription card.

Trudy brushed this possibility aside and visualized Mrs. Lansing as stepping gracefully into the shop. "Here I am. Now, what can you do for my arm and hand?"

Trudy located the record room, secured the case history and muscle chart from the filing clerk and sat down at a table with them. She turned first to the history. "Emily Lansing, husband civil engineer, children none." The polio had struck six months before. Severe. In iron lung for three weeks. Resulting disabilities—Trudy turned to the muscle chart for these, and when she grasped their extent, caught her breath in pity. Emily Lansing, twenty-two, would perhaps never walk again. The muscles of her legs and feet were rated as zero, which meant they were practically destroyed.

How would I feel if I knew I might never walk again? For an instant Trudy visioned how, in such a situation, the wings of the spirit might beat against the walls of the flesh. Perhaps Mrs. Lansing doesn't know, she said to herself. Still, even if she did not know now, she would have to know sometime. Trudy shuddered to think of the agony of that realization.

But Mrs. Lansing may be able to walk, after a while, and after a fashion, with crutches and braces, Trudy tried to console herself. What dreadful walking it would be, creeping along, balancing, taking step after careful step. Cold comfort to a young woman who had moved freely.

And how did her husband feel? His heart must be wrung every time he saw his helpless young wife. Or had her invalidism opened an abyss between them? This was worst of all to contemplate.

Oh, dear, I'm going to cry on these papers. I'm a fool to let my imagination run ahead so. I must get myself in hand. Trudy bit her lip and hoped that the filing clerk did not notice her emotion. Get down to business, she told herself savagely, and dug her pencil into the first sheet of her notebook with so much force that the point broke. She sharpened it again and began her notes. The process calmed her, but when she had completed them and gone back to the workshop just before closing time she still felt shaken. She was glad that as she and Meta walked home together—the two girls had discovered they roomed within two blocks of each other—Meta proposed they stop at the corner drugstore and have a cup of chocolate.

"It'll perk us up," Meta said.

"And I need to be perked," Trudy commented as they found an empty booth and settled down gratefully in its relative seclusion.

"You're tired," Meta observed.

"Yes, and then I let myself agonize over a new patient I'm to see in the morning. I know it doesn't pay to do that."

"No, it doesn't," Meta agreed. "Of course you can't be Hard-hearted Hannah, but neither can you burn yourself up with pity. In our profession, like the nurses, we have to keep our eyes on the bright side of our job, have to remember that we really help. Why, sometimes we help people who thirty years ago would have been left to sit in wheel chairs or lie in beds the rest of their lives!" Meta's expression had grown almost exalted. Suddenly it changed. "Well, well," she said as if surprised at herself, "I've read you quite a lecture, and I'm not given to 'em. Mm, this is good." She sipped the steaming cream-topped drink that the waiter brought just then.

For a few minutes the two girls did nothing but absorb chocolate.

"We're like two kids. Can't even stop to talk," Meta was commenting when a man's figure blocked their view of the store and a low voice said: "At it again, Meat-eater."

"Hello, Sam," Meta said without looking up. "I know who it is," she explained to Trudy with a wink. "Nobody but Dr. Bradford would dare address me in such disrespectful terms. Dr. Bradford"—suddenly she put on the little act of mock decorum which she did so well——"Dr. Bradford, I'd like you to know our new therapist, Miss Wescott."

"Glad to know you." Dr. Bradford held out a surgeon's well-cared-for hand. "Had a tough day?" He gave her an appraising glance which, she knew, took in her fatigue. "Keep up your courage. The first hundred years are the hardest."

The sympathy in his voice, added to the hot chocolate, raised Trudy's spirits considerably. She laughed and Meta joined her.

"Nice little thought to keep in mind sometimes, that hundred-year business," Meta commented; then changed the subject. "By the way, Sam, that patient of yours in Three A, burn case, is showing marked improvement these last few weeks, isn't he? Congrats."

"Thanks." Dr. Bradford turned professional. "I'm going to give Miss Swift an order for functional work for him. We want to develop his upper-arm muscles so he can handle crutches and get to walking."

"Yes, Doctor." Again Meta's decorum was mocking.

"Oh, you!" Dr. Bradford dropped his formality and gave her a twinkling glance.

"And oh, you!" Meta answered. "You'd better run along. Aren't you on duty at six?"

"Yes, I am. I'd have liked to have a coke or a malted with you. Well, so long!" He turned regretfully away.

Meta's eyes followed him as he moved toward the door. "Isn't he nice?"

"Yes, I like him," Trudy said.

"Maybe we can have a date some time." Meta voiced what Trudy had been thinking the day before, only she gave it a different turn. "Sam has a friend who might make it a foursome."

CHAPTER III

TRUDY'S first check was a thing of wonder to her. She received it with such a radiant smile that, she realized afterwards. Mr. Bell who handed it to her must have felt a little uneasy as to whether he personally was involved. The sum of money, which the check stated in cold stiff letters was to be paid to the order of Gertrude Wescott, seemed fabulous, yet when she calculated her expenditures she realized she could send less than a third of it home. Her living expenses were proving to be higher than she had foreseen. Still, she smiled at the thought as she mailed a money order, that third was something. Her mother would deposit it in the bank, and later when enough had accumulated, it would be drawn out for some nice thing, a heating plant for the little farmhouse, a new truck for her father, maybe for Susan's higher education. Who could say?

That night Trudy slept really well for the first time in the little cubicle which she called home. It was a third-floor front-hall bedroom in a typical old city house, and she had taken it because it was cheap, of course. Her bed, a studio couch, was comfortable, but so far she had slept in snatches. The city's heavy air had come sluggishly through the window, the light from the street lamp outside had filled the room with what, to Trudy's country eyes, seemed glare. The distant roar of trains, the whistles from the river, and the rush of automobiles on the avenue had wakened her at short intervals.

On this night, however, with her money order dispatched and the balance of her salary under her pillow, she slept in a fashion which she thought of as fathoms deep. Her first tension about the new job had relaxed, and the sounds, the light, the close air, fell into unobtrusiveness. She woke refreshed, ready for the day, and especially eager to begin it when she remembered that it was to include the patient whom, if she were successful with her, she might be able to call her very own. Mrs. Lansing had had some little setback which had kept her from the shop, but she was coming this morning.

Meta's words and Trudy's own reasoning powers had long since adjusted her to Mrs. Lansing's tragedy. Her profession dealt with those who were ill. She must accept her patients' disabilities. Besides, Mrs. Lansing's situation might have been worse. Much worse. Trudy applied her own philosophy to it. Mrs. Lansing might not only have been unable to walk, but unable to use her hands. Think what that would have meant. In this fashion Trudy talked to herself as she bathed, dressed, snatched a light breakfast at the same corner drugstore where she and Meta had imbibed the hot chocolate, and arrived at the hospital at five minutes to nine as she had decided to make her habit.

Miss Blaine was the only member of the staff ahead of her, and as the two girls put their outdoor wraps in their lockers and slipped on their uniforms Trudy studied her a little curiously. She realized that while the red-haired therapist smiled very sweetly the gaze of her greenish eyes was cool. Trudy was not quite sure that she liked her unreservedly now. Of course her having spoken out of turn about Meta's acquaintance with Dr. Bradford had something to do with her feeling. Perhaps you had to be a little cautious with Miss Blaine. The thought flashed through Trudy's honest head and vanished, for she was not given to undue suspicion of her fellow man.

"How do you like your job, Miss Wescott?" Miss Blaine asked pleasantly now, and Trudy answered without reserve.

"Oh, ever so much. It's a grand department and a grand hospital."

"I think so." Miss Blaine went to the mirror and rearranged an auburn curl. "How do you like Miss Swift and Miss Compton?"

"Oh, they're grand, too."

"Yes," Miss Blaine agreed. "Miss Swift is so friendly and Miss Compton's so capable."

"Oh, Miss Swift's just as capable, I'd say," Trudy said loyally, "but you do think first about how friendly she is."

"You mean you think Miss Compton isn't as friendly as she should be?"

Before Trudy could answer Meta came breezing in. "Greetings, fellow toilers! How's everything this morning? You look rested." She turned to Trudy. "You're not getting as tired as you did.

"Like your job?" she asked when Miss Blaine, who had hesitated as if she would like to hear the rest of the conversation, had left the locker room.

"Like my job? Oh, yes!" Trudy said wholeheartedly.

"Don't regret the greasy grind of all that studying and training?"

"Oh, no!" Again Trudy spoke enthusiastically, while through her mind, like a movie film, ran a series of tiny pictures—college classes; then classes in special subjects, anatomy, pathology, psychology, and the crafts which O.T. used in its work.

After the classes had come her clinical training, served in five different types of hospitals—general, orthopedic, children's, T.B., mental—to familiarize her with all the lines of work.

"Come along!" Meta cut short her recollections. "We minions must hasten to the mill."

Was there ever anyone who was better fun than Meta, Trudy wondered as she sat down for a minute at one of the work tables and reviewed the projects which she considered might be within the limits of Mrs. Lansing's strength. She had given them much thought and had decided on four: knitting, weaving—using a small hand loom—plastic jewelry, or finger painting. Of course it would be either Miss Swift or Miss Compton, leaning as much as they could toward the patient's preference, who made the final decision.

Despite her qualms as to her ability to approach her patient, Trudy waited eagerly for Mrs. Lansing. At ten o'clock as she traced a giant cat head on a bit of plywood for a child who was to come in that afternoon, she found Miss Compton at her shoulder. She was beginning to find the assistant's sudden appearances a little disconcerting, although they were entirely logical. They saved time, and to be as efficient as she was—Miss Blaine had certainly put her finger on Miss Compton's outstanding quality—she had to be everywhere, have everything under her eye. Perhaps it was just that she moved so quietly and quickly that she startled one, Trudy thought. This time, however, she turned with pleasure, for she was certain that Miss Compton's appearance meant that Mrs. Lansing was in the shop.

True enough, with an inclination of her head toward the far end of the room, Miss Compton said, "The patient Miss Swift directed you to handle has come," and Trudy saw that an attendant had just swung a wheel chair into place beside one of the work tables. "Miss Swift will be with you in a moment," Miss Compton added as Trudy put away the plywood.

Trudy's pleasure was almost overbalanced by suspense as she crossed the room. She had quite convinced herself that Mrs. Lansing would be amiable and responsive. But, oh, would she be? Suppose—

"Ah, here you are, Miss Wescott." Miss Swift had been ahead of Trudy in reaching the wheel chair and now she turned with her ready smile. "This is Mrs. Lansing, the patient I spoke of several days ago."

"How do you do, Mrs. Lansing?" All Trudy's doubts vanished like mist before the sun. She thought the face before her one of the loveliest she had ever seen. The skin was as softly colored as a pink-lined seashell, the eyes were sea-blue and wide apart. The lashes which shaded them were dark, yet the soft roll of hair above the face was gold-colored.

Trudy knew that part of the build-up of morale for patients who were long-term inmates of the hospital was to keep them well groomed, to avoid an appearance of invalidism. In line with this, Mrs. Lansing's lips and fingernails were tinted just the right shade to be harmonious with her delicate coloring. To complete the picture, her bed jacket was patterned in the blues and greens of summer water.

As Mrs. Lansing smiled up at her, Trudy realized that it was not only her appearance which was so attractive. The wide forehead and the gentle expression of her eyes told that here was a truly lovable person.

"May I see how much motion and muscle power you have in your hand and arm, Mrs. Lansing?" Miss Swift asked in her friendly way.

"Certainly." With a slowness which seemed like languor, Mrs. Lansing lifted her hand.

Miss Swift took it in hers and made a skillful examination. She motioned to Trudy to examine it also and, when she had finished, asked with a tactful avoidance of discussion of the patient's infirmities, "What do you think Mrs. Lansing might do?"

Trudy knew that Miss Swift's years of experience enabled her to gauge far more accurately than she herself could the disabilities of the arm and hand, also that she knew perfectly well what work Mrs. Lansing might do. Yet here was her tact again. Trudy was to handle the case, so Trudy was to make the suggestions and appear, at least, to be in charge. Trudy's admiration of Miss Swift was almost worship at that moment. A little breathlessly she named the projects which she had listed, leaving out the plastic jewelry which she now knew was beyond her patient's strength.

"Yes." Miss Swift nodded. "Any of those would get the motions we want. Which appeals to you, Mrs. Lansing?"

"Well, I don't think I want to knit," Mrs. Lansing said candidly. "I did so much of it before"—her voice grew low on the last word and Trudy knew that she meant before she was ill—"I'm sort of tired of it."

"We're glad you are." Miss Swift laughed. "We'd infinitely rather teach you something new."

"Well then, the weaving, if it isn't anything too big." Mrs. Lansing's gaze went to the foot looms in their row along the floor. "I don't feel strong enough to handle anything very large now."

"Oh, no. We'll use a small loom that can stand in front of you on the table," Trudy said, and Miss Swift nodded.

"What would you think of weaving a bit of material for a handbag?"

Mrs. Lansing was responsive. "That would be nice. I might give it to my sister for Christmas. She has everything you can think of, but she might like something handmade. She's wearing browns this season. We could make it brown with a bit of the right red or green? But may I choose the colors?"

Mrs. Lansing looked up and smiled again. "Here I run on, and your work may all be standardized."

"Of course you may choose." Trudy saw that Miss Swift was delighted with Mrs. Lansing's attitude. It was so much better than the indifference they sometimes met. "Miss Wescott will show you the wools." Miss Swift turned as the telephone began to ring. "I must go. My master's voice." She waved toward her office. "See you tomorrow, I hope."

Trudy brought the wools and, as she had expected, Mrs. Lansing selected a charming combination of colors. "Not those browns. They go too much toward green. My sister's suit has a reddish tone," she said and Trudy realized that she had that rare gift, the ability to carry a color in her eye. "This is right." Mrs. Lansing unhesitatingly made a selection when Trudy brought another group of wools. "And this is exactly the right red to go with them."

Once the wools were selected, Mrs. Lansing began to show unmistakable signs of fatigue. Her eyes looked strained and not only her disabled hand but her normal one, too, lay listlessly in her lap. Trudy was glad that the attendant came promptly after she had put through the call for her.

"Good-bye. See you tomorrow. I'll have the little loom in condition," Trudy said, and Mrs. Lansing, reviving for the moment, waved almost eagerly as the attendant wheeled her through the door.

And now, what for the rest of the day? It would seem somewhat desultory, Trudy knew. She wished she might have begun work with Mrs. Lansing at once and gone on for hours, but of course that would never have done. One of the worst things a therapist might do was to overfatigue a patient.

Trudy went back to tracing the cat head, and although it and other tasks which Miss Compton assigned to her did seem anti-climactic, the morning passed quickly. At noon it happened that Trudy and Meta finished their lunch with especial dispatch. Trudy realized afterward that possibly Meta had engineered their speed. As the day was mild and golden, true Indian summer, they went out into the roof garden which opened from the opposite end of the corridor. The view was very lovely today. The November haze softened the glimpse of the river and the distance beyond it until it looked like an old faintly tinted print.

Trudy spoke of it to Meta who nodded a little absently. "Yes. Say, Trudy, how about that blind date we were talking about the other day?"

"Blind date?" For a moment Trudy could not make the connection.

"Yes, a foursome, Sam Bradford and me. You and Sam's friend. Sam likes you. You made what is known as a good initial impression." Meta laughed. "I saw him for a minute again yesterday and he suggested it. Not for a week or two, so you needn't feel you're being rushed," Meta added. "The fellows like to make the dates ahead, because often they have to do some swapping to get the same free evening."

"Why, I don't know." Although Trudy had thought favorably of the idea beforehand, now that she was faced with it she felt a little hesitation. She was shy, and the thought of two doctors seemed overwhelming. Besides, she'd never met the second one.

"Sam's friend is just as nice as he is. Much the same type." Meta sensed Trudy's hesitation. "He's considered one of the coming men around here. His name's Kerr," she added.

"Dr. Kerr? Oh," Trudy's face brightened, "I had a patient of his this morning." It wasn't logical of course, in fact it was a silly idea, but it did seem as if any doctor who had as nice a patient as Mrs. Lansing must be nice himself.

"Think it over," Meta said. "We can let them know in a few days. It won't be so much of a date," she added, "probably a good movie and a bite afterwards at some little place. They haven't much money to spend."

"Oh, that's all right. I'd rather they didn't—" Trudy had begun when Meta unobtrusively pressed her hand where it lay on the coping aud Trudy turned to see Miss Blaine coming through the door.

"Secrets, and so soon?" she asked.

"No. View and fresh air," Meta said abruptly. She turned the conversation with an ease of which Trudy knew she herself would have been incapable. "Do you know if Miss Swift was able to find that blue ribbon the patient in Four C wants? She was asking me about it this morning. I suppose such an unusual shade is hard to match."

The three girls talked in desultory fashion for a moment or two; then the clock on a nearby church tower gave a preliminary whirr and struck the hour.

"One. We'd better backtrack." Meta led the way to the door.

Trudy thought over Meta's proposition all through the afternoon. It appealed to her. If the two doctors liked her and she liked them, it would mean that an occasional date would keep her from being too lonely in the city. Of course she had originally thought that Chet Fielding might make up the foursome, but she knew that he, a busy young lawyer, could not make the trip to the city very often.

And there was another angle to this blind-date proposition, Trudy was thinking as, late in the afternoon, she put the warp on the little loom for Mrs. Lansing. It would be very interesting, valuable, to have a first-hand contact with the doctor who had charge of one of her cases. She might learn —Here a voice, high pitched and tense, broke in on her thoughts.

"But Miss Compton!"

Trudy looked up to see that the shop had emptied of patients. Miss Swift's office was closed. Neither Meta, Miss Blaine nor the student whom Trudy liked were in sight. The other student, the aggressive one, stood before Miss Compton at the far end of the room. It was this student's turn to put the shop in order at the end of the day, so of course she would be the last to go.

It was evident that the girl was being reprimanded and Trudy, her sympathies entirely with Miss Compton, wondered what she had done now. Trudy's later observation of the student had strengthened her first impression that she was inclined to be tactless and to exceed her authority. The girl had probably annoyed a patient, or worse, overfatigued one.

She has it coming to her, Trudy thought, as the student

said again, "But Miss Compton," and the assistant director cut her short.

"There are no extenuating circumstances. Your directions are perfectly clear." Miss Compton's voice, in contrast to the girl's, was calm but it was exceedingly firm. "You are to put the shop in order. That includes putting away all materials. Suppose this pin had been lost." Miss Compton motioned toward a silver pin which lay, along with the tools used in making it, on the table beside her. "The patient has put a great deal of work on it. She would have been distressed if it was missing, especially as she was making it for a Christmas present. We would have had to replace it, and it would have made a great deal of trouble all around. There is no excuse for such carelessness."

Later when Trudy went to the locker room to take off her uniform and get into street clothes, she found the girl who had been reprimanded huddled with her fellow-student in a corner. Trudy glimpsed them beyond the rank of lockers which ran down the center of the room. If they saw her they gave no sign. The one who had been disciplined, all aggression gone, was sobbing brokenheartedly. She was so abject, so shaken, so the reverse of her usual self, that Trudy felt a thrill of pity for her even before she grasped what she was saying.

"It isn't fair." The girl's voice caught between sobs. "It was Miss Blaine's patient who was making the pin. Miss Blaine said to leave the pin out. She wanted to give it a couple of finishing touches herself. But Miss Compton wouldn't let me explain."

Trudy changed her clothes and slipped from the room as quietly as she could. What a disciplinarian Miss Compton was, and the student really was right. It wasn't fair not to let her explain. Well, of course, the student was an annoying person, and had done so many wrong things that it was natural enough for Miss Compton to assume she was wrong this time.

Still, Trudy thought, as she walked toward the elevator, it wouldn't be any fun to get into a jam with Miss Compton. As the car bore her downward she added to herself, And I hope I never do.

CHAPTER IV

"GOOD MORNING!" Mrs. Lansing's golden head shone in the November sunshine as her attendant wheeled her past the shop's great windows to a place at one of the work tables. She had been occupied with Physical Therapy and exercises in the pool for two days, so this was her first appearance to do any actual weaving.

Trudy was delighted to see her, and Mrs. Lansing herself seemed happy to be in the shop. "Here I am, all ready to do a big morning's work," she said cheerfully. "It must be big if I'm to weave a handbag before Christmas. Isn't Thanksgiving just a week away?"

"Yes, it is," Trudy agreed as she set Mrs. Lansing's small loom on the table before her.

"You're going home for the holiday, I suppose." A shadow fell for an instant on the young woman's sea-blue eyes.

"Yes, Mrs. Lansing." For her patient's sake Trudy tried not to show the thrill those simple words gave her. Home for Thanksgiving. There was magic in them. They conjured up the little farmhouse under the hill, her lively mother, her

45

work-hardened father, brown-eyed Susan, and even Duzenbury, the dog.

Mrs. Lansing brought Trudy back to the hospital by saying with charming plaintiveness, "Why don't you call me
Emily? I've been here so long, 'most everybody does."

"That would be nice." As she went for the shuttles which
she had wound at the same time she prepared the loom,
Trudy intercepted Meta who had returned from the wards
for some article she had forgotten. "Is it all right to call my
patient Emily?" Trudy whispered.

"Of course," Meta answered with her head in a cupboard.
"Has anybody seen the button for Mrs. Bronson's beanie?"
She raised her voice and caused a general laugh.

"Isn't Miss Tripp good fun," Emily Lansing commented
when Trudy went back to her, "and in fact, isn't this whole
place fun?"

"I think so." Trudy looked about the shop for a moment.
In the sunshine which had brought such a glow to Emily's
bright hair, a dozen patients were stooped over work which,
at the same time it interested them, helped them to conquer
the disabilities from which they suffered. Saws buzzed, looms
clacked, and the rocking horse swung back and forth exercising a four-year-old boy who squealed with delight at each
forward swoop. Miss Compton stooped beside him, smiling
and intent. Noting the gentleness of her expression, Trudy
could hardly believe her capable of the severity which she
had witnessed two days before. The aggressive student was
gone, her two months of training at Hillhaven completed.
Trudy remembered that she had been very subdued during

her final days. Her voice had been properly pitched, her manner less assertive. In this direction the reprimand had done much good, but Trudy imagined that its injustice would always rankle. Still, Miss Blaine might have set the matter straight. Trudy had no way of knowing, but she had seen Miss Compton speaking cordially to the girl at the moment of her departure. At least it was "exit with a smile," Trudy thought. The student's very sensitiveness proved her better material for O.T. than she had at first believed.

Trudy's attention returned to her patient to find her exploring the little loom with her normal hand.

"This looks intricate." Emily brushed tentative fingers across the warp and touched the levers which were designed to lift alternate threads so that the shuttle could be passed between them.

"It isn't, though." Trudy put her own hand to the levers and pressed down the first and third. The threads of the warp obediently separated. "We'll begin at the right side," she explained, "because we want to exercise your weak hand most, and each time counts."

"Now, this is it." She picked up the shuttle of brown wool. Taking Emily's hand gently in her own, she slipped its cool limp fingers under the shuttle. Emily's thumb dropped automatically in place on top and Trudy, using her own strength to hold it there, pushed the shuttle through the warp. "Now you can pull it out on the other side with your strong left hand," she said, "and we already have woven one thread." She pointed to the strand of brown wool which now lay between the threads of the warp.

"Next, we have to beat it." She laughed at Emily's puzzled expression. "Oh, that doesn't mean we run away. We just press the thread tightly into place with the beater." She indicated a movable bar which stretched across the warp from one side to the other. "When we pull the beater toward us, it jams our threads tight against each other. Otherwise"— Trudy thought of an expression her mother had used about a piece of inferior muslin—"otherwise our weaving would be so coarse we could shoot peas through it."

"I see." Automatically Emily lifted her left hand toward the beater. Of course she would, Trudy thought. It was natural she should have formed the habit of using the hand which had most strength. Trudy checked her now, however. "Let's use your right hand for this, too," she said. "Every time we make it work is just that much gain."

It was the old old process, the universal process, of Occupational Therapy, Trudy thought as Emily's weakened fingers and arm fumbled through the movements of weaving. You repeated an exercise numberless times, as the little boy was doing now on the rocking horse, and one day you found that your patient was better, perhaps that he was well.

Trudy soon saw that she need plan no additional exercise for Emily's shoulder. Just the effort of holding it up so that the arm might swing the beater was enough. She watched her patient's face closely for signs of fatigue. That was all-important in this first work.

It wasn't long before two tiny spots of additional color came to Emily's cheeks. It was time to stop, and Trudy was about to shape the thought into tactful words when Miss Compton paused beside her.

"Your patient is tired, Miss Wescott," she said bluntly and took the situation entirely out of Trudy's hands. "Don't you want to go down and rest a little, Emily? Miss Wescott will call the attendant." Miss Compton gave Trudy a nod which was a command.

"I was just going to suggest that Emily stop," Trudy explained to Miss Compton after Emily had gone, for she felt that she had better make it clear she had not been careless of this important point. She spoke a little stiffly because it seemed to her that Miss Compton had almost, if not quite, corrected her in the presence of a patient. This was never considered good practice. It not only humiliated the therapist but lessened the patient's confidence in her.

Miss Compton did not answer, and looking at her out of the corner of her eye, Trudy saw that a quizzical expression played about her mouth. Instantly Trudy was annoyed on a second count. It wasn't fair to assume that she was trumping up an alibi, trying to gloss over an error. Why, that was the way Miss Compton had treated the student, had condemned her without allowing her to explain. Well, if this is the way it's going to be, Trudy was thinking, her cheeks burning, when fortunately Miss Swift came along. She had just been on "rounds," a tour of the wards with the doctors which took place weekly. Whether she had overheard the conversation Trudy did not know, but consciously or unconsciously, she poured oil on the troubled waters. "Did Emily get along nicely?" she asked; then turned the current of Trudy's thoughts. "Miracles never cease. Dr. Worthington is sending us a patient, and he's never done that before. It's a feather in our cap." Miss Swift made a little gesture which indicated cap and feather above her smiling face, and Trudy thought, Oh, never mind Miss Compton. This is the gal I really work for.

Toward the end of the day as work slackened and fatigue crept in, her resentment returned, however. As she and Meta sat over their usual cups of hot chocolate, Trudy wondered if she might speak about it to her new friend. She didn't want to be petty, it didn't seem to be just the thing to talk about the staff, but—

"Out with it," said astute Meta. "What's on the mind?"

"We-ell," Trudy said gratefully, yet still with hesitation, "I was just wondering about Miss Compton."

"Get in a jam with her?" Meta ate a cracker with gusto.

"Pretty nearly. I might have if Miss Swift hadn't come along."

"She straightened things out, didn't she?" Meta asked.

"Well, it didn't really come to that."

"I'll tell you about Miss Compton." Meta sipped her hot chocolate thoughtfully. "She's new to her job, was promoted just before I came here, and it makes her officious. Then I don't believe she ever was the most tactful person in the world. That doesn't make her easy to work with, but there's nothing to be done about it, and the less we think about it, the better. Maybe she'll improve with age." Meta screwed her face into a comical grin.

"We'll hope she will," Trudy said drily, for in spite of Meta's explanation the affair still rankled a little.

"It's been my experience," said Meta who claimed preaching was not her line, yet really did a good deal of it, "it's been my experience in two years of training that it takes all sorts of people to make an O.T. director. Most of 'em are nice. A few aren't. And, as that girl used to say on the radio, you have to take the bitter with the better."

Yes, that was true. Trudy, too, could remember the directors she had worked under in her student days. Only one out of the five had been difficult. Meta was exactly right. How wise she was, what a grand friend!

"And now," said Meta as if she guessed what Trudy was thinking, "now before I say some silly thing that wipes that look of wonder from your eyes, suppose I change the subject. Could you consider a date with our two doctors next Monday night? Just a movie and a snack afterwards. No grand affair."

"Oh, I'd love to." Trudy felt no hesitation now. Anything that Meta suggested was all right.

Accordingly on the following Monday evening the two girls, dressed in their best bib and tucker, as Trudy's mother, who loved old-fashioned expressions would have put it, waited in the hall of Meta's rooming house for the young doctors.

"You look simply radiant." Meta scrutinized Trudy admiringly.

"Maybe it's the light." Trudy indicated the rose-colored globe which swung above their heads. "But I feel radiant," she added. "Do you realize this is the first time I've really had a date since I came to Sayre City?"

"That's so," Meta said. "Didn't you say that at home you went about a good deal with your friend, Chet Fielding? Wasn't that his name? It must have seemed dull here."

"It has," Trudy said, and felt a thrill of anticipation run through her. "This is going to be fun."

"It sure is." Meta nodded. "Sam Bradford's always joking. Don Kerr's the quiet type, but don't let that worry you. He gets around."

Trudy didn't mind the idea of Donald Kerr's being quiet. It might be a welcome change from Chet. Chet wasn't quiet enough, talked too loud, laughed too much, and made you conspicuous sometimes. His sense of humor wasn't always Trudy's either. Yet he had qualities which she liked a great deal. His mind was as keen as a razor. He was kindhearted. He danced well. Things around him always moved fast and amusingly. Oh, she wasn't a hypocrite in going with him, didn't go just for a chance to get out, Trudy said to herself. She'd had some very good times with Chet.

And she was going to have a wonderful time this evening. In spite of her expectation, Trudy discovered that her hands were a little cold. Perhaps it was because she stood in awe of going out with a real M.D. She had a great reverence for the profession. Naturally enough her own work had given it to her. During her two years of O.T. training she had become keenly aware of the knowledge and fineness of judgment which a physician must have. She worshipped accordingly, and tonight in addition to this admiration, she hoped keenly that she would like Dr. Kerr and that he would like her. Oh, nothing romantic, she brushed the thought impatiently aside. She just hoped he and she would like each other enough to want to join Meta and Dr. Bradford once in a while and break the deadly monotony of the city evenings.

"Here they are." Meta rose from the hall settee as the bell trilled. She glanced at her watch. "They must have hustled, for they didn't come off duty until eight."

Meta unlatched the door. "What ho, Doctors!" She swung it wide.

"What ho!" Sam Bradford responded, and the four young people found themselves in rather close quarters in the narrow hall.

Meta had said that Donald Kerr and Sam were of the same type, and Trudy saw in the instant before the introductions that this was so. They had pleasant, intelligent faces, an assured manner, a quiet taste in clothes, while an indefinable something about them was so alike that anyone might have told they belonged to the same profession.

Even if Sam hadn't been Meta's special, Trudy would have liked Donald Kerr better because his eyes, dark and well set under his wide forehead, were so very kind. His mouth, slightly full, yet firm, bespoke a capacity for emotion well under control. In fact his whole face was controlled and grave in repose—as befits a good surgeon, Trudy thought—

yet it had the happy faculty of breaking into a sudden radiant smile. Young as he was, only seven or eight years older than herself, that smile had already creased delightful little lines at the outer corners of his eyes.

Oh, he's nice and I do hope he'll like me. Sam Bradford's voice roused Trudy from her thoughts.

"Get on the job, Meter"—she realized Sam had a pocketful of variants of Meta's name—"introduce your friend."

"Give me time. Give me time," Meta said equably. "Trudy, I'd like you to know Don Kerr."

"How do you do, Dr. Kerr." Trudy's awe would not allow her to be anything but professional.

"Glad to meet you, Trudy." Donald Kerr didn't seem to mind her formality. Sam and Meta had started down the steep front steps and Don took Trudy's arm. "We'd better follow our leaders. We haven't too much time."

The four young people took the bus at the corner and jolted to the opposite side of the city where the picture they had selected was showing. The bus was crowded and they had to stand. In a way, Trudy was glad, for it relieved the necessity of talking very much.

Nice to have a little time to let my awe wear off; why, I'm almost shy, and I shouldn't be. Chet Fielding certainly has taken me over the jumps often enough. She thought, as she had earlier, that an evening with Chet was a practical lesson in "How to Overcome Shyness." Chet never allowed such a feeling near him. He—

"Here we are." Donald Kerr tightened his hand under

Trudy's arm and helped her to step from the bus into the dazzle of Sayre City's White Way.

The picture, a mystery, had begun when they reached the movie house, and again there was no chance for conversation. In fact Trudy lost herself at once in the maze of clues the film portrayed. When she came back to reality at its end, she began to feel more at home with Donald Kerr. After all, people who had laughed together as they had, who had been swept away together in suspense as again they had, were bound to feel easier with each other, she thought.

"Like it? Is it too cold here?" Don pulled the collar of her coat up about her shoulders in friendly fashion. "This next number ought to be good, too. I'm a little foolish about Disneys myself."

He laughed so boyishly at Donald Duck that by the time the feature was ended, Trudy's awe had vanished. Donald—coincidence—Kerr was a human being, and a nice one. The last of her stiffness was gone.

At the end of the program the foursome, or rather, Meta, Sam and Don held a consultation. Where should they go for supper, Tony's or the Club Bleu?

"I think Trudy would like Tony's best," Don said, and she realized that already he felt he knew her tastes. That was fine.

Later, as they sat around a table in Tony's little restaurant and lingered over an after-theater snack, Trudy agreed that what Meta had said about the two men was true. Sam, like Meta, had the gift of fun. With Meta's help he kept the

party in a small uproar of laughter. Donald Kerr seldom made
a sally, but like Trudy herself was on the quiet side.

See him now, Trudy thought, glancing unobtrusively at
him. Don was leaning back, smoking in long calm puffs, his
eyes moving observantly from one to the other, his smile
illuminating his face at each of Meta and Sam's jokes. He
never misses a trick, and she realized that he was a relief from
Chet Fielding. Sam was more like Chet. Well, let Meta have
him.

After a time the conversation took a professional turn.
Trudy did not know who started it, but she found herself
saying to Don, "I have one of your patients, a Mrs. Lansing."

"Isn't she charming?" Donald Kerr leaned forward at
once. "And to see her now, you don't realize half she's been
through. Her physician told me he thought he was going to
lose her a dozen times. Then when she had the polio licked
and came to Hillhaven I thought we might still lose her. She
got into a very bad state of mind, a psychosis, really."

"Oh, no." Trudy thought of Emily's cheerful manner.

"Yes, and it took her a long time to pull out of it. I don't
wonder," Don went on. "You see, she's been married only
two years. Her husband's in South America. She was taken
sick after he left, and he hasn't seen her since she was paralyzed."

Trudy looked surprised and Don explained. "He was so
far back in the wilds on some engineering project when she
was at the worst that the message didn't reach him. Then
when she was better she insisted that we cable him not to
come. She didn't want him to see her. That's her horror, the

thing that got her down, and still does at times. How's he going to feel when he sees her? Is everything going to be over between them? You can't blame her." Donald Kerr's grave face softened into a very tender sympathy.

"Will she ever walk again?" Trudy asked.

"No, except with the greatest difficulty, with braces and crutches." Don voiced what Trudy had surmised from Emily's chart. "I have great hopes of her arm and hand, though. I think you O.T.'s and P.T.'s will be able to restore it just about one hundred per cent."

"Thanks for those kind words," Meta put in. "I wish they could be broadcast on the radio. It might help in some quarters where we O.T.'s are thought merely to play. And as Trudy and I will have to 'play' eight hours tomorrow, and it's tomorrow right now"—Meta motioned toward Tony's clock whose hands stood at one—"I think we'd better adjourn."

The young people took a taxi back to their section of the city. Sam had suggested it and Meta abetted him. "Why worry about expenses? We have plenty of 'em. See you tomorrow," she added as they left Trudy at her vestibule.

"Yes, but on what a different footing!" The smile lines showed at the corners of Don's eyes. He pleased Trudy greatly by adding, "We'll do this again sometime soon," and she ran up the steps thinking that the foursome had been a great success.

Next morning, in the light of what Don had told her, she looked at Emily Lansing with tender eyes. Emily's tragedy was even greater than she had thought. Little older than

Trudy herself, so very much in love as she must be, and to have to wonder, to fear, that she might be cut off forever from her happiness. That seemed more than any human being should be asked to bear.

CHAPTER V

A T LAST, at long last, Trudy thought as the crowded bus rattled its way out of Sayre City on Thanksgiving Eve. It had seemed as if the day would never come. Each hour had dragged, at her lodging house and in the busy hospital. Even when she had worked with Mrs. Lansing, Trudy had been in a ferment of expectation; but now, here she was, nearly breathless with happiness that she was really on her way home. She could stay until Sunday evening, too. The hospital left such matters to its director's discretion. Wise Miss Swift, knowing that the first weeks of a new job were especially wearing, had said Trudy might be the one of the staff to have the long vacation. The others would report on Friday morning; then on some later holiday Trudy would work while another member had the long leave.

In her anxiety not to miss the bus Trudy had been a half hour early at the terminal and had found that in preparation for the holiday rush the company was sending out a special bus in fifteen minutes. She was delighted. That meant fifteen minutes more at home, and even that little bit of time counted, she thought, as she sat down beside a girl at whom she hardly glanced. As the lights of houses thinned and the calm dark of the country fields took their place, she looked at her seatmate a second time and said, "Why, Elsie Hayes," just as the girl exclaimed:

"For goodness sakes! Aren't you Trudy Wescott?"

"I am. And I haven't seen you in ages. Not since high school, I guess. That's five years ago. I've been away at college and training most of the time since." Trudy found that she was glad to have someone to talk to. It would help the time to pass. "You don't live in Knolton any more, do you?" she asked.

"No." Elsie shook her elaborate hair-do. "My folks moved to Garville. I have a job in the big knitting factory. You know, the one right by the highway?"

Trudy knew the factory. The bus always passed its great wall with a slam-banging reverberation of sound which meant that she was only five miles from Knolton. Home, home. Again she began to float away on a rosy cloud when Elsie brought her back to the moment by saying in a voice suddenly hollow, "It's awfully close in this bus. I wish somebody'd open a window."

Trudy turned to see that her seatmate had grown pale under her vivid rouge. She leaned across her and, with the aid of a man who had overheard Elsie's remark, managed to lift the sash.

"That's good." Elsie drew a long breath as the fresh air streamed over her face. "I'll be all right now, but I'll just take one of my pills to make sure. They're all right," she explained rather apologetically, "my doctor gave them to me."

Trudy refrained from asking questions, and Elsie, fumbling in her handbag, brought out a pillbox and slipped a tiny pellet into her mouth. She leaned back afterward, the box held loosely in her fingers, and Trudy couldn't help scrutinizing it, for it was the prettiest one she had ever seen. The box was square, and its hinged lid was decorated in what her knowledge of metalcrafts told her was a very fine kind of enamel work. French, English, Norwegian, she couldn't say, but its pattern and coloring, a girl's head surmounted by a wreath of flowers done in delicate tints, were unforgettable.

"What a perfectly lovely box," Trudy said as soon as she saw that Elsie felt like talking again.

"Yes." Elsie nodded; then smiled. "My boy friend gave it to me. It set him back some, too. He says it's gold. I told him he ought not to spend so much, but he wanted to, so it's up to him. Well, he might as well spend his money on me as somebody else," she added. "He's got plenty.

"My folks don't like him," Elsie went on with a lack of reserve which Trudy found annoying, "but I do. And it's my business, isn't it?" She appealed to Trudy for corroboration.

"Well, I suppose it is," Trudy said noncommittally and speculated about how she herself would feel if her people said they didn't like a young man who interested her. Of course no girl liked out-and-out interference, but they would have been so fair in their judgment that she surely would have thought over what they said. She barely listened to the rest of Elsie's conversation which ran on about John, his handsome clothes, his fine car and how he was always taking her here and there. Trudy was glad when the slam-bang of the factory wall announced their arrival in Garville and Elsie left the bus.

" 'Bye now. Be seeing you," Elsie called over her shoulder, and Trudy answered with a conventional yes. But not too soon, she added to herself, as the bus picked up speed again. And now for home.

The bus station at Knolton was jammed with people, but above all the shoulders Trudy was able to pick out Chet Fielding's striking blond head. He was talking animatedly to a girl she did not recognize, probably a newcomer in town, and wasn't it just like Chet to be one of the first to get acquainted with her? As he did not expect Trudy for a good ten minutes yet, he paid no attention to her bus as it slid to a stop at the platform.

He's using his old line, Trudy thought with considerable amusement as she saw him lean toward the girl, concentrating his attention on her in a way she knew he thought irresistible.

Well, maybe it was, Trudy smiled, but it had never made so much as a dent on her. She liked Chet, liked to go about with him, but that was as far as her feeling for him went, or was ever likely to, she added to herself.

"Well, good-bye, darling. Got to meet a bus." Trudy smiled again as she caught his voice above the crowd. He turned from the girl and was surprised but entirely unabashed when he saw Trudy.

"Hi, sweetheart!" he said in a voice a little too loud to suit Trudy's taste, for it made heads turn to look at her. "Hi, sweetheart, you're early."

"Yes. Do you have a different pet name for each one of us?" she teased as he took her bag and led her to his car.

"Sure."

"How do you keep us all straight?"

"Oh, my trained lawyer's mind does that. Jealous?" he asked in mock hopefulness.

"Not a bit." Trudy laughed.

"That's too bad, because you're special. I can't make you believe it," he added as she laughed again, "but you are."

"Tell that to the Marines." Trudy forgot Chet for the moment as the car threaded its way out of the bus station and through the familiar streets. There was the movie house, Tate's drugstore, the municipal building. Soon the houses grew scattered; then a familiar crossroad and a sharp curve told her that she was only a mile from home. They should see the light any minute. Yes, there it was, not one light, but an illumination. All the windows were shining, in the living room, the dining room, the kitchen ell. Trudy's heart beat a tattoo of happiness as Chet stopped the car in the drive and she descended into the sweet leaf-smelling air.

Her family was waiting for her at the steps. "Oh, Mother! Oh, Daddy! Oh, Susan! Oh, Duzenbury," she added with a choky little burst of laughter as the big dog leaped up at her. "It's so good to be home!"

"Isn't it!" Trudy felt tears on her mother's cheek as she

kissed her. "You must come in the front door. You're company tonight."

The family trooped into the long narrow hall; then into the living room. A fire burned on the hearth, and the old Victorian furniture which Trudy had hated as a young girl, but now knew was in style again, looked not only comfortable but a little smart. The room was not the heart of the house, however, and when her mother turned toward the kitchen, Trudy said, "Come on. Let's go with her."

It occurred to her as they crossed the hall and went through the dining room that Chet had never been in the kitchen before and that he might think it beneath his dignity, which was considerable at times, to sit and be entertained there. Let him think what he pleases, Trudy said to herself. She wasn't going to be separated from her family for an instant more than she had to be.

"Come along," she said again, and saw over her shoulder that Chet was following with no displeasure apparent on his face.

The kitchen was the largest room in the house. It had three outside walls with windows that were curtained in turkey red. Against the inner wall stood a great stove, polished until it shone like jet. On either side was a Boston rocker, together with a small chair for Susan. Trudy left the rockers for the two men and squeezed herself into Susan's chair while her mother busied herself between oven and counter.

"Let me look at you, Suze." Trudy drew the little girl to

her side. "You're all right." She brushed Susan's fair hair back from her forehead and studied her candid brown eyes. "And I believe you are, too, Mother and Dad." She noticed that her mother moved as energetically as ever, and that her father, although he leaned back in his rocker as if tired, nevertheless looked well.

"You seem to be all right." Trudy's mother turned to scrutinize her with love and warmth.

"Maybe you've lost a little weight, or perhaps you've sort of firmed up," her father commented.

"She has firmed up, hasn't she?" Chet began his teasing again. "Maybe she's firmed too much. She refused to be jealous when she saw me talking to another girl at the bus station."

"As if, from what I hear, that is unusual," Trudy's father said with a chuckle. He turned toward his wife. "What's for dinner, Mother? It was all right to wait for our big girl, but I'm hollow to my toes now."

Chet's expression showed that he was hungry, too, also that he didn't mind the kitchen. Trudy had seen him give it a sharp scrutiny when he entered, then drop easily into a rocker. That was nice of him, to make them feel he was at home. Still, it might be part of his professional attitude. He always said a lawyer should be able to make himself at ease anywhere. It gave him control of situations.

"We'll be dished up in a minute," Mrs. Wescott said, and her husband laughed.

"She's still at it, Trudy." He turned to Chet to explain,

"Mother collects old-fashioned expressions as some women collect china dogs. They have the best of her nowadays and she uses them herself."

"Yes, and nobody can stop her," Trudy said, but she really didn't care. Her mother's vivid old sayings had long since become a family joke.

"Glad you realize you can't stop me. Now maybe you won't pester me. And there's a good old-timey word for you." Mrs. Wescott laughed as she lifted the plates from the warming oven and carried them to the table in the dining room. "Bring the roast, Dad, and the rest of you each carry something."

A minute later the family was seated around the table, Mr. Wescott at one end with the roast before him, Mrs. Wescott at the other with the coffee service at her hand. Mr. Wescott would have seated Chet on his right, but Susan, who sometimes asserted herself too positively and could be very persistent, insisted that Trudy and not he was the guest of honor.

"She's going to sit by Dad." Susan pulled Trudy toward the chair.

"Very well," the family conceded, partly from affection, partly from the wish to avoid what Trudy knew her mother would have called a tow-row before company.

In the quiet of the little country farmhouse they bowed their heads while Mr. Wescott asked the blessing.

"Dear Lord, we thank Thee for this food. Bless it to our use and to Thy ends." He added an extra line because of

Trudy's presence. "We thank Thee that our dear daughter is safe under our roof tonight. Amen."

What a beautiful blessing, Trudy thought, and was there a happier family anywhere this Thanksgiving Eve? She doubted it as she looked about the table at her smiling family, and at Chet who seemed so much at home.

The evening was just as pleasant as the supper hour, and when it was ended and Trudy climbed the creaking old stairs to her little room she thought, Maybe this is the peak of my vacation.

Thanksgiving was a wonderful day, however. It seemed as if all the gold of the autumn's harvest, the wheat, the corn, the pumpkins, had centered in its sunshine. Warm and yellow, it poured down on fields and woods, poked long fingers through Mrs. Wescott's freshly laundered curtains, and even laid one on the great turkey on the table.

"Look! The sun wants a drumstick!" Susan exclaimed, and the family laughed.

There was no one quite like Susan, Trudy thought, and there was no doubt her mother and father felt so, too. Brown-eyed Susan, they often called her, and the little girl with her fair hair and dark eyes did resemble the flower, yet she made Trudy think of a butterfly, too. Perhaps it was because she was so light on her feet, always flitting here and there. They'd probably spoiled her a little, for instance giving in to her about the seating at supper the night before. She must have seemed pert to Chet. But never mind her faults—she's my darling, Trudy said to herself as she had numberless times since her little sister had been born.

After the turkey and all its trimmings, not to mention pumpkin pie, had been eaten and the dishes washed, Trudy's parents sat drowsily before the fire. Trudy felt like exercising, however, so as Chet was not coming—Trudy suspected he had another date—she suggested to Susan that they take a walk to Pike's Peak. That was what, years before, they had named the fairly high hill which rose behind the farmhouse.

"Susan and Duzen"—Trudy laughed as the big dog joined them in the lane—"race you to the gate!" A moment later she thought that had been a great mistake, for Susan and Duzenbury were there long before her.

It didn't matter, however. Trudy and Susan toiled up the steep slope while Duzenbury detoured to one side and the other in search of woodchucks.

"They're out of season, Duze," Trudy called when he met with no success, and Duzenbury seemed to agree, for he joined them on the crest of the hill, and, as it was still warm, the three of them sat down on an outcropping ledge and watched the early-setting sun.

"The old man's going to bed. He's poking his way right between the blankets," Susan said as the sun's edge disappeared behind the distant hills. "This has been the nicest day, with you home." She turned and touched Trudy's cheek. "I miss you," she said with a gesture of affection which was rare for her.

"And I miss you." Trudy was too deeply moved to say more.

"You'll always come home for holidays, won't you?" Susan asked.

Trudy nodded.

"And we'll always climb Pike's Peak, won't we?"

"Yes," Trudy promised, "we'll always climb Pike's Peak."

The vacation days went by as if some unseen force speeded the sun. More walks, a talk about finances with her mother and father—Trudy's contributions were enabling them to accumulate what Mrs. Wescott called a nice little nest egg in the bank—a dance at the country club with Chet, and suddenly it was Sunday afternoon. In four hours Trudy would be in the bus on her way back to Sayre City.

The nearness of her return directed her thoughts to the hospital and her job.

"Funny," she said as she and Chet took a last ride through the country. "I'm both glad and sorry to go back."

"That's natural," Chet commented. "You've had a good time here, and you're interested in your work there. If you stayed here, though," he added, "it would grow dull. I find it so sometimes, even though my professional interests are in the town."

"Have you ever been sorry you came to Knolton?"

"Not since I met you," Chet said with a chuckle. He became serious, and not a little boastful. "No, I think I can do a lot of good around here. The present incumbents of the Bar Association in this county are a set of old fogies. They need new blood to stir them up, and I'm their man. You don't like me to talk that way, do you?" he added shrewdly, and Trudy shook her head.

"No. You sound conceited."

"Well, I am conceited," Chet said unrepentantly. "I have a right to be. I've had a thorough training, I'm quick on the pick-up, I have a strong personality and I'm not afraid to make it felt. If everybody was a mouse like you"—his lack of temper made Chet's words stingless—"if everybody was a mouse like you, no lawsuits would be won. But I like you, Mouse," he added with a smile.

Trudy laughed, "Well, I suppose you do like me," she conceded. "If you didn't you wouldn't date me. But as to my being your one and only"—she waved an unbelieving hand—"I have my doubts."

"Aw, Trudy, don't say it." Chet drew his face into mournful lines.

"No? And you going with every girl in town? Mother writes that she sees you with this one and that one—"

"Wicked woman," Chet put in.

"I see you myself," Trudy continued, "and even Dad, who's as blind as a bat about such things, is on to you. Don't get the idea that I care," she added.

"Oh, yes, please care," Chet coaxed. "I always go with you when you're home, don't I?"

"That's because I'm a novelty." Trudy was so full of amusement at her idea that she burst out laughing. "Besides, I'm not home enough to put any great strain on you."

"Go ahead. Mock my tender sentiments—Hi, lookout there!" Chet's voice changed suddenly. He steered the car with quick skill around a kitten that had dashed from a farm gate into the road.

Ah, here was one of his finest qualities. Trudy watched him admiringly. Let him blarney if he would. Behind his bold flashing front was a kind-heartedness that was like a vein of gold. Trudy had seen many manifestations of it; a lost dog restored after much searching to its owner, a trek of several miles over rough roads to take someone with a heavy package home, lawsuits undertaken for people in poor circumstances around the community. Trudy's father said Chet never gave a thought to being paid. His sympathy, his warm-heartedness, impelled him to see wrongs righted. Trudy, along with her parents, considered that it showed a very fine spirit in him.

The clock on the municipal building in Knolton reminded Trudy again of the swiftly passing time. Only three hours now.

Chet read her thought, and cleverly, instead of helping her bewail the situation, turned her attention toward its silver lining, her job. "Tell me," he said, "exactly what's the first thing you'll do tomorrow at the hospital."

"Well, tomorrow morning"—Trudy was interested at once—"I'll be going on the wards with Meta. I dread it just a tiny bit," she confessed.

"Why?" Chet asked.

"Oh, I expect it's because in the workshop we O.T.'s are boss. When we get out into the hospital we have to rub shoulders with all departments. We're bound to get in the way sometimes, bound to make a little extra work for somebody, especially the nurses. I know exactly how they feel." Trudy remembered the days of her clinical training. "They want their wards to look as neat as wax, and the work we leave with the patients means things around, knitting needles, wool, pieces of leather, maybe a weaving frame. Then, too, hospital hours are full. Perhaps our time on a ward corresponds to the time the nurses have to take temperatures and pulses. They come to a patient just when we've got his hands full of knotted work or something, and it takes us a minute to get out of the way. We O.T.'s try hard not to have that happen, but it's unavoidable sometimes."

"Do you think the nurses understand the value of your work, know the good you do?" Chet asked sagely.

"Better than they used to," Trudy answered. "These days part of their training is an orientation to O.T., so that they'll know what it's all about."

"Which, as I understand it, is to keep up the patient's morale, even if the work itself doesn't benefit any special muscle."

"That's right. And ninety per cent of ward work is just that. Diversional, we call it. It's in the shop that we do most of the work strengthening and restoring motion to poor muscles. Of course Physical Therapy does that also. The two sort of overlap."

"And you like the shop best," Chet commented.

Trudy nodded. "Except when Miss Compton goes off the deep end. Well, she doesn't really go off," Trudy modified her statement. "She's just too quick sometimes. She's one hundred per cent efficient, but you can't warm up to her as you do to Miss Swift." Trudy knew that her face grew bright. "I could love Miss Swift," she said.

"Couldn't you love me, Trudy?" Chet gave her a teasing glance from the corner of his eye.

Trudy wrinkled her nose at him.

CHAPTER VI

"GOOD GRIEF! Ten o'clock already. We'd better hustle." Meta picked up her gay red market basket on Monday morning, and Trudy followed with her blue one. Both baskets were filled almost to overflowing with wools, pieces of leather, strips of plastic, pads of drawing paper, pencils, a small weaving frame, and a few games; materials in which Meta thought the ward patients might be interested, or would need to complete projects already started.

"I think we have everything." Meta gave a last glance through her notebook as they waited for the elevator. "Everything we could get," she added. "Mary Nelson wanted some light-blue felt, but we couldn't find it in any of the stores."

"Yes?" Trudy spoke absently. She had turned to look back toward the shop. As she had told Chet, she would have preferred to stay in it rather than go to the wards. It was because she always felt more at home in the shop, and this morning she had a second reason for wishing to stay. Any moment now, she thought as a clicking in the shaft announced the approach of the elevator, any minute now, perhaps on this very trip, Emily Lansing would be coming, and Trudy would miss the morning's work with her. Miss Blaine would have charge of Emily, Miss Swift had said, and Trudy, not caring for Miss Blaine in any case, felt a twinge of regret mingled with something like jealousy.

Well, it was all a part of the job, the bitter with the better, she said to herself as she and Meta entered the car.

"Third floor, please," Meta directed, and a moment later they stepped into the boys' ward.

How it shone in the morning sunlight, immaculate and polished; not a wrinkle in a bed cover, not a pin, not a patient's hair, out of place. Trudy appreciated how hard the nurses had worked, and did not wonder that some of them resented any disturbance of this almost exquisite order. Only one nurse was in sight, giving a ten o'clock medication to a patient at the end of the ward. Meta went immediately to the bed nearest the door.

"Hello, Tommy. Here's our new therapist, Miss Wescott, to see you."

"Hello, Miss Wescott." It took Trudy a moment to locate Tommy, for all that presented itself to her in the bed was the back of a great white cast which had, roughly, the shape of shoulders and a head.

Suddenly a mirror gleam caught her eye. Tommy, lying on his stomach in the cast, was looking at her in reflection from a small round mirror which he held in his hand.

"Hello, Tommy." Trudy spoke quickly to cover her pause and Tommy smiled up at her. What a charming small-boy face, pointed chin, clear bright eyes, she thought as he asked in a voice entirely undaunted by the mass of cast which surrounded him:

"Have you brought me that leather this morning?"

"We have. Tommy's a worker," Meta explained to Trudy as she took from her basket two pieces of leather shaped to make a change purse. "Think you can punch the holes for the lacing around the edge, Tommy?"

"Sure." With surprising adroitness, considering the hampering cast and his awkward position, Tommy took the leather and a punch, which Meta handed him, and began to punch holes in the places she had marked.

"Isn't Tommy handy," Trudy commented, and Meta laughed.

"He's used to that cast. How long have you been in it, Tommy?"

"Five months. One more op"—"Meaning operation," Meta put in—"and I'm through," Tommy said casually. "I hope," he added.

Because most of the patients were flat in bed, some of them on their faces, there was a certain privacy about the center of the ward.

"Tommy's a scoliosis, caused by polio," Meta explained with no fear of being overheard so long as she kept her voice low.

She and Trudy approached the next patient, a boy of Tommy's age, in a cast which apparently encased the lower part of his body and legs under the bed covers. What a difference in the two boys, Trudy thought. Where Tommy was plump, almost rosy, this child was the color of paste and pitifully thin. His hands lay like claws on the coverlet.

"Would you like to make a case like Tommy's? We could punch the holes for you if that was too hard. Or an airplane model? Or a belt?" Meta asked. Each suggestion brought no light to the boy's dark eyes.

"No." His head moved infinitesimally on his pillow, and Meta nodded cheerfully.

"O.K. Maybe tomorrow, then. 'Bye." She turned to the next bed.

On down the long row Meta and Trudy went, leaving work at some beds, nothing at others. As they left the ward, after having made a complete circuit of it, Trudy estimated roughly that thirty per cent of the patients were doing some sort of O.T. work.

"Do you call that a good percentage?" she asked Meta as they went along the corridor toward the girls' ward at its far end.

"Yes, considering that quite a number of the patients are in for short terms. It's the long termers who get really interested, and you can do something for. Tommy was in the dumps at first. It took quite a while—but look at him now. And after he has this last 'op,' as he calls it, gets out of that cast and up to the shop, won't he make things hum?"

"He certainly will," Trudy agreed as they came to the door of another shining ward.

"Good morning." Trudy remembered Miss Connor to whom Miss Swift had introduced her on their round of the hospital.

"Good morning." Miss Connor, pausing at the door of

her office, smiled pleasantly as Trudy and Meta stepped into the sunny room. Here, casts similar to Tommy's showed in some beds, but on the pillows of others lay heads with pretty hair-dos, bright ribbons encircling many of them to keep curls in place. How nice, Trudy thought, that in a hospital girls could be fixed up just as they would be at home.

"Hi, Louise." The patients in the first two beds had declined work, and Meta was now standing by the third.

Louise, too, was lying on her face, but she managed to turn a little to her side and Trudy saw that she was pretty.

"Hello." She disengaged her thumb from a loop of elastic which was pinned to the bottom sheet. "I've been pulling on this, trying to strengthen my poor old thumb."

"Think it's any better?" Meta asked, and Trudy saw that Louise's left hand was drawn slightly out of shape.

"I think so. I found I could weave for quite a while yesterday. Isn't this going to be pretty?" She held up the small frame which Trudy had warped that first morning at the hospital. Louise had used narrow satin ribbon as weft and had woven a mat in soft blue and rose. The work was nicely done in spite of her handicap and Meta was generous with praise.

"Grand. In another couple of days you'll have it finished. Need any more ribbon?"

"I think some blue." Louise reached with difficulty and fumbled in the drawer of her bedside table. "Yes, that's right."

"I thought you would." Meta took a length from her basket. "We'll soon have to be talking about a new project. How about—" she began when she was interrupted by a low sobbing.

"My hand," a girl's voice said. "My hand's never been bad before. My back was bad enough. I just can't bear it if my hand's going, too." The sobs began again.

Trudy, aware that one must never make a sudden move or sound in a hospital, turned cautiously. Two beds away a girl a little younger than Louise lay with her left hand across her eyes. Her right was stretched in a position of helplessness on the coverlet. Above her stooped Dr. Kerr.

"Janet"—he stroked her hair, and Trudy thrilled at the deep tenderness of his voice—"it's going to be all right. You've just leaned too much on the edge of your cast. We'll cut the edge away and massage your arm and hand. It will be all right. You must believe me."

The sobs were softer, but they continued.

"Won't you believe me?" Dr. Kerr's voice was persuasive now. "You trusted me to operate on you. You know I wouldn't tell you a fib, not even a little white one?" He drew Janet's hand from her eyes and smiled into them. "Won't you?" he coaxed.

Janet wavered for a moment, like a needle before a magnet; then she, too, smiled. "Yes," she said just audibly.

"Good!" With a reassuring pat on the affected hand Dr. Kerr straightened and, before she could turn away, met Trudy's eyes. "Good morning," he said perfunctorily, and when he did not add her name, Trudy had a sudden realization that he was so absorbed in his profession, he did not recognize her.

There was a doctor for you, she thought as, erect and tall, he walked away, and a voice at her elbow echoed her feeling, "Isn't he grand?"

A smiling nurse, a bottle of alcohol in the crook of her arm, stood beside Trudy. "Janet's been crying ever since we noticed that her hand was affected," she said. "We nearly stood on our heads to bring her out of it. We couldn't do a thing with her, and here Dr. Kerr has her smiling in just one minute." The nurse turned to the nearest patient and proceeded to give her an alcohol rub, talking to Trudy over her shoulder as she worked. "That's lovely wool you have in your basket. I've been trying to persuade Nellie"—she nodded toward the patient—"to knit me a bed jacket. Cold weather's coming on and I haven't one." The nurse made a little face at Nellie and winked at Trudy. "She doesn't love me enough," she sighed comically.

"Well, now, maybe she does." Trudy knew that as a rule patients were not allowed to make articles for hospital employees. However, in the case of a patient difficult to interest, an exception could be made. She played up to the nurse's lead. "How about it, Nellie?"

"A sweater's too big to start with." Trudy saw a gleam of interest come into a face which had been apathetic. "I haven't done any knitting in, oh"—the gleam began to dull—"I don't know how long."

"Well, then"—Trudy was quick to catch the last glow—"how about a beanie, some color Miss—"

"Ericson," the nurse supplied.

"Miss Ericson would like. A beanie's not a big job "

"I'll pay for the wool," Miss Ericson said swiftly, and Trudy blessed her, for sometimes this was the reef on which a patient stranded. As a rule patients paid for their own materials, the hospital supplying them only to the needy. These cases, however, were often reluctant to admit their lack of funds, and in this way denied themselves O.T. work.

Nellie apparently had funds, for she said without hesitation, "Oh, that's not necessary." Her eyes turned toward Trudy's basket. "What colors have you?"

"Powder blue, Kelly green, a sort of pomegranate red, just samples, you know. We can get whatever color you want."

"Kelly green," said Miss Ericson whose coloring ran to auburn. "It'll set me off. And start Nellie with the sample, will you? I'm in a hurry for that beanie. Better strike while the iron is hot," she murmured in an aside, and later as they left the ward, Meta agreed.

"We've never been able to get Nellie working before. She's been a hard nut to crack."

"That's a grand nurse; so friendly and co-operative." Trudy's heart felt warm when she thought of Miss Ericson.

"Yes, she understands O.T. Then, too, she's just naturally kind."

"And now, my dear colleague"—Meta's manner took on its untrammeled gaiety as she and Trudy found themselves alone in the corridor—"it's almost twelve o'clock and time for nourishment. Come along. We'll leave our baskets at the mill."

Trudy began the afternoon with much less regret for the shop. The morning's work had been extremely interesting, and the recollection of Miss Ericson lingered happily in her mind. Such a nice person. Maybe she lived in the neighborhood. Maybe Trudy could see her outside the hospital. Trudy hoped she might, for she still found the city lonely. Meta was grand, but of course she couldn't be with her all the time.

"Women's ward first." Meta led the way to the fourth floor, and Trudy found herself in another long room, not so bright as the morning wards had been because the afternoon sun did not touch it. It shone with the same order and spotlessness, however, even though drawn curtains around two beds interrupted its uniformity. From one of the beds came low moanings and an incoherent voice.

"Patient coming out of ether," Meta commented. She nodded toward a bed in a corner. "That's Emily Lansing's."

"Oh, is it?" Trudy looked with immediate interest. How nice that Emily Lansing had a corner. That gave her greater privacy, since she would have a patient next her only on one side. Emily Lansing's table held several books, some stationery, evidence of a person who had resources within herself.

Several nurses were in the ward, beginning to take pulses and temperatures near the door, so Meta began work at the opposite end of the row of beds. Many of the women had projects under way, and one Trudy admired especially, partly because its pastel colors were so pleasing, partly because it was so well adapted to the limitations of a person working in bed. It was an afghan made up of small squares which were crocheted separately, to be joined later. This meant that the patient need have only a small amount of material in her hands at a time.

"Did you choose the colors?" Trudy asked the woman who, bolstered up in a sitting position, was working on a pale-orchid square.

"Yes. They're my favorites. Miss Tripp"—she turned a bright face to Meta—"I've had an idea. Wouldn't a white square every so often bring out the colors better?"

"I think it would, and I'll get you some white wool tomorrow." Meta jotted the item in her notebook.

"Very encouraging," she said when she and Trudy were out of hearing. "That patient is thinking for herself."

Trudy and Meta maneuvered themselves around the nursing schedule and turned down the corridor toward the men's ward. As Miss Compton and a student were taking care of the nursery, this would be the last ward of the day. It, too, was serene with order. Several of the men were sitting up in bed, two or three—ambulatories, they were called—were walking about in pyjamas. One was exercising in a walker, a circular waist-high framework on small wheels, which supported him while with great difficulty he learned to walk again after some accident or illness which had disabled his legs. Two other patients, in an earlier stage of cure, lay supine under an elaborate rigging of ropes and pulleys which held their legs in desired positions.

"Good afternoon, Mr. Duncan." Meta went directly to a man who was sitting up. "How's the belt coming?" Mr. Duncan immediately and with justifiable pride exhibited the belt he was knotting from plastic strips. The work was beautifully executed, so evenly that each strand lay perfectly in place.

"That's really something," Trudy began in honest praise when a voice at her elbow snorted:

"Women's work," and she swung about to face a little dried-up man. One glance at him, and she knew that he was cantankerous, probably the pest of the ward.

"Hiya, Nick," Meta said imperturbably. She studied Nick with a professional eye. "I'd say you'll soon be well enough to come up to the shop."

"The shop!" Nick snorted again. "Why any red-blooded he man would mess with that kind of stuff." He pointed to Mr. Duncan's belt, but Mr. Duncan met him very neatly there.

"Better have Nick make a belt, Miss Tripp," he said with a grin. "He'll need one when he gets into pants again."

The men in the surrounding beds chuckled and Nick retreated in blustering haste.

"We're rid of him for today," Meta murmured as she and Trudy left Mr. Duncan and turned to a patient above whose bed was slung, of all things, a typewriter. A stout metal frame held it at such an angle and height that the young man in the bed could reach its keys.

"How's the touch system coming, Nat?" Meta asked in the voice which Trudy admired so much. Its warm easy pleasantness always gave the impression that she was genuinely interested.

"Well, I'm having a little trouble minding my p's and q's." Nat said jokingly.

"We all do." Meta's eyes twinkled at Nat; then she turned

to Trudy. "Isn't this set-up something? The Simmons bed people made it, and it helps Nat kill two birds with one stone. The reaching and typing strengthen his arms and fingers, and as he's going to be a secretary when he gets out, he can use the skill he's gained.

"Nat's spirits have risen a lot since he got the typewriter,' Meta commented when they reached the center of the floor. "He was in an automobile accident that nearly killed him. He was terribly bitter at being disabled, especially as at first it looked as if it might be permanent.

"The patient in the next bed is Jack Selby. Disabled hands, among other things. I usually play a game of ticktacktoe with him to exercise his fingers. I'll introduce you, and suppose you do it today while I go ahead with some of the others."

"O.K." Trudy took the little board with its pegs. It had only eight pegs although there were nine holes. You didn't need the ninth, Trudy reflected, because you knew who was licked when you played the eighth. The idea was, of course, that you had one less peg to look for when you left a patient's bed.

"Jack, this is our new therapist, Miss Wescott," Meta said, and Trudy found herself looking down at another young man. It was just about all he could do to grasp the pegs and put them in the holes of the board, but she soon found that she faced a keen adversary. Five times running, Jack beat her, and Trudy was laughingly commenting that she was a dead duck when she looked up to see that a nurse was approaching.

Oh, yes, it was time for afternoon temperatures and pulses. In addition to the fact that nursing care came first, Trudy was anxious to be courteous and not get in the way, so she made haste to gather up the game.

At the moment one of the pegs was in Jack's half helpless fingers, and as he tried to assist her by placing it in the box, it fell into a fold in the bed cover.

"I'll get it," Trudy reached for the peg, but it eluded her fingers, and in the moment before she secured it the nurse arrived at Jack's bed. She was forced to wait and gave Trudy a steely glance. "Too much stuff around here," she said caustically.

Trudy saw that Jack would have been glad to explain, but the nurse silenced him by thrusting the thermometer into his mouth.

That left Trudy to make the apology. "I'm sorry," she began, but when she saw that she was met with silence, there was nothing to do but step quietly away.

"Is that nurse usually so impatient?" she asked Meta as they returned to the shop at five.

"Miss Blanchard? That's her reputation. Permanently dislocated temper." Meta grinned.

"It's tough on us, tough on the patients, too," Trudy said. "I know Jack Selby felt bad that the delay happened and she didn't let him explain."

"Those things always do happen with the peppery ones," Meta said. "Well, forget it. The pepper pots are few and far between."

"I've had one of each today"—Trudy remembered Miss Ericson—"a nice nurse and a cross one."

"So everything's even," Meta commented. "And that's not such a bad ending for your first day on the ward, is it?"

Trudy granted that Meta was right, but nevertheless she felt a little depressed, possibly from fatigue. She took her time as she walked down the hill from the hospital, and was not surprised that someone, pacing swiftly behind her, overtook her.

It proved to be Donald Kerr, and he fell in step at her side.

"Come in the drugstore and have a chocolate. It's a good bracer, and you walk as if you needed one. You were surprised to see me in Three C this morning, weren't you?" he asked after they were seated in one of the booths.

"Well, not really." Trudy smiled. "After all, the resident doctors do go around the wards once in a while."

"I was surprised to see you, or something close to it," Don confessed. "At least I didn't recognize you for a moment. Hardly flattering, was it?" His smile lines crinkled as the waiter brought Trudy's chocolate and his malted milk.

"Under the circumstances, it was very flattering. To you," Trudy added as he looked up in surprise. "To be so absorbed in your profession that you don't recognize your friends is something."

"Thanks." Donald Kerr's eyes showed that he appreciated Trudy's compliment. "Well, of course Janet Wood's case is very interesting. She's a scoliosis like Tommy and Louise, only her case was worse. Why, her back was like an accordion when we started. Like this." Don drew the menu card toward him and began to sketch on its margin. "We had to perform a three-stage operation."

As Trudy listened he went on to describe how at three month intervals he had inserted wedges of bone on one side of the vertebrae, had incised the muscles to stretch them and compel them to allow the curvatures to straighten. She realized that for a second time he had forgotten who she was and that much of what he was telling her must already be familiar to her as a graduate O.T. However, he was so interesting and she liked him so well that she didn't care.

"It's a wonderful thing," Don went on, "the way the body's built on a series of balances. From the top of your head to the soles of your feet, two opposing sets of muscles, the flexors and extensors, hold you steady, your arms, your legs, your fingers, even your spine."

Very true, Trudy thought. She remembered the little girl on the rocking horse. Her foot, because polio had weakened the muscles on one side, had become unbalanced.

"Of course that's what scoliosis is, loss of balance in the spine. The muscles on one side in a given area are weakened by disease or injury. They can't do their part. Then the strong muscles on the other side pull the vertebrae over and you have a curvature. Janet had three such areas, but as I told you, we got them pretty well straightened out."

"And you think she'll walk again?" Trudy asked as Don pushed aside the ruined menu card and returned to his forgotten malted milk.

"Oh, sure. She won't have just the posture of a normal

person. We can't perform miracles, but she'll be all right. We're only waiting now for complete calcification before we get her up. After you O.T.'s and P.T.'s have strengthened her arm muscles so she can use crutches, she'll get around and gradually learn to walk again. Her arm's nothing," he added. "You heard what I said to her this morning."

"Yes." Trudy drew a long happy breath in contemplation of Janet's recovery. O.T. would have had a part in it, and she, Trudy, would have had a humble little share in that O.T.

"Say!" Donald Kerr leaned forward and looked at her closely. "You're just as pepped up about this as I am, aren't you? Your eyes are shining like—Well, this is no place to be poetic"—he indicated the cluttered drugstore—"so I won't say stars. Instead I'll say like electric-light bulbs. How's that?" He chuckled and Trudy laughed.

"Light bulbs it is. And you're right." She had been ready to admit her enthusiasm when she saw Meta coming toward them across the store. Meta was moving deliberately, yet Trudy sensed a strange tenseness about her. Was something wrong?

She knew that there was when Meta would not sit down in the space Donald Kerr made for her.

"No, thanks," she said automatically and turned to Trudy. "There's a 'phone message for you."

The tenderness in Meta's voice told Trudy better than words that it was bad news. "It's not Dad!"

"No."

"Not Mother!" Trudy exclaimed before Meta could say more.

Meta shook her head.

"Oh, don't tell me it's Susan!" Trudy could not bear the thought.

"You must be brave," Meta said. "Susan's had an accident. She's in the hospital, and your folks thought you'd want to come home."

CHAPTER VII

"OH!" TRUDY, aglow the moment before, felt icy cold now. The cold seemed to numb her brain and her voice. "I wonder what happened," was all she could say.

"Automobile." Meta, too, seemed to be short of words, and Donald Kerr stepped into the gap.

"Trudy will want to take the next bus." He drew her gently to her feet. "We'd better help her get ready."

It was Don who telephoned the bus company and made sure of time and reservation, he who telegraphed to Knolton, since the Wescotts had no telephone, and told them that Trudy was coming.

Trudy did automatically whatever he and Meta directed her to do. As they pressed her into the seat on the bus which they said was hers and Don put her bag into the rack overhead, Meta kissed her unexpectedly. "Take it easy," she counseled.

"Yes." Donald Kerr took her hand in his for a moment. "Don't allow yourself to imagine the worst. Until you see Susan you can't know."

How can I help imagining? Trudy did not know whether

or not she spoke the words aloud. You know perfectly well, she looked up at Donald Kerr reproachfully, you know what terrible hurts she may have, spinal injuries, brain injuries, internal injuries which would not show at first. Trudy's professional knowledge made the possibilities all too real.

"Yes, I understand," Don said gravely, so Trudy thought that perhaps she had spoken aloud, "but until you see Susan it's useless to speculate. You can help more at home," he added with a final pressure on her fingers, "if you keep cool and don't wear yourself out beforehand."

Excellent advice, Trudy admitted to herself, as the bus pulled out of the terminal, but who could follow it, when all the time there was a vision of a little brown-eyed girl on a hospital bed, under a sedative, no doubt, yet even in her drugged dreams aware that something was terribly, terribly wrong. Trudy remembered the soft moanings of patients she had seen, some of them drifting back to consciousness, some drifting into that deepest sleep of all. Oh, not that! We couldn't live without Susan. At the thought her tears came and brought her some relief. I'm a fool. She dabbed them away, and set herself resolutely to take Donald Kerr's advice.

Nevertheless the journey which had been such delight less than a week before was agony now. If there'd only been someone to talk to, even an Elsie. There was no one, however, and she was deeply thankful when the lights of Knolton showed. A minute later she saw the silhouettes of Chet and her father in the door of the terminal.

"How is she?" she asked before she was down the last step of the bus, and they both reassured her.

"Pretty good," Mr. Wescott said. "She's suffering from shock, of course, but she's under an opiate and resting quietly. Her most serious injury is a broken pelvis. I understand they don't put that in a cast. She's in what they call a binder and the preliminary examinations don't show any other injuries, except two broken fingers. They're just nothing, of course."

"Can I see her tonight?"

"Yes, Dr. Billings said you could if you wouldn't disturb her—"

"Of course an O.T. would know enough not to do that," Chet put in, and Trudy knew he did it purposely to relieve the tension.

"Mother's waiting at the hospital for us," Mr. Wescott went on. "We'll go right along there."

Mrs. Wescott's arms seemed the dearest things in the world to Trudy. Her face, too, showed unspoken fears, but they were under firm control.

"They tell us there isn't a thing we can do tonight," she said, "so we'll just take a peep at Susan and go home."

A shaded lamp filled Susan's room with peaceful twilight. The little girl was peaceful, too, but oh, so pitiful, Trudy thought. No imperious little ways, no pertness tonight, she lay straight and still, one hand with a temporary cast on its broken fingers, stiff at her side, the other flung emptily across the coverlet. A bandage about Susan's head made Trudy start, but a smiling nurse indicated that it was nothing. "Just a scratch," she whispered.

That was something to be grateful for, no head injury. Trudy leaned forward to scrutinize Susan's sleeping face.

The child's dark eyes were closed, but her slightly rapid breathing and cold moist skin told that she was in a state of shock.

"She'll be better in the morning." The nurse's nod meant it was time to go, and after all, what use was it to stay? Until the morning light showed through the window there would probably be no change in this quiet room.

With Chet following in his roadster Trudy and her parents drove home.

"It happened here," Trudy's father said as they passed the crossroad a mile from the house, but in the darkness they could see nothing. Automatically they gathered around the stove in the kitchen. Susan's rocking chair by the hearth gave them a sharp pang, and with a set face Mr. Wescott took it into the dining room; then they pulled their chairs up to the grateful warmth of the stove. Trudy realized from the way Chet warmed his hands that even he was chilly with anxiety. No bravado tonight. All his tenderheartedness had come to the fore.

"What happened?" Trudy asked as soon as they were settled.

"Hit-run driver," Chet answered and added with a savage edge to his voice, "I'll handle your case and I'll get him, or her, if it's the last act of my legal life."

Trudy barely heard Chet. Her thoughts were all on Susan. Let her live! Let her be well again. Never mind the hit-run driver!

Her father's voice brought her back to the conversation. "It may have been partly Susan's fault. She hasn't always been careful on her bike, you know; and she may have come out onto the highway from behind that hedge at the corner pretty suddenly. If you were coming fast you'd be on her before you knew it."

"Yes, but the driver could have stopped after he hit her. He could have stayed and taken care of her. The rotten heel," Chet's teeth gritted. "He needn't have run away."

"Maybe we can ask Susan the details in the morning," Mrs. Wescott said quietly. "Of course we couldn't question her this afternoon."

"She was on her way home from school when she was hit." Mr. Wescott turned to Trudy as if in spite of her question he only now realized how little she knew of the facts. "Apparently she turned off on the side road to get some pine cones from that big tree at the edge of the pasture. The ground's covered with cones where she was hit."

Poor Susan, so happy at getting a little present for her mother. Trudy remembered the numberless afternoons Susan had come in with some small gift—"Here, Mummy dear!"— a flower, a handful of berries, a shining apple.

Perhaps Susan had been careless, but the man, if it was a man, the dreadful, heartless driver, to leave a little girl, hurt and bleeding, lying in the ditch.

"Amos Black found her. He's our R.D. man, does a bit of insurance on the side," Mr. Wescott explained to Chet. "I guess it couldn't have been long after she'd been hit. She lay where she'd been flung, and he didn't know who she was until he wiped the grime off her face. He was going to pick her up, when a man came along and yelled, "Don't touch her!" The man gave her first aid, and sent Amos down the road to the next house to 'phone for an ambulance. Then as soon as Amos had 'phoned he came for us. I was out in the field husking corn. Your mother called me, and we hurried as fast as we could, but when we reached the crossroad Susan was already in the hospital."

"Good quick work," Chet commented. "I arrived a minute later, and the State Police were already there."

"What did they find?" Trudy held her breath for Chet's reply.

"Not much," Chet said tersely. "Just Susan's bike with a damaged front wheel, her shoes—they'd been jerked off her feet—and the glass from a headlight of the car that hit her. They gathered that up, of course. They've probably got it pieced together by now and can tell from it what make of car it was. That may help, but it isn't much to work on.

"Still, it's something," Chet continued as he saw how Trudy's spirits had dropped. "The State Police will notify all the garage and repair people in this section to report to them if anyone with that make of car comes in to have a headlight replaced. Ask them, too, to notice if there is a small dent in one of the front fenders. There almost always is one in a car that's struck a person," he explained.

"Is that all the police can do?" Trudy asked. It seemed so very very little to her.

"That's all at the moment," Chet answered gravely. "I wish there was more we could do, for until we locate the driver, aside from seeing that he gets his deserts for leaving Susan, we can't make any claim for damages."

Damages! At the word Trudy's spirits dropped still lower. Concerned with Susan's injuries, with her very chance for life, Trudy had not thought of this angle of the case, of the expense it involved, and how difficult it would be for her family to meet it. It seemed almost wicked to think of it now while Susan's life still hung in the balance, but she couldn't help it. The hospital, the private room, the special nurse, all absolutely essential at the moment, and perhaps for some time to come, she knew well how much these things cost. The little bank account, the nest egg, would have to go, and much more besides.

Suddenly Trudy blamed herself that her people were not in better financial shape. If she hadn't wanted such an expensive education, hadn't demanded it, she reproached herself, they wouldn't have found it half as hard to meet this emergency.

Still, that's not quite fair, Trudy's common sense told her. Her education was an asset, not a liability now. If she were working in a store, in an office, at a mill, she wouldn't have as large a salary with which to help the family, and of course she would help all she possibly could.

"Let's not speak of damages tonight." Mr. Wescott's voice had the sweetness of faith in it. "There will be a way. Instead let us thank our Heavenly Father that our little girl is alive."

Trudy did so with all her heart when she had gone up to her sloping-ceilinged room, and afterwards she slept better than she had thought she possibly could. She woke to find a square of sunshine on the whitewashed ceiling above her head. The day was bright, and surely it offered hope. "A broken pelvis and two fingers aren't so bad," she murmured, and remembering Dr. Kerr's advice, held to that thought.

Trudy went downstairs to find that her father had already gone to a neighbor's and telephoned the hospital for news of Susan. It was good. She had awakened refreshed and no new symptoms had developed. Trudy knew that her father would have liked to spend the day, as she and her mother would, mostly at the hospital and at Susan's bedside. However, this was one of the days when the factory had work for him, and the wages were important. A drop in the bucket, in one sense, in another they would mean that the family had just that much more with which to meet the emergency. So, quietly directing Trudy to give his little lamb his love and tell her he'd see her on his way home that evening, he took his lunch box and steered the old truck out of the drive.

Trudy and her mother hurried through the morning's work; then caught the eight-thirty bus and were at Susan's door by nine o'clock.

"Hello!" Susan caught sight of them almost before they saw her. She was flat on her back, but she held out her unin-jured hand. "Hello, Mummy. Trudy, what are you doing here?" she asked.

"Oh, Mummy 'phoned me you were in the hospital." Trudy giving her a gentle kiss, tried to be casual. "I just thought I'd come out and see how you were."

"I wish I was in your hospital. Then you could take care of me." Susan's ideas about Trudy's profession were some-times vague.

"No, the nurses have to do that."

"Well, I hope you can stay a long long while." Susan changed the subject. "Have they caught that fellow who hit me?"

"Oh, was it a man, Susan?" Trudy asked after another kiss.

"Yes. A man and a girl," Susan stated. "I heard the girl scream, just before everything turned red."

Trudy shuddered.

"Everything turned red, and it was a red car that hit me." Susan nodded her head as much as she could.

"Oh, then it'll be easy to find. There aren't so many red cars," Mrs. Wescott said soothingly, and answered Susan's original question. "No, they haven't caught the fellow, as you call him."

"But they will," Susan said confidently, and then, suddenly exhausted, closed her eyes.

She slept, or at least lay quiet most of the morning. It did not seem wise to question her further. After all, what more could she tell? The circumstances of the accident were apparently just as Chet and Mr. Wescott had deduced. Susan had turned into the side road to get the pine cones, had put them into the basket on her handlebars; then had come racing out onto the highway and the car had struck her almost before she realized one was coming. She hadn't known anything until she was in the ambulance and heard its bell clanging. At first she had thought it was her bicycle bell. She had tried to hold the handlebars steady and had found her fingers hurt; then everything was "sort of foggy" until this morning.

"She insists that the car that hit her was red," Trudy said

to Chet at noon. He came to take her and Mrs. Wescott to lunch.

"I'd discount that." Chet shook his head. "A blow to the head or jaw gives an impression of red, you know. How is Susan?"

"All right," Trudy said. She almost added, "so far," thinking of the very real possibility of injuries which might not become evident for even forty-eight hours yet. Her mother did not know of them, however, and it was only merciful not to alarm her.

"She was as bright as a button when we first went in this morning," Mrs. Wescott commented.

"A little too bright, maybe," Trudy said. "Probably the shock hadn't quite worn off." She changed the subject. "What steps will you take next, Chet, to locate the car and driver?"

"Well I, personally, can't do much as yet. The police are still looking for the car, of course. They've found from the pieces of the headlight lens that it's a De Soto."

That might help, but to Trudy it seemed very little, and thinking how few and slight the clues were she felt depressed. She hardly wanted her dessert, finished before her mother and Chet, and waited impatiently for them.

At last they crumpled their napkins, and Chet turned to Trudy. "One of the things I did think I'd do was run out and look over the scene of the accident again. Want to come with me?"

Trudy did and did not want to go. That morning in the bus, she and her mother had passed the spot with averted eyes. Still, she had a feeling that because of their love for Susan she and Chet would investigate the place more closely and painstakingly than even a trained state trooper. She also knew her mind would not be at rest until she had gone over the ground. So she said yes, and she and Chet drove away from the hospital at once, leaving Mrs. Wescott to come home with Mr. Wescott at supper time.

The day reminded Trudy of Thanksgiving. It was bright and still, also relatively warm for the time of year. Above the silhouettes of the December trees Pike's Peak showed its rounded dome and Trudy wondered with a pang how long it would be before Susan would race up its slope again. Poor little girl, she thought as she had so often, and Chet, reading her expression, said, as many people had:

"It might have been much worse."

Chet parked his car at the edge of the highway, and he and Trudy walked to the intersection on foot. Two things only showed there had been an accident there; the dark streaks on the concrete where the driver of the car had burned his tires in trying to avoid hitting Susan, and a scuffed area on the shoulder of the road where her bicycle had been flung by the force of the collision. The bicycle itself was gone. Trudy thought that her father had brought it home in his truck, but Chet said no, the police had taken it as evidence. As her father had told them, pine cones were scattered about, and Trudy picked up one with another sharp pang; the innocent present for her mother which indirectly had been the cause of so much trouble.

"I can't see a thing, and I have a pretty good eye for this

sort of set-up," Chet said. "As I told you, the police got the glass, Susan's shoes and the bicycle. There simply isn't anything else."

"Well, let's look along the gutter and the hedge on the side road anyhow," Trudy said, and Chet complied. Together they stooped and scrutinized the ground for thirty feet in each direction, brushing the leaves and an occasional weather-stained paper aside. At the end of the search, Trudy had to admit that there was nothing.

"Something might have been flung into the field." She looked over the fence to where the stubble of a wheat crop showed.

"That's a fact," Chet said good naturedly, yet with a skeptical undertone.

Solely to please her, Trudy knew, Chet squeezed himself between the strands of wire and searched a considerable area as conscientiously as she would have herself. He came back, flicking bits of stubble from his trouser legs with his handkerchief.

"Not a single thing," he said. "I'm sorry."

"Oh, dear." Trudy again looked about her, and suddenly the landscape took on a stubborn tone. We know, said the hedge, the woods, the fields. We know, and we won't tell.

CHAPTER VIII

"HELLO THERE!" Meta greeted Trudy on her return to the hospital two mornings later. "How's Susan?"

"Yes, how is she?" The entire staff, especially busy in preparation for the annual Christmas sale of articles made by the patients, the proceeds to be used to buy materials for the O.T. work, paused and turned toward her in sympathetic concern. "We've been so anxious about her."

"She's doing nicely, thanks." Trudy felt a warm glow to think they cared so much. "That is, she has a fractured pelvis, and two broken fingers on her left hand; but she hasn't developed any complications."

"And that's a great deal to be thankful for," Miss Compton said, with the feeling which she expressed only for a patient.

"Yes, indeed." Miss Swift's face lighted with her lovely smile; then grew serious. "When you think how some of the children in the wards have been smashed up by such an accident, it makes you shudder."

That was the way Trudy felt when she accompanied Meta around the wards an hour later. Here was a child whose mind had been affected by head injuries. Here was another who would never walk again. Here was one whose arms were paralyzed.

Yes, it could have been much much worse, Trudy thought, although she was haunted by a picture of a Susan whose morale had broken down, more from being closely confined to her bed than from actual pain. It did not make it any easier for Trudy to know that this was a typical reaction in children.

"Don't go! Don't go!" Susan had sobbed bitterly when Trudy left. "Take me home. I want to go home."

It wasn't pleasant to remember and in the succeeding days Trudy tried to turn her thoughts to other things, but did not succeed too well. A daily bulletin from her mother was both encouraging and discouraging. Dr. Billings said that Susan's physical condition was good, she was making satisfactory progress. On the other hand, Susan was restless and unhappy, and pleaded continually to go home.

"Because of her bad fingers," Mrs. Wescott wrote, "we haven't been able to arrange anything for her to do. I know an O.T. could, but there is none in this little hospital. Perhaps you can suggest something we could carry out."

Trudy wrote at once, outlining several projects which could be executed with one hand; a book for coloring clamped to the bed, a frame for finger weaving fastened in the same way, a storybook, a writing pad.

Oh, if she could only go herself and get Susan started on these things. She knew just how she would handle the little girl; get her mind off herself by telling her about the dollhouse which the patients at Hillhaven were making for the

Christmas sale; get Susan to laughing by asking what she thought Duze would like in his stocking, all the while skill-fully guiding Susan in the use of her uninjured hand.

When the week end came, the urge to go to Susan was almost unendurable, but Trudy felt she ought not to spend the money for the bus fare. She had sent her mother most of her last check, and was cutting her expenses wherever she could. On Saturday afternoon she went into the drugstore for a toothbrush, and as she turned away, wishing that she might work during the entire week end rather than face its idle hours, she almost collided with Donald Kerr.

"Hello, there," he said. "I've been hoping I'd see you. How's your sister?" As he spoke he guided Trudy toward one of the booths. "One chocolate, one malted," he directed the waiter, and Trudy was happy to accept.

It wasn't the chocolate, it was his company, she thought as she answered his question, described Susan's fracture, and spoke of her low spirits.

"Poor child." Donald Kerr's eyes were warm with sympathy. "She has a long stretch ahead of her. I'd say that type of fracture might take eight to ten weeks in the hospital." He seemed to think, as Trudy did, of how much all that hospital care would cost. "Can you collect damages from the person who hit her?" he asked.

"No, that's the worst of it." Trudy described the circumstances of the accident, the hit-run driver. "Chet Fielding—he's a lawyer friend of ours—is attending to things for us and he hasn't come on a single clue as yet."

"Tough luck." Donald Kerr had finished his malted, but

he seemed in no hurry to go. Instead he leaned back as much as the booth would allow. "What are you doing tomorrow?" he asked.

At his words Trudy's spirits rose. To have something to do, a date to help her over this terrible week end would be—well, simply heaven!

"Nothing special." She made her voice as casual as she could. "I wanted to go home, but—it didn't seem best."

"I haven't anything to do either, for I thought until about an hour ago that I was to be on duty. I'm not, though, so what would you say to a concert at the Academy? I think I can get tickets, but if I can't there's the movies to fall back on. I'd like to run you out to see your sister," he added, "but I haven't a car, so that's that, and nothing to be done about it."

"Yes, I know, and either a movie or a concert will be lovely." Trudy felt as if a weight had fallen off her spirits. Now she had something to look forward to. "I hope you know you've helped me no end," she said. "I had the blues."

"And no wonder. Well, maybe I had the blues myself." Don smiled. "We all get 'em now and then."

Now what could Donald Kerr have been blue about, Trudy speculated as she dressed for the concert next day. She knew that doctors felt very bad when they lost a patient. It might have been that. Or was it some personal affair? For of course he had personal affairs. Maybe he had financial troubles, a family like hers which had strained its resource to help him get his education. Maybe, worse still, he had someone dependent on him. Not a wife—she knew he wasn't married—but perhaps a widowed mother, a younger brother. Aside from the fact that he was single, and was country bred like herself, she knew almost nothing about him.

The concert was pure joy, a program of popular classics which Trudy, who had little knowledge of music, could understand. It was wonderfully pleasant to sit by Donald Kerr and listen to melodies which carried her off to happy countries where little girls didn't have automobile accidents and fractured bones. She came back to earth with rather a bump when the program ended. Now, after the brief bus trip back to her rooming house she would be faced with a lonely dinner and an empty evening. Of course she could write to Susan—

"How about a bit of nourishment?" Donald Kerr interrupted her thoughts. With no apologies, he took her to an inexpensive little place with checkered tablecloths and heavy earthenware. "The food's good," he said, and over lamb chops and French frys they grew better acquainted. Don told her about his Ohio boyhood, his setting his dog's leg when he was just a boy, and his subsequent ambition to be a doctor. He showed her snapshots of his mother and father, kind-looking people like himself; then Trudy in turn told him about her life at home on the farm, and brought out the snap of Susan which she always carried.

"She's our darling," she said, and Don nodded.

"I don't wonder you're all broken up over her. Look at those beautiful eyes."

Susan's eyes haunted Trudy constantly during the two weeks which, for the time being, completed her work on the wards. She felt that she had not done too well, for she had been distrait and depressed. However, Meta, who was responsible for the work and was always candid about shortcomings, had made no comment, so Trudy judged that her performance must have been passable. She realized that, despite her preoccupation, the ward work had helped her a great deal. In approaching so many patients, one after another, she had gained more ease and tact. She did not hesitate so often for an opening word now, and found it less difficult to establish a pleasant relationship with her patients. As this was one of the therapist's chief goals, she knew that she had made a distinct advance.

Encouraged by her progress, Trudy felt so light hearted on the morning of her return to the shop that for the first time since Susan's accident, she hummed a tune. She felt a little set back when Miss Compton told her that she herself would take over Emily Lansing while Miss Blaine did her stretch of ward work. On the other hand, Trudy was consoled by the fact that a new patient, a Mr. Tobin, was being assigned to her. His card was on Miss Swift's desk, Miss Compton said. Miss Wescott had better read it at once; then run down and look up his history and muscle chart, for he would come to the shop at about ten.

Cheerfully Trudy did as she was directed. The case was one of arthritis, of several years' standing. "Disability—reduced degree of flexion of wrist, fingers and elbow of right hand, of fingers and wrist of left hand."

Trudy's trained mind suggested the treatment. Weaving would be one of the best exercises for that. Second best, perhaps, if the patient's hands were pretty painful and the skin tender as it so often was in arthritics, would be light carpenter work of some sort. Trudy hoped she could persuade her patient to do a bit of weaving. Men didn't always take kindly to it, but with her new skill perhaps she could inveigle this Mr. Tobin into doing it. Not wishing to keep him waiting, Trudy made a few notes and ran back to the shop.

She entered its door, humming her tune again, and was confronted by Old Nick.

Old Nick, the pest of the ward! He and Mr. Tobin were one and the same!

Completely nonplussed, she stared at him while he glared at her. Nick's whole attitude was truculent and there was fire in his eye.

"The doctor ordered me to come up here, and here I am," he snapped. "But don't you give me no women's work. I won't do it! I warn y'!"

Trudy could have laughed aloud at her hope that she could persuade this patient to do some weaving. She dropped the idea as quickly as if it had burned her. At the same time she blessed the sound judgment which had led Miss Swift to relegate the sewing machine, the dollhouse and other articles of feminine employ to the far end of the room; and instead place the very masculine-looking work bench prominently in front of the entrance door. In this position it could not fail to impress just such patients as Old Nick.

Trudy saw his eyes turn toward the bench, and said at

once, "How about a bit of carpentry—er, Nick? Perhaps you'd like to make a cigar box."

There, she congratulated herself. That was finesse.

"Cigar box is as good as anything." Nick was unimpressed. His whole look said, Get this over with, and let me get the dickens out of here.

"Come over to the bench and I'll show you some models." Trudy led the way and Nick followed reluctantly. She leafed through a book of patterns and it was really she who made the selection, for his eyes barely followed hers.

"Do you—" Trudy broke off the question. No use to ask a patient of Nick's type if he had much pain. He'd say yes, of course, in the hope that it might get him out of doing any work. A chronic case like his wasn't apt to have a great deal, Trudy speculated, yet he might suffer from what her profession, as well as the medical, called psychological pain. Arthritics as a group had an overwhelming dread of pain and often imagined it where it did not exist. It was just as real to them, poor things, Trudy said to herself, and with this thought in mind used the greatest gentleness and care in examining Nick's hands and arms.

Nevertheless Old Nick flinched and ouched until she was almost at a standstill. She worked slower and slower with the arthrometer, an instrument with one movable arm like a compass, used in measuring the degree of motion of which a joint was capable. As Nick bent his right elbow under her direction so that she might measure it, he let out the worst yelp of all. It caused everyone in the shop to turn his head, and Trudy felt greatly embarrassed.

Was Nick's distress real? Was it psychological? His card had not said, and Trudy, not knowing her patient well, had no way of determining. Her examination had shown her that his skin was like tissue paper, and there was little strength in his fingers and wrists. He would have to begin with the thinnest plywood, and his work would have to be carefully graded in order not to overtax him. You can do an arthritic more harm in two minutes than can be undone in two months, she remembered a precept that had been drilled into her during her training.

Perhaps Nick had better begin by doing a bit of sandpapering, the lightest work of all. Trudy built up a sanding block with some pieces of sponge rubber to fit his hand.

It was a long process, all this examination, preparation of the tool and planning of work. Trudy, careful and methodical, both by nature and training, was capable of no short cuts or quick decisions, and Nick's moanings and groanings held her back.

A glance at the clock showed her that it was almost lunch time, and a sixth sense told her that it would be better to have Nick do some actual bit of work before he went back to the ward. Otherwise he would undoubtedly tell his fellow patients with infinite scorn, "Nothing but women and a lot of shilly-shallying up there."

As quickly as she could Trudy located a piece of thin plywood approximately the size of the box bottom and fastened it in the vise.

"There. Now the sandpaper, Nick."

Whether his distress was real or imaginary, Trudy's heart

went out to the old man when she saw him flinch as he grasped the sanding block. Nevertheless it had to be done, and she put out her hand to help him.

"Don't touch my elbow!"

"No, I won't." Trudy knew well the tenderness of arthritic joints. She put her hand under his forearm and supported it.

It was all an insult, Old Nick's eyes said as they met hers in helpless rage.

"Just one side of the plywood, Nick." Trudy knew that a minute's work could not harm him. "Just one side, and we'll call it a day."

Fine, said Old Nick's glare, and I wish there'd never be another one! In just as great a rage as when he had come he stalked to the elevator.

"Whew!" Trudy expelled a long breath of relief as she turned to help the staff close the shop for the lunch hour. "That was certainly something."

"Yes, I noticed you had drawn our prize porcupine." Meta laughed. "I thought you did very well. I expected the air to be full of flying quills, but it wasn't."

Trudy thought herself that she had done well. In fact, she felt triumphant. She'd had a cantankerous patient, perhaps the most difficult one she had ever handled, and while she had not made a dent in his resistance, she had succeeded in getting him to work on an actual project.

One of Miss Swift's feathers in my cap, she thought, and was so happy that she again hummed a tune as she entered the shop next morning. She had put her first patient, a man with weak wrists, to work caning a chair when Miss Compton spoke to her.

"Miss Wescott, you don't need to be with Mr. Leeds every moment. Take on this little girl of Miss Blaine's. She doesn't need constant attention either. I have to send Miss Blaine down to the X-ray department."

"Surely." Trudy gave a glance to see that Mr. Leeds was all right; then turned to the twelve-year-old girl who was seated at a foot loom. Miss Blaine stood beside her.

"Alice is making her very own rug." She smiled and motioned toward the loom on which a gay rag rug was half completed. "She paid for the materials and it's to be hers when it's finished. She has a stiff elbow," Miss Blaine indicated the right arm. "Be back as soon as I can." She smiled again; then hurried to the elevator.

Trudy understood at once. Moving the loom's beater forward and back would compel Alice to extend the elbow and thus stretch and exercise it.

"How did you hurt it?" she asked as Alice began weaving.

"Oh, I fell on my roller skates. It didn't take a second to smash myself up"—she laughed—"but it's taking weeks to get me well again."

"That's the way it goes." Trudy nodded; then turned because Mr. Leeds asked her to untangle one of his strands for him. A minute later she heard Miss Compton's voice behind her, sharp as a razor's edge.

"Miss Wescott, you have left this child without seeing that

she is properly prepared to work. She is leaning forward and using a shoulder movement instead of an elbow movement to operate the beater. She should have been tied in her chair so that she could not use her shoulder."

"Oh, Miss Blaine didn't tell me," Trudy said before she thought.

"She shouldn't have needed to tell you," Miss Compton said tartly. "You should have known for yourself."

Yes, that was true. Trudy felt abashed. Of course she knew. The fact was so simple it was fundamental. She felt an impulse to say that, attending to two patients at once, she had not thought of it, but that was no excuse.

"Get a wide strip of goods, pass it around Alice's body and through the chair back. Tie it," Miss Compton commanded, and Trudy was glad to slip away for a moment and go to the cupboard for the material.

"Wasn't she cross," Alice said candidly when Trudy came back. "I s'pose I ought to have told you to tie me, but you see I hate it. It makes me feel like a baby in a high chair "

With difficulty, Trudy smiled. She was ablaze with indignation. The correction itself was justified; yes, she tried to be fair, but the way it was done! That was all wrong. Corrected before a patient! It had nearly happened once before, that first day with Emily, when Emily got so tired, but this was the real thing.

"It was lucky it was before Alice, a child. She didn't think anything about it," Trudy burst out to Meta at noon. She had been thankful that after lunch Meta had suggested they go to a little park at the river's edge to get away from the hospital's atmosphere for a few minutes.

"Suppose it had been Old Nick," Trudy went on. "I'd probably never be able to do anything with him again."

"No, it was all wrong," Meta agreed, "and I'm just as burned up about it as you are."

The sympathy in her voice made Trudy's tears come, and for a moment the winter landscape was as blurred as if she saw it through frost-patterned glass.

"I don't know a thing to do about it, Trude," Meta went on a little sadly. "It's just a part of the toughness of working with Miss Compton. And of course you were at fault."

"Yes, I admit that," Trudy agreed. "Wasn't I dumb not to fasten Alice in the right posture! I know perfectly well that even a grownup will unconsciously use a good joint instead of a lame one I don't see why I didn't think of it."

"That comes with experience," Meta said wisely. "You have to have patience with yourself as well as with Miss Compton, Trude. And now, come on," she added as the clock on the nearby tower whirred before striking one. "Pack up your troubles and smile, and remember that Miss Swift's really our boss."

Trudy was glad Miss Swift took charge of the shop that afternoon and she did not have to confront Miss Compton until she felt steadier.

"You're to work with Emily Lansing." Miss Swift smiled at Trudy and at once she felt more cheerful.

"Emily asked for you. I heard her," Meta said out of the

corner of her mouth as Trudy passed her on her way to Emily's chair.

Oh, that was fine. Emily wanted her, preferred her. It off-set her error of the morning, and meant a bit of professional success. Trudy's step was light as she approached Emily.

"Hello! I'm so glad you're back at shopwork!" Emily held out her normal hand and smiled radiantly. "I've missed you."

"And I've missed you." Trudy returned the pressure of Emily's fingers warmly; then examined her hand and arm. The muscles were less flaccid. She could feel a stronger contraction in them "How you've improved!" she said. "And your weaving! It's almost done."

"It had better be. Christmas is just around the corner." Emily's blue eyes grew shadowed as they had when she mentioned Thanksgiving several weeks before. "Are you going home?"

"Yes, I'm going home." Trudy had resolved that despite the expense she would go. "I simply must see my sister," she said.

"Of course you must. My husband—he's in South America, you know—wrote for a while about coming home, but decided that he'd better not. Flying would be too expensive and boats take too long. I know you'll think it strange"—Emily's eyes met Trudy's in a look which begged for understanding—"but I'm glad he's not coming." Her gaze dropped to her half-helpless hand. "I must be better, a lot better before he comes home."

Did Emily think, too, of the motionless limbs, the motionless feet, concealed by the blankets of her wheel chair? Undoubtedly she did.

Torn with pity, Trudy knew that she faced a tragedy far greater than Susan's, perhaps as great a one as she would meet in her whole life.

CHAPTER IX

"Hail to thee, O Februeer,
Lemon month of all the year!"

TRUDY intoned as Chet's roadster slipped and splashed through the slush on the highway. She had gone home for Christmas, but now she was going again on an equally gala occasion. Susan had been discharged from the hospital three days before and was reported to be progressing nicely.

"Susan's her old self," Chet commented. "Full of—er—pep. Your mother's going to have a job of it, keeping her in bed."

"Yes, I suppose she'll have to stay there for two weeks or so yet," Trudy said. "That's the usual time with a broken pelvis."

"She's improved a lot since Christmas." Chet, who had been very quiet and done no blarneying while Susan's condition was serious, was his old self again. "Glad to see me, sweetheart? You are my sweetheart, aren't you?" he asked as he maneuvered the car around a curve.

Trudy ignored his query. "Suze should be a lot better," she said, and remembered the holiday which had been far pleasanter than anyone had expected, both because Susan's condition was satisfactory and because her morale had improved. She had been very happy with the inexpensive presents for which Trudy, her mother and their friends had scoured the five and dime shops.

All the presents had been inexpensive except one, a gorgeous doll with trousseau complete which had arrived at the hospital by mail, in a typewritten wrapper and without the address of the sender. The whole family had wondered who might have sent it.

"Maybe your rich ol' Aunt 'Lizabeth, Daddy," Susan had said to her father.

"Maybe, except that she moved to California when I was knee-high to a grasshopper and nobody's ever heard from her since," he said drily.

It might have been a mistake, the doll might have been meant for some other little girl, Trudy and her mother had thought, yet had hoped not, for to take the doll away from Susan would have been a major operation. But no, the name on the wrapper was clear, Miss Susan Wescott. They all grew tired of speculating after a while, and decided that probably some sympathetic person who had read of Susan's accident in the paper had sent it. Chet suggested that they name the doll Mystery; Susan agreed and they let it go at that.

"Here we are." Chet slowed the car to a snail's pace before he made the turn into the drive. "I don't know whether she'll climb the slope through this slush, and the question also remains, if I get her up, can I get her back?"

"Leave her here." Trudy jumped happily to the slushy

ground, slipped, but recovered herself and raced toward the house.

"Hey, let me help you," Chet called, but she reached the door long before him.

"Hello, darling!" She gave her mother a close yet hasty hug. "Where is she?" she asked.

"In the dining room where it's warm and I can take care of her easily. Also where she can see what's going on. That's important, for she has to boss things, you know," Mrs. Wescott said with a laugh, and Trudy found Susan ensconced on her own little bed between the sunny windows and the big coal-burning stove. She saw at once that Susan was infinitely better, healthier in color and stronger. Her injured fingers were practically well. Witness that in them she held up her doll.

"Her husband's come," she said after a perfunctory hug and kiss. "Look, Trudy." She poked another doll in Trudy's face. "Here he is."

"Her husband?" Trudy felt completely bewildered for a moment; then saw that the second doll was dressed in boy's clothing and was an exact counterpart of Mystery, the Christmas doll.

"She's Mrs. Mystery now, and he's Mr. Mystery," Susan said complacently. "They're very fond of each other." She clanked the dolls' two hard noses together in a would-be kiss.

"What's going on here?" Chet had followed Trudy into the room. He stared at the boy doll with eyes that Trudy thought bulged a little. "What's this?"

"Mr. Mystery," Susan said again, and Chet threw down his hat.

"Well, for gosh' sake. Now where did he come from?"

"Same place as the other one," Mrs. Wescott said. "Type-written address, sender not named." She brought the wrapping paper and they scrutinized it together. When they had finished, Chet's professional look came over his face.

"Girls," he said, "this is a clue, a clue to who struck Susan. I believe the dolls were sent by the person who did it." He sat down in front of the stove and sank into deep thought, and Trudy, although she was agog, compelled herself to keep quiet until he came to some conclusion. She brought a chair to the edge of Susan's bed and stroked her hair. Susan, too, was excited, but Trudy motioned her not to speak, and after a moment Chet came out of his abstraction.

"Yes, sir. I believe the person who hit Susan isn't far from here. He or she keeps track of the case by means of the news-papers. He or she—"

"Sending dolls sounds like a woman's work to me," Mrs. Wescott commented, and Chet nodded.

"Well, then, *she* sent Mrs. Mystery as a Christmas present; then she saw in the paper that Susan was discharged from the hospital and sent her Mr. Mystery, as a coming-home present. She—"

"It was a he that hit me," Susan interrupted and they all laughed.

"Well, whatever the sex, I'm going to follow this up, right away. If you'll excuse me"—Chet picked up his hat—"I'm going back to town to the hospital and see if I can find out anything further there. This gives me a new slant on things. I'll be back in an hour," he said over his shoulder.

"Do you suppose he can find out anything?" Mrs. Wescott asked as they heard the outer door slam. "He's kept in touch with the police, and watched everything so closely all along."

"I haven't the slightest idea. We can only hope. I suppose you've searched the doll's clothes." Trudy turned to where Mr. Mystery sprawled beside his wife on Susan's pillow.

"Oh, yes, we've been over them forty 'leven times," Susan answered for her mother. "There isn't a speck of writing or anything."

Chet was later than he had thought he'd be. Dusk had set in and Mr. Wescott had come from work before he turned into the drive again.

"I think we're on the track of something." He came through the kitchen door and into the dining room where Mrs. Wescott was giving Susan her supper.

"You are?" Susan's eyes were like stars in the lamplight. "Aren't I right, it's a he?" she asked.

"I'm not close enough to tell that yet," Chet answered and joined in the general laugh. "But what I found seems to fit together. I got hold of the hospital's 'phone operators and asked them if they remembered anyone in particular who 'phoned concerning Susan. At first we didn't get anywhere. They said a lot of people 'phoned, some of them several times. Some people left their names, some didn't, and that was that. Then I asked if anyone who seemed especially nervous, especially anxious, and, well, sort of secretive, had 'phoned several times. With that one of the girls said, 'Why, yes, you might say so. There was one person who 'phoned—a woman—who always ended by saying, "You're sure she's all right?" I got sort of tired of it, and that's why I remember,' the operator said, 'her taking up my time with that kind of thing when I'd told her exactly what I had been instructed to say.'

"I asked her if the calls were locals or out of town," Chet went on, "and she said sometimes they were the one, sometimes the other. But that's no matter. My original idea holds good; whoever hit Susan isn't far off and keeps track of the case; has a conscience of a sort, you might say."

"A fine sort," Trudy commented bitterly.

"Right you are," Chet said. "Of course in addition the person may want to keep track of what charges might be brought against him or her. I mean that if Susan had been fatally injured the charges would have been very serious."

Trudy understood that.

"You can collect damages from him when you find him, can't you, even if you don't locate him right away?" she asked.

In her own mind she did not like to admit the possibility of not finding the hit-run driver at all, for this matter of damages was becoming important. Although the hospital had allowed the family to take advantage of its system of deferred payments, there had been many extras which required cash, and the bank balance which they had built up so happily was rapidly being depleted.

"You can collect damages, can't you?" she asked again.

"That's a tough one to answer," Chet said thoughtfully. "It depends on information that I don't have. First, is the driver insured? Second, if he isn't insured, has he means of his own on which we might collect? Third, if he *is* insured, has he notified his insurance company about the accident? There's a clause in every policy that says the assured agrees to report any accident promptly. If he does not, after a certain length of time the insurance company is not responsible. And," Chet added, "you can bet a hit-run driver isn't reporting, especially as the insurance company is forced by law to notify the police or become accessory to the crime."

Oh, dear. Trudy said it to herself, but her depression must have shown on her face.

"Let's skip it," Chet said, "and go out for supper and a bit of dancing. How about Johnny's Place? That's near and you like it."

"It's all right with me." Trudy was glad to go.

She and Chet slipped and slid down the drive to the car; then Chet drove cautiously and soon the lights of Johnny's shone across the snow.

"Come along, gal." The orchestra was playing as they stepped in, and Chet embarrassed Trudy for a moment by whirling her onto the floor, coat, hat, boots and all, while the guests and waiters laughed. However, they soon had a table and were dancing properly; and as Chet guided her smoothly through the steps of a rhumba Trudy forgot herself in pure pleasure. No one danced like Chet, she thought as the music ended, and they sat down again at their table.

Chet ordered, not supper but a table d'hôte dinner and they ate it leisurely, dancing between the courses. As they sipped their coffee he asked, "How are things going at the hospital?"

"Oh, fine," Trudy said automatically. A tinge of her depression returned. There had been another unpleasantness with Miss Compton. Trudy had moved a patient from the loom where she had been directed to work with her, because it was short of warp, and Miss Compton, without making any inquiries had scolded sharply. Obey orders or else! It had been a bad time. Involuntarily Trudy sighed, and Chet, always astute, leaned forward and took her hand.

"As bad as that?" There was a tone in his voice Trudy had never heard before. "Why don't you drop it all?"

"Drop it all? You mean give up my job?" Trudy looked at him in bewilderment. "I can't."

"Sure, you can. Marry me," Chet said. "I can afford to get married now, and I love you."

Again Trudy looked at him, this time with incredulity. Chet, the blarneyer, who had girls by the dozen, called them darling, sweetheart, whatever came into his head, was asking her to marry him, said he loved her. Did he mean it?

"You don't believe me, do you?" Chet's laugh was a little forced. "I've fooled around so much, I don't wonder. But I do mean it. I've known for a long time there was nobody for me but you."

Tell that to—Trudy never spoke the words. Suddenly she believed Chet. There was no mistaking the sincerity of his voice. She was moved, touched, but not for a moment had she any doubt about her own feeling. She would never know anything but liking for him.

"I'm sorry," she said in a low voice, "but the answer's no."

"Well, maybe you'll change. I'm willing to wait." The

music began again and Chet drew Trudy to her feet. "Come on, let's dance."

As they twirled and turned about the floor he was his old teasing self again. "You're taking an awful chance not saying yes, sweetheart. One of those other girls'll get me. Then you'll be sorry." He sang a snatch of a popular song, "You'll shed a bucket of tears."

Trudy, not so volatile, could think of no gay rejoinder. However, it wasn't necessary, for Chet rattled along about this and that, and at the end of the dance suggested they go.

"If this slush is freezing, it's going to be some drive, taking you home and getting myself back to town.

"You understand, I'm not going to give this up on one try." Chet squeezed Trudy's arm as he helped her across the slippery ground to the farmhouse. "Lots of gals change their minds and I'm quite a persuader."

"I'm sorry, but it's no use, Chet," Trudy said. As she stepped into the warm kitchen, she added, although Chet had turned away and she supposed she had no audience, "I hope he believes me."

"Believes what?"

Trudy found her mother sitting beside the stove. "Susan wanted a drink," Mrs. Wescott explained, "and I felt chilly after I got it, so I thought I'd warm myself before I went back through the cold hall to bed. Believes what?" she asked again.

"Believes I don't care for him." Trudy spoke a little incredulously. The whole thing seemed like a dream now. "Chet proposed to me this evening."

"He did?" Mrs. Wescott, too, was incredulous. "I didn't think he was the marrying kind."

"Neither did I."

"You said no?"

Trudy nodded, and there was a long moment of silence, broken only by the ticking of the old clock and a whimper from Duzenbury, deep in dog dreams, behind the stove.

"Who's not the marrying kind?" Trudy and her mother jumped as a voice piped from the dining room. They had forgotten Susan.

"Little pitchers," Mrs. Wescott said, and Trudy thought how awkward it would be if the news of Chet's proposal got about Knolton.

"Didn't you want me to know, Trudy?" Susan's voice came with unexpected sweetness. "I won't tell. Cross my heart and hope to die if I do."

CHAPTER X

"WANT TO TAKE the nursery this afternoon, Trudy? You like little kids." Meta Tripp and Trudy were sitting in the park by the river's edge as they so often did in their noon hour. The hills on the far shore were growing green now, and an April breeze, soft as a kitten's paw, touched their faces.

"Hmm," Trudy answered absently. She was thinking about Chet. He certainly didn't give up easily, and had meant it when he said, "I'm a great persuader." Since that night of his proposal he had written several times, once indignantly because Trudy had not let him know she was coming home for a week end, and only this morning a letter had come from his asking her to go to a Kiwanis Club dance with him.

Of course she wouldn't go. If you turned a fellow down, you turned him down. If you didn't care for him, you didn't go around with him or give him any encouragement. It hardly seemed fair even to allow him to continue with Susan's case. However, Trudy knew that Chet's kindheartedness would make him want to, and it did seem as if that matter could be put on a business basis. Trudy and her parents had talked it over and agreed that if Chet was successful in solving the case and collecting damages they would pay him in full at the time of settlement. If he was not successful they would pay him in installments as they had the hospital. That should make it right.

Trudy came back from her thoughts to realize that Meta was laughing at her. "I don't believe you know what I asked you," she said. "And I'll bet I know what you were thinking about," she added, for Trudy had told her about Chet's proposal.

Trudy ignored Meta's second remark. "Yes, I do know what you asked," she affirmed. "You asked me if I wanted to take the nursery this afternoon, and the answer is yes."

"O.K. Then it's you for the surrey with the fringe round the top." Meta referred to the tall old cabinet phonograph which had been set on wheels and which the O.T.'s trundled wherever there was need of music.

The two girls, having completed their three months' round in the shop, were back on ward work. A few weeks earlier Trudy would have been glad to get away from the shop because of the friction with Miss Compton. Things had been better of late, however. Probably Miss Swift had noticed the tension, for she had taken over more of the shopwork and directed the staff herself. Of course it could have been that at the moment Miss Swift was not so busy with administrative matters and had more time for the shop. On the other hand, so good a director as Miss Swift must always have been keenly aware of what was going on in her department, of its emotional make-up. Perhaps there had been some tactful guidance of Miss Compton as well, for the assistant's attitude seemed to have modified considerably.

Altogether Trudy had been a little sorry to leave the shop for the wards, not only because she preferred the shopwork, but because it meant she would be separated from Emily Lansing and Janet King. Both patients were continuing their good progress and Donald Kerr had told Trudy at the last meeting of the foursome that he was greatly pleased.

Trudy had no regrets at leaving Old Nick. He was the same cantankerous old codger, and not an inch had she advanced in conquering his snarling resistance. On the other hand she felt what she called "unholy glee" that he had been handed over to Miss Blaine in her absence. Let that smooth person make little or much of him.

As to the ward work itself, familiarity with the hospital and its routine made her feel more at home in it on this, her second round. A speaking acquaintance with the nurses helped, too. Of course there was a Miss Blanchard here and there, but there were also Miss Ericsons. In any case, Trudy's increasing realization of how much the O.T. work meant to the patients, and of the fact that it was a legitimate part of hospital routine stiffened her self-confidence. She moved about the wards with ease now, and as Miss Duncan, in charge in the nursery, was especially pleasant, quite looked forward to an afternoon there.

"Time to hit the trail," Meta said as the clock in the church tower gave its familiar whirr.

"So it is." The two girls sauntered through the warm mild air back to the hospital.

As soon as the hospital's afternoon rest period was over, Trudy collected the phonograph, the student who was to help her, and a hamper of simple games and toys; then made her way to the long bright room which housed the one-and-a-half to five-year-olds.

Poor little souls, she thought as she entered the door. Here, as everywhere in the hospital, were the great casts which, while their objective was cure, locked their occupants in rigid white prisons. How anyone who suffered from claustrophobia, the dread of being confined, could stand them! Well, perhaps little children didn't suffer from it. However, Trudy knew that some of the older patients did, and went through periods of terror so severe that they felt faint and nauseated when they first found themselves encased in these unyielding forms.

A number of the children were sheathed in casts which began at their waists and extended down their thighs, spreading their legs in a gentle V. These were the cases of congenital dislocation of the hip. Pitiful, Trudy thought. For no known reason the hip socket was too shallow in these children and the surgeons tried to build it out by means of bone grafting. When they failed, as they did occasionally—well an O.T. mustn't dwell on that angle, she told herself sternly.

"Oh, here you are," a pleasant voice said, and Miss Duncan came toward her. "The children have been asking, 'When will she come? When will she come?' "

"Yes, yes!" Sweet high voices filled the room. "We want to sing *London Bridge! They're Changing the Guard! Farmer in the Dell!*"

"*Farmer in the Dell?*" Trudy put on the well-worn record, and she and the student sang, clapping their hands to the rhythm. The children clapped and sang, too; and oh, Trudy thought, this was one of the times when you saw at once the good you did. The children's faces glowed, their little hands came together in pure delight and the ones whose disabilities allowed them to sit up in bed, bounced up and down.

Moving unobtrusively about on small duties Miss Duncan smiled at their happiness. What a pleasant atmosphere. You almost forgot you were in a hospital, Trudy thought. She and the student distributed gay blocks, wooden beads to be strung on shoelaces, picture books and little games. and there was more joy.

Since she was in charge, Trudy kept an eye on everything Looking across the ward after a time, she realized suddenly that all was not well. The student had given an active little girl crayon and paper; then had turned to help another child, and the little girl, left to herself, instead of coloring her paper was drawing great zigzags on her sheet.

Oh, dear, just when things were going so beautifully! Trudy dashed across the room. "On the paper, sweetie," she directed the child; then motioned to the student to return to her bedside. "We aren't supposed to leave a patient with crayons," she reprimanded her as gently as she could, and the girl, her voice shallow with fright, said:

"Yes, I know. I forgot for a moment."

That's just how I would have felt not so very long ago, and could again—Trudy thought of Miss Blanchard. "I'll tell the nurse," she said, and the student looked at her with eyes that were moist with gratitude.

Pleasant though the nurse was, Trudy approached her with some trepidation. "Accident, Miss Duncan. I'm afraid we forgot," she said and showed her the ruined sheet.

"Let the laundry worry about it." The nurse was calm and Trudy blessed her luck that it was not Miss Blanchard.

After a time the children tired. Some grew noisy and restless and flung their blocks to the floor. Others dropped the toys and lay back on their pillows. The baby of the group, a two-year-old who was lying on his face in his cast, put his head down on his chubby hands and frankly went to sleep.

Trudy looked at the clock. Its hands stood at four. "Time to go," she said, and she and the student collected the toys, counting each set of blocks, each string of beads, so that no stray article should be left behind.

"Good-bye." Trudy guided the old phonograph to the door.

"Good-bye!" Some voices shouted while others murmured sleepily.

"Good-bye," Miss Duncan said gratefully. "You do us so much good."

"We really do," Trudy commented to the student as they went down the corridor. "They tell me that the children were very dull and listless before this work was begun. Almost like a mental retardation.

"Yes, I guess children just have to play," the student answered.

"Have to is it," Trudy said and was reminded of Susan. In fact Susan had been in her thoughts all afternoon. One little yellow head in the nursery had looked so much as Susan had at her age.

Poor Suze. Trudy was absent-minded as she and the student returned to the shop and put away their paraphernalia. Susan had made a fair recovery, but as yet had been unable to go back to school. She had tried once, but her accident had left her both weak and lame. There had been considerable contusion, bruising of the muscles of one thigh, and the ride to school was too much for her, aside from the fact that she became overtired. Susan followed the lessons at home, but she missed the other children and all the fun.

Yes, Susan was bored, Trudy thought, although she had arranged plenty of diversional work for her, and some exercises for the affected leg as prescribed by Dr. Billings. On a week-end visit which, despite the financial stringency, she had made in March because Susan was so depressed, Trudy and her father had rigged Susan's old bicycle on a stationary platform. Susan was supposed to mount it and turn its pedals several times a day, thus exercising the weakened muscles of her thigh.

Another device was to arrange the farm grindstone so that Susan could turn it. Mr. Wescott had taken off the handle and arranged a foot treadle instead. Trudy had measured Susan, and he had built a stool just the right height to stretch the tight muscles of Susan's thigh as she sat and worked the treadle.

The little girl did enjoy this exercise. "I'm really helping, aren't I?" she asked each time she turned the stone while Mr. Westcott sharpened his tools.

"She wears her daddy out," Mrs. Wescott wrote later. "She wants to turn the stone all day, and besides, there's nothing left to sharpen."

Well, that was one bright spot, but the rest of the picture was pretty gray, not only Susan's low spirits, but the fact that after four months she was still lame. Trudy was glad that Easter was near and she would soon see for herself how Susan was getting along. Expense or no expense, she must do that. Suppose, later on, it should develop that the child was permanently disabled. Trudy, with her professional knowledge, would know that Susan might have exercised too much instead of not enough. She needed supervision, and no matter what the cost, Trudy must give it.

When the time came, the expense was not as great as Trudy anticipated. One evening a week before Easter, Meta came to Trudy's room all agog. "What think?" She flung herself on Trudy's couch. Then, too excited to relax, sat up abruptly. "I just saw Sam Bradford."

"As if you didn't every day in the week!" Trudy laughed. "What's so unusual about that?"

"Hold the sarcasm." Meta herself laughed. "You're in on this."

"I? How?" Trudy simulated complete bewilderment.

"Well, it's this-a-way." Meta settled herself among the pillows. "Sam's borrowed his brother's car and he's going to take me home for Easter. I told you ages ago that we come from the same town. I looked it up on the map and your place is only about thirty miles out of the way, a mere nothing." Meta waved her arm and swept the miles aside as if they were inches. "So! Sam's going to take you home. And! As Don Kerr's going home with him for the holiday, the foursome's complete, isn't it? *Oh, frabjous day. Caloo, callay,* Come soon and take us on our way!" Meta improvised.

With her long upper lip, and her rolling eye, she was so irresistibly funny that Trudy burst into peals of laughter. Meta joined her and they laughed until they were almost helpless.

"It *will* be a frabjous day for sure," Trudy said when they had quieted down. She thought what Meta had been too tactful to say, that the ride home would cut her traveling expenses in half. Then, too, coming home with friends would bridge what she thought might be an awkward situation with Chet. He would expect that she would come for Easter, would undoubtedly try to make a date to bring her home from Knolton, and was entirely capable of settling himself at the terminal and meeting every bus until she arrived, if she said no. Chet was being very persistent. Trudy thought it might be due in part to the conceit that sometimes filled him. He just couldn't believe anyone would turn Chet Fielding down. In any case, if he kept on, it could be annoying.

As soon as Meta had gone, Trudy sat down to write to her mother. Could she please have a nice afternoon snack ready —some open-faced sandwiches, a crabmeat salad, something like that, she suggested, thinking that Meta, Sam and Don

might not care for the heavier meal her mother would be apt
to provide.

Trudy felt a little out of things until the Easter week end
began. All the girls she knew went shopping. Meta bought
a leaf-green suit and a wisp of a hat made entirely of violets.
Miss Blaine expected to be resplendent in powder blue, while
even Miss Compton spoke of a new outfit. The best Trudy
could do was to have her old suit cleaned, and buy a fresh
spray of rosebuds for what her mother would have called her
last-year's bird's nest. When the day came, however, she was
so happy she didn't care about her clothes. She felt like Cin-
derella, transfigured not by a fairy godmother, but by her
own joy.

"All this peps you up, doesn't it?" Donald Kerr waved his
hand toward the blooming forsythia and the greening fields
as the long gray sports car zoomed out of town.

"Oh, yes!" Trudy smiled at him and saw that he, too, was
deeply happy. "I always feel as if I could breathe better in
the country."

"I do, too. And then, you're going home. There's nothing
like that," Don said with a tinge of wistfulness.

No, there was nothing like going home. Trudy watched
the turns in the road and the villages grow more familiar.
Soon they were moving through Garville where the long factory wall bordered the road. Next would be Knolton. Five
miles from home! Trudy was so absorbed in the idea that she
hardly noticed when the car was blocked by a truck and
stopped for a moment opposite the factory entrance.

"I think someone waved to you," Don Kerr said.

Trudy looked back to see that a knot of employees stood on the steps and that a tall girl had stepped from the group and lifted her hand.

"I don't know anybody there. Oh, yes, I do. Elsie Hayes. I met her on the bus Thanksgiving time and she told me she worked at that factory. I can't tell now if it's she." Trudy strained her eyes to look back, "but it might be. Still, several other Knolton girls work in Garville."

Trudy forgot Elsie and almost everything else as the car rounded the last turn. Yes, there was the little farmhouse under the hill. The lilac by the front door was in soft purple bloom and the old place had never looked sweeter. Beside the lilac stood her father and mother, and yes, Susan, without any support. Susan tried to run down to the gate. She made a clumsy job of it, but she managed to reach it by the time the car had stopped.

"This is Susan, and this is Duzen, short for Duzenbury." Trudy was forced to introduce the dog because he cavorted so wildly. "Down, Duze," she commanded. "You've had your turn. Now let Mother and Dad have a chance."

As soon as everyone was acquainted, Trudy's mother proposed that they have their snack. "With a hundred miles to make I know you won't feel you can stay too long," she said, "so let's eat while we don't have to hurry."

"I'm willing," Susan said so promptly that they all laughed. She led the way past the Victorian living room, and Meta, glancing through its door, exclaimed, "Out of *Harper's Bazaar*, eh, Trude?"

In the sunny dining room Susan went directly to her place.

"Come sit by me, Dr. Kerr." She patted the chair beside her and Trudy saw that he had quite won her fancy. "Now, you on the other side, Trudy," she waved her hand imperiously. "The rest of you may sit wherever you want to."

"Well, I never! Seems to me you're pretty fresh, Miss Susan." Mrs. Wescott paused in the doorway with a tray of tomato juice. "We've spoiled her since her accident. I hope you'll excuse her," she apologized.

"Queens will be queens!" Sam Bradford laughed and Mrs. Wescott put the rest of the meal on the table. Despite Trudy's suggestions it was a good substantial country supper, slices of rosy home-cured ham, a great bowl of potato salad, pickles and jams and biscuits; a sponge cake that was light as a feather and home-canned peaches, golden in their syrup.

"What food!" Sam Bradford sighed happily after a few mouthfuls, and Meta and Donald Kerr echoed him.

Did they really like it, and what did they think of her old home? Especially, what did Donald Kerr think? Unconsciously Trudy asked herself that question.

Don did not seem to be thinking about it at all, for he was absorbed in Susan. Trudy saw that his interest was partly professional, for between discussions of various subjects she caught an adroit question. Could Susan put her foot squarely on the floor without discomfort? Did her back ever ache? Did she feel stiff sometimes? Trudy wished Don might examine Susan, but knew that would be unethical. She was Dr. Billing's patient. Besides, it wasn't really important, since Susan, slowly to be sure, was getting well.

The two hours that Meta, Don and Sam could stay flew on

wings. After good-byes all around, and much barking from Duzenbury, they were on their way. The family turned back toward the house.

"No supper to get tonight," Mrs. Wescott said, and Susan gave a clumsy skip of joy.

"Oh, goody! Let's have a picnic."

"After all we've eaten! And all we've talked! And as tired as we are?" The three adults gave one simultaneous groan.

"Yes, sir! I want a picnic." Susan set her feet in a stance more than familiar to the family. "I haven't had one since my accident, and that's months and months. I can walk now." Her face took on the pleading look which her elders were so little able to resist. "I think I ought to have some fun."

Trudy and her mother and father looked at each other. We ought not to give in to her, but—their eyes telegraphed to each other.

"Well," Mr. Wescott said slowly, "where would you like to go?"

"To White Brook Glen," Susan said positively.

"Not just up to Pike's Peak? That's near. Daddy could carry you," Mrs. Wescott suggested.

"No, I love White Brook Glen. The water's so pretty, and maybe there'll be arbutus there." Susan looked almost ready to cry.

"All right. White Brook Glen it is," Mr. Wescott gave in with a sudden readiness which was soon explained. "I might catch a trout while you girls are spreading out the picnic," he said a little sheepishly.

"We're done for, Mother." Trudy laughed. "I'll get the baskets and thermos. We'll make some sandwiches out of the ham."

Once they arrived at White Brook Glen, which was about five miles distant on the highway and was reached by an additional mile of wood road, Trudy was glad they had come. The April sun was still warm, and the Glen was a golden bowl of light. Susan could not walk far, but while Mr. Wescott fished and Mrs. Wescott arranged the picnic things on an old log, Trudy wandered farther along the wood road looking for the elusive arbutus.

At last she found a spray and was lifting it to her nose to catch its heavenly fragrance when ahead of her, half out of the road and half in it, she glimpsed an automobile. She walked toward it curiously. It had been there a long while. Leaves had drifted higher than its running boards, and the bushes about it had scraped against it in the winter winds until they had marred its paint.

It was a De Soto, the same make of car that had hit Susan, Trudy thought idly, and then she stiffened. As she stepped to the front of the car she saw something which made her give a shout that brought even her father from the brook.

"Look!" she cried. "See the dent on the right mudguard! See the broken headlight. Could it be the car that hit Susan?"

"It is! It is!" Susan skipped about as well as she could, but Mr. and Mrs. Wescott jumped to no conclusion.

"It might be, and it might not," Mr. Wescott said, "but it's well worth looking into."

"Let's go right away," Susan cried and started back along the road.

"Hey, I thought you wanted a picnic," Trudy called after her, but Susan did not so much as turn her head.

"Well, we really didn't want anything to eat," Mrs. Wescott said as she and Trudy gathered up the picnic things while Mr. Wescott made a further investigation of the car.

"The license plates are gone," he said when he joined them, "but the car can be identified by the serial and engine numbers. I suppose the thing to do is to get in touch with Chet. He'll know just what steps to take," Mr. Wescott added as they jounced back to the main road.

"Yes," Trudy agreed. "The 'phone's quickest." Even in her excitement she thought of her present situation with Chet. "You do it, Dad."

Mr. Wescott let the family out at the house, then drove to their next neighbor's where there was a telephone. He came back in a very few minutes.

"I got him," he said, "and he's calling the state police. They ought to go by here any time now."

"Then he thought there was something to it," Trudy said. She watched the road, and while the clock said only ten minutes, in her suspense it seemed an hour before Chet's roadster and a police car shot by. Chet honked his horn and waved, and after an actual hour this time drove up to the house.

"Hi, folks. Hi, sweetheart!" he greeted Trudy with a significant twinkle. "Well, I think we may be on the trail at last. That car had hit someone, all right, and, coincidence, that car was stolen from where it was parked on the street in Knolton"—Chet paused and let that fact sink in—"on the very day that Susan was hit. Oh, now, it may not mean a thing." He held up a protesting hand as Susan squealed. "But it is an interesting coincidence."

"Who owned the car?" Mr. Wescott asked.

"Fellow by the name of John Marston. I don't know him personally but I've seen him around town. Your Amos Black —he's the man who found Susan, isn't he?—issued the insurance on the car. We got in touch with him and he said the car belongs to the insurance company now. They paid the theft claim on it long ago, and Marston bought a new one. Amos is going to have the car towed out, and I suppose the company'll sell it second hand and get what they can for it. All that part has nothing to do with us."

"Well, just where do we stand," Mr. Wescott asked, "supposing this is the car that hit Susan? I judge," he went on before Chet could answer, "finding it doesn't improve our chances of apprehending the hit-run driver, since he was a thief."

"It makes 'em worse," Chet said. "There's no way of discovering who he was now. And the probability of collecting damages is out, too," he added.

Trudy's heart sank. "How's that?" she asked.

"Because it's an act of the King's enemies. Lawyer's lingo," he said as Trudy showed her bewilderment. "It's a legal term that comes down to us from Old England. This is the way it works in this case. The owner, and that goes for the insurance company, too, can't be held responsible for a car that is in the hands of a thief, an outlaw or King's enemy."

Trudy felt depressed, and saw by their faces that her mother and father did, too. It was fortunate that Susan made them all laugh by saying, "I don't see where the King comes in. We don't have one in our country."

"The State takes the place of the King with us. You might say it's an act of the State's enemies here," Chet said after the laugh had subsided. "But, you know," he went on, "the more I think about that stolen car, the more I think there's something wacky about its being hidden. Two classes of people steal cars, joy riders and professional thieves, and neither one of 'em would hide a car. Joy riders want a car to get some place. When they get there they abandon it, at the curb usually. Professional thieves want the car itself. They put distance behind them; then roll into a garage their ring operates, repaint the car, chisel off its serial numbers. Then after it has cooled off—they call it hot at first—they sell it. Now. Why did whoever hide the car?"

Despite the tension, Trudy laughed. "That's good, that 'why did whoever?' "

"Huh? Maybe." Chet was abstracted, "Yes, that's it," he repeated. "Why did the driver hide the car?"

"Because he was scared," Susan volunteered.

"Out of the mouth of babes," Chet said. "'That may be it, and it will bear thinking about."

"We didn't think to look, but weren't there any clues?" Mrs. Wescott asked. "A hairpin, an old envelope, something. There always are in books."

"Oh, books!" Chet said indulgently. "No, there weren't.

We all searched. Who's that?" he added, for a rattling old car had turned into the drive.

"Amos Black," Mr. Wescott said.

"Humph. I'm certainly getting well acquainted with him, had him on the 'phone only two hours ago. Now what's he got on his mind?"

With her head full of the discovery of the car, Trudy thought for a moment that Amos had come with some additional information about it. But no. Amos' call was strictly in the line of business. From behind the enormous package which he took from the back seat he called, "Parcel post for Miss Susan Wescott. It come on the last mail, and I thought she'd like it for Easter.

"Thanks for findin' the De Soto, folks," he added. "I've had it towed in and the company'll be glad to git a penny or two out of it. Well, so long. I'll let you know if anything new turns up about it." He rattled away and the family clustered around the package. Susan cut the strings and opened it; then because she wasn't strong enough to, her father reached into the box and drew out a tremendous Easter rabbit.

"My goodness," Trudy said. "He makes you think of the rabbit in that stage play, *Harvey*."

"Harvey's his name." Susan skipped around the rabbit.

"Who sent him?" Even as Trudy spoke she knew that the question was superfluous. An Easter gift, sent by parcel post, no name of sender. Harvey, like the dolls, came from this anonymous person who they all thought was the hit-run driver. Now this person might be a thief. Maybe the dolls were stolen. Her mind fiddled with the idea. Chet brought her back.

"Confound it!" he almost kicked Harvey. "Clues around here thicker than blackberries, and I can't make anything out of 'em." He put his hand to his head in mock despair. "I ought to be a boiler maker instead of a lawyer."

CHAPTER XI

"HOW BEAUTIFUL the view is today." Trudy lifted her eyes from the belt of knotted work which Emily Lansing was making. The river and the distant hills had taken on the blue which only June can give, and Trudy and Emily, sitting in the hospital's roof garden, had an unobstructed view of them. Trudy was especially lighthearted this morning. She had finished her round of ward work the day before and Miss Swift had re-assigned her to her favorite patient.

"There's nothing like June." Emily, too, looked at the view for a long moment; then returned to her work. "How would you say I'm doing?"

Trudy checked the tautness of the knot Emily was making. Knotted work always reminded her of braiding except that instead of simply crossing the strands you tied them in a knot each time. "I'd say you're doing wonderfully. Your knots are tight and even, and that means your hand is stronger."

"Yes, and I can work much faster than I used to. I really could have had this belt done a couple of days ago except that Miss Blaine couldn't find the knotting frame. It's nice,

isn't it?" Emily stretched the belt across her lap, and Trudy
saw that with her usual taste she had selected pleasing colors.

"It's very attractive." Trudy answered a little abstractedly,
for the significance of Miss Blaine's not having been able to
find the frame had just struck her. Of course she might mis-
judge her, Trudy knew, but she did not think she did. Was
there anything meaner one O.T. could do to another than
hand over a patient at just the moment that patient was
ready for a new project? All the work of planning and preparation—

"How's Susan?" Emily interrupted Trudy's conjectures.
"I haven't had a chance in some time to ask you about
her."

"She's pretty well," Trudy answered, "back at school and
walks without a limp. She still tires easily," she added, and a
flicker of worry touched her mind. "Her back aches once in
a while, too, but we think she's going to be all right."

"That's fine. And what about that car you found, and you
thought might be the one that struck Susan? Did anything
come of that?"

"Not a thing." Trudy shook her head, remembering the
excitement and hope that had finally dropped to dead level.
Chet had made all possible inquiries but had discovered
nothing.

"What a pity," Emily said. "Janet King and I were so excited about it. In fact, when Janet went home she made me
promise I'd let her know what you found."

"That's right. Janet has gone home, hasn't she?" Trudy
thought for a moment of her former patient. "I remember

now. Don—Dr. Kerr said she was proud as Punch of the way she was beginning to walk without crutches."

"You might say she was practically walking on air, she was so happy." Emily laughed; then returned to her former subject. "She and I thought you were going to solve the mystery right away. That means you haven't been able to collect any damages, I suppose, and your family must have been put to terrific expense."

"We were. Susan had to have P.T. up until just a few weeks ago," Trudy said. As she helped Emily to tighten an unusually stubborn knot her thoughts wandered to the effort she and her people had made to keep out of debt. Of course there was still a balance to pay on the hospital bill, but she did not call it debt since it could be met in deferred payments. But this wouldn't do. Trudy brought herself back with a jerk. "What project would you like to take up next?"

"Oh, weaving, of course," Emily answered with enthusiasm. "I love it, the materials, the colors, even the names of the patterns, *Rose Path, Double Snowball, Rings and Chains, Monks' Belt*. I'm planning to devote myself to weaving. Didn't they tell you I've bought my own loom?"

"No, I hadn't heard, but it's grand," Trudy said and smiled. "It makes you the living exponent of one of Miss Swift's pet ideas, that of giving a patient a permanent interest that she can take home with her."

Instantly Trudy regretted her speech, for at the word home, Emily's eyes dropped to her work and the corners of her lovely mouth trembled. When will I go home? And will I have a home? Will my husband want me?

Trudy knew that Emily's husband had written reassuringly from the very first, yet the doubt was always in Emily's mind. Trudy changed the subject.

"What do you want to make on your loom?" she asked, and Emily with the courageousness that was so much a part of her, responded instantly.

"I want to make a runner for a beautiful old chest of drawers my sister has in her hall. The handmade material will just suit it. Greens must predominate; green, russet, maybe a thread of gold"—Trudy could see Emily's mind working on her color scheme—"and I want a pattern that's pretty and has one of those lovely names, isn't there one about chariots?"

"*Chariot Wheel?*"

"Yes. That's it. What ought the warp to be?"

"Beige-colored cotton, I think. And I suppose you'll use wools for the weft. Their colors are so rich. Well—" Trudy was considering the proposition when a light hand touched her shoulder. She looked up to find Miss Blaine's face close to hers.

"Miss Compton asked me to stop on my way to Four B and tell you that your next patient is waiting," she said in her low bland voice.

"Oh, dear, I've kept you too long." Emily Lansing was all contrition as Miss Blaine moved away.

"No, I kept myself," Trudy said. "I suppose, just getting back from ward work I sort of forgot the schedule," she explained, but she knew that that would mean nothing to Miss Compton.

"Run!" Emily said. "I'll stay here. You can ring for my attendant on the way. I'll be all right."

"I'll take your work with me"—Trudy took the knotting frame and belt from Emily's hand—"and I'll get your loom threaded for you as soon as possible."

"Good!" Emily added some remark which Trudy could not quite catch as she hurried toward the door, but it sounded like, "Don't take this too seriously."

But I have to take it seriously. I'm at fault, Trudy said to herself. Oh, dear, why did this have to happen, just when I've come back to the shop, and things were going so smoothly?

Trudy entered the shop as swiftly as she could, put Emily's belt in the cupboard, gave a hasty look for Miss Compton who was not about; then got old Nick's case card, for she knew he was next on her schedule. She turned to find him waiting for her, and if ever resignation to abuse and neglect was written on a man's face it was on his.

Here I come up to this confounded place—because they make me. It don't do me no good—and when I get here the young whipper-snapper that's supposed to look after me is off gallivantin' somewhere, his look said. Probably he would have walked out if he'd dared, Trudy thought. But he didn't dare, for he was scared to death of his doctor who happened to be Sam Bradford.

"Hello, Nick." Trudy spoke as casually as she could; then examined his hands. Like Emily's they had improved, although not as much as they should have. Also like Emily he had just completed a project. Miss Blaine had been entirely successful, from her point of view, Trudy thought sarcastically.

"So you finished the book ends, eh? Now what would you like to do next? Don't you want a change? I see by your card you've done nothing but woodwork."

"What would the change be?" Old Nick asked craftily.

Trudy knew that he was only waiting for her to suggest some craft which he considered women's work, to explode.

"Well, leather work. A wallet? A cigarette case?"

There. I guess that'll hold you, she said to herself.

Old Nick looked nonplussed. He had hoped for a fight, or at least a skirmish, and there wasn't a chance for one. "I suppose that'll do as well as anything." He resumed his look of resignation.

"Wallet or cigarette case?" Trudy forced him to choose.

"Wallet," he said grudgingly.

"We can't start it today. I'll have to cut the leather." Trudy reflected that with Emily's loom to thread and the leather to cut she would have plenty to do in the next few hours. Meanwhile Nick must do some exercising. She took a board from the stock pile at the end of the workbench and fastened it in the vise. "You don't want to lose any time, of course," she said with secret glee, "so suppose you plane this board for a while. The motion will be good for your elbow."

The handle of the plane had been padded for another patient and fortunately fitted Old Nick's hand. He grimaced as he took it.

"Now, Nick, you're not as bad as that," Trudy said. "I can tell," and she stood over him until he had worked for the twenty minutes which his card said was now his fatigue level. Rather, he had gone through the motions of working, she thought as he stalked stiff-legged to the elevator. He was a most unsatisfactory patient.

Miss Compton was still absent from the shop. "She's gone on rounds for me," Miss Swift, who looked extremely tired, explained. The city had been sweltering in a typical June hot spell and she seemed to have been exhausted by it. She directed Trudy to work with a young man, an out-patient, who had had a tendon transplant on his right hand. What an interesting case, Trudy thought. In fact there was something almost miraculous about it. The young fellow had been ill with polio. The muscles of his thumb had been paralyzed and the thumb become helpless. Then the surgeons had opened his palm, detached a tendon from his third finger, transplanted it to the thumb, let it heal thoroughly and lo, after P.T. exercises, he had a useful thumb again. Hallelujah, Trudy sang softly to herself as she directed the young man in modeling a bowl from clay. It involved just the motions he needed to strengthen the muscles, and she watched to see that he used his third-finger flexors and the muscles involved in opposition

After lunch Miss Compton returned, but perhaps because the shop was extremely busy, she did not speak to Trudy. In fact she did not so much as glance in her direction.

I'm certainly in the doghouse. And I deserve to be, Trudy added honestly to herself, but I do hope she'll let me say I'm sorry and that I'll be careful not to let it happen again.

The heat returned that afternoon. The sun glared in the

great windows and the breeze which had attended the morning died. Patients and therapists perspired. Tools, materials, everything they touched, stuck to their hands, and weariness filled them.

Trudy was as uncomfortable and tired as anyone. She longed for the relaxation of a shower and her couch, but nevertheless she determined to make a good start at threading Emily's loom, and to stay a little late at the shop to do it.

At four-thirty, when the patients had thinned to one or two, she turned to the cupboard and got out the material for the warp. Fortunately the cupboard contained a quantity of beige-colored cotton which had been purchased ready warped on spools. These spools could be slipped quickly in place on the loom. Then the threading could begin, Trudy was thinking, when she found Miss Compton at her shoulder.

Miss Compton's face was flushed, her eyes bright with fatigue, and Trudy thought, I'm in for it.

The assistant's first words were not reassuring. "Why are you beginning a job of this sort at this hour, Miss Wescott?" she asked. She did not add, "Are you trying to make up for your delinquency this morning?" but Trudy felt that she thought it. It seemed to her that her explanation sounded pretty thin.

"Well, Emily Lansing's so enthusiastic about her loom," she said. "I thought I'd get it ready so she could start weaving as soon as possible."

"I see." Miss Compton's glasses gleamed sharply in the late sun. "Miss Wescott, you have brought up the very matter I wanted to speak about, Emily Lansing. I've noticed that you were very attentive to her. Today you overstepped. You gave her time which belonged to your other patients. That I cannot and will not allow.

"I don't understand you," Miss Compton went on before Trudy could speak. "You seem to be enthusiastic about your work, yet at times you certainly don't have your mind on it. The very first time I saw you, you were standing daydreaming instead of coming to see what I had for you to do."

Trudy remembered that time. It was her first morning at the shop, when the little girl had swung happily on the rocking horse. She, Trudy, had been so interested in Miss Compton's skill. Well, call it daydreaming if you would! She came back to herself to hear Miss Compton saying, "You must have been in some sort of dream this morning to forget all about time, forget that you were on a tight schedule, that your next patient must be waiting."

"I wasn't dreaming, Miss Compton," Trudy, confused by the unexpectedness of the accusation, its injustice, as it seemed to her, still tried to speak fairly. "I was working hard with Emily Lansing. She has to start a new project. But I did forget the time," she said, "and I'm sorry."

"Being sorry never got anyone anywhere," Miss Compton said acidly. "Nor does it help to run an O.T. department. Don't let it happen again." She turned away, and her slow step told that she was fully as exhausted as Trudy herself was.

Even if she was tired, she ought not to have reprimanded me like that, Trudy said to herself, when her hurt and resentment had died to a point where she could think. She discovered that she was beginning to have some definite ideas about being an executive. A wise director wouldn't reprimand her therapist at the end of a long hot afternoon. She'd wait until next morning. Then, when they were both rested, she could handle herself better, and her therapist would react better.

That's what I'll do when I'm a director. Trudy had to laugh at herself. It was a fine thing for a beginner who had just been bawled out for something in which she really was at fault, to be thinking about being a director.

Trudy's flash of humor helped her over her first hurt, but nevertheless, and in spite of Meta's advice to forget the whole thing, she felt constrained toward Miss Compton during the next few days. Apparently Miss Compton felt the same toward her, for she was sparse with words, and Trudy was aware that she watched her constantly, especially if Emily Lansing was in the shop.

It was wearing. Trudy did her best and was meticulous in giving Emily only her allotted time. Miss Compton watched just the same, and at last Trudy grew so nervous under the flash of those keen eyes that she was not as efficient as usual.

Emily noticed that something was wrong, for she said once, "You don't feel like yourself, do you, Miss Wescott?" Miss Swift, too, was undoubtedly aware of the strain, for, as she had in the winter, she directed Trudy herself and made several adjustments to ease the situation. One of them was to appoint one of the students to work with Emily when Trudy's time was ended, in this way providing Emily with the extra assistance she needed to start her new project.

Wonderful Miss Swift, Trudy thought as she had so many times, what would she do without her? She saw that Miss Swift was not standing the hot weather well and thought she looked especially haggard on a morning when she told Trudy she was to have a new patient. They were sitting in her office, and she leaned back in her desk chair, an unusual thing for her to do.

"Your patient's a darling," she said. "He's a C.P."—Trudy knew that Miss Swift meant a case of cerebral palsy—"four years old and his name's Robin."

"Is it a bad case?" Trudy asked.

"No"—Miss Swift pushed Robin's card toward her across the desk,—"and he's had six months of P.T., so he has a good idea of how to relax. He's to begin O.T. as an out-patient on Thursday afternoon at three o'clock."

Trudy, thoroughly familiar with procedure now, took Robin's card and went down to the record room. "Robin Brent," she read, "cause of disability, injury at birth."

Probably a brain hemorrhage, Trudy said to herself. Already she liked Robin—because of his name and because Miss Swift had said he was a darling—so she looked anxiously to see what his disabilities were. "Lower extremities in fair coordination." That meant he could walk fairly well. "Upper extremities, medium amount of involuntary movement, also medium amount of overflow movement. Facial movements fairly well trained and under control."

Well, Robin, Trudy said to herself, that's not too bad. Probably you twist your mouth a little when you talk, you reach too far and swing too wide when you move your hands and arms. Probably they jerk a little when they're idle. We'll fix you up in fine shape, or at least we'll make a good try at it.

Trudy waited eagerly for Thursday. Not only was she anxious to meet Robin, but she had worked hardly at all with C.P.'s, and felt that the case would be interesting.

There was little to do before Robin actually arrived at the shop except to see that the special relaxation chair and table were set in a quiet corner and the toys especially designed for cases of this sort were at hand; standards with holes for pegs which could be removed and put back again, little wagons with rows of removable pegs which were shaped like tiny men, a set of unbreakable dishes, a game with a central post and rings which reminded Trudy of ringtoss.

When Thursday came Trudy was thankful that it was cooler. She knew well that children reacted like barometers to weather. Even a gray day could set them off mood.

Ah, there he was, the little Robin. At three o'clock Trudy saw him coming with his mother from the elevator. She forgot his slightly toed-in walk, the faintly grotesque swing of his arms, in the charm of his head and face. Curly haired, blue eyed, a mouth like a Cupid's bow, a voice as sweet as a bell. "Is this the place?" He looked up at his mother.

"Hello, Robin. Yes, this is the place." Miss Swift had come to Trudy's side. "Come right in. This is Miss Wescott who is going to help you. You're to have a chair and table of your very own, just the size to fit you."

"Here's our corner, Robin." Trudy led Robin toward the place she had arranged while his mother retired discreetly to a distance. Robin, grown accustomed to this procedure during physical therapy treatments, took it as a matter of course.

"What are we going to do," he asked, and Trudy noticed that his mouth twisted a little as he spoke.

"Well, first of all we're going to fit your chair to you. Did you ever hear of *Goldilocks and the Three Bears?*" Trudy summoned all the ingenuity she had acquired when Susan was his age, as she adjusted the relaxation chair until it was right for him in height and angle, and until its arms gave his elbows just the support they needed to stabilize them and make a relaxed movement possible. She told the story with many embellishments and concluded with, "A wee little chair that just fits Robin."

"Isn't there a wee little table, too?" Robin helped her out.

"Yes." She brought the table which had a concave curve in one side deep enough to fit closely around his body and keep him in a good posture. "Now we're going to have some fun." She decided to use the ringtoss game, so she set the standard with its central post on the table. Instead of rope rings, this game, made especially for cerebral palsy cases, had a graded set of brightly painted wooden rings, each one large enough in diameter for poorly controlled fingers to grasp.

Robin knew at once what it was all about and made a wildly erratic reach for the top ring.

"Let's relax first, Robin," Trudy said and blessed the P.T. work which had made him familiar with the term. She saw that he understood, for his small hands went limp on the stabilizing arms of his chair.

"Now, reach again, Robin. Easy does it." The top ring was

red and Trudy searched her mind for some object within his ken which it resembled. "Let's make believe it's a big red apple ring and you wouldn't want to crush it," she said and, although he fumbled, Robin made a much better motion than he had before.

"I do'od it," he said in his high sweet voice, and Trudy saw several heads about the shop turn in amusement.

"That's good. Let's rest a minute," Trudy said. She knew how fatiguing was his effort to concentrate, his struggle to control his muscles.

"O.K." Robin leaned back in his chair, his eyes roving about the shop. "What's this? What's that?" he wanted to know, and Trudy answered his questions until she saw that his fatigue had disappeared.

"Now let's try the green ring," she directed.

Despite the rest, Robin did not do so well this time. Possibly some object about the shop still held his attention. An involuntary jerk of his arm and the green ring clattered to the floor.

"That was dumb," Robin scolded himself. Of his own accord he relaxed his hands on the chair arms.

He's a good worker anyhow, Trudy thought, grand to get along with, and he'll make progress, too. "Let's rest again. And now try the yellow ring," she suggested after she had brought him a drink of water. "We'll make believe it's a ring of pumpkin for a pie."

At the end of thirty minutes, at least half of them having been spent in rest, Robin had succeeded in lifting the rings from the post.

"All do'od," he said, and Trudy, observing that despite her care he was tired, said:

"Yes. All do'od for today. And you'll come next Monday, won't you?" she asked as his mother came forward to claim him.

"Sure. You'll save my wee little chair for me?" Robin's voice held a note of anxiety.

"The chair will be here," Trudy promised. She gave his curly head a pat which held much tenderness. "Good-bye, Robin. You've been a good boy"

Miss Swift and Miss Compton were both near by as Trudy turned from her small patient.

"Nice work, Miss Wescott," Miss Swift commented, but Miss Compton was busy adjusting a suspension sling to a patient's flail arm. Trudy, remembering the dangling end of the old-fashioned flail her father used in threshing grain, thought flail arm a clever name for an arm which was entirely helpless. The suspension sling kept this flail arm out of the way while the patient worked, and Miss Compton smiled perfunctorily as she finished the adjustment.

"Seems to me she might have warmed up a little," Trudy fumed to Meta later as they changed from their uniforms to new sport dresses in the locker room. They were going to Sand Beach with the two doctors that evening. "I really did a good job, even if I do say it myself. I remembered just how we used to handle Susan. I used the same technique and it worked."

"I know it did. I kept an eye on you across the shop. Congratulations!" Meta bowed even as she slipped her dress over her head. A second later her wise, twinkling eyes appeared above the dress collar. "But, my dear Trude, hasn't it occurred to you that, compared with Miss Swift's, our dear assistant's smile is always a wintry gleam? Besides, you say she was busy with a patient. You know how absorbed she is in her work."

"Yes, I know," Trudy admitted. "I suppose I imagine a lot."

"If you ask me—" Meta adjusted her belt. "You don't, but I'll tell you anyhow. At times you have too much imagination. Sometimes it works for your good; for instance it helped you with Robin. At other times it raises the very dickens with you, as in your upsets with Miss Compton. You let it run wild."

"I suppose I do," Trudy agreed humbly. She felt quiet and subdued as she and Meta, Don and Sam, made the bus trip to Sand Beach. Apparently Dr. Kerr felt quiet, too. Compared to Sam or Chet he was never exuberant, but this evening he had almost nothing to say, and as they rested against an old driftwood log after their swim Trudy realized that not once had she seen his pleasant smile.

She did not ask what was wrong. She knew doctors well enough now to realize that such questions were out of place. Perhaps a patient was very ill, perhaps they had lost a patient. They felt that the responsibility of life and death was theirs, and it got them down. After all, doctors were human beings.

Yes, there was no doubt Donald Kerr was depressed.

They were very good friends these days, and Trudy pushed her own low spirits aside in an effort to cheer him. She told him about her new patient, about the keen interest Emily Lansing had developed in weaving, about Old Nick's having refused to punch holes in the leather of his wallet, although she had seen him that same afternoon, jabbing the elevator bell with about a hundred pounds' force behind each punch because he was mad when it did not come.

Don was unresponsive, and at last, thinking that since he was fond of Susan, her case might interest him, she spoke of how easily the child became fatigued, and of the pain which persisted in her back. "Do you suppose she has some complication the X-rays haven't shown?" she asked.

"I don't know." Don was curt. "I haven't examined her. She's not my patient."

Why, he's actually cross! Trudy felt only sympathy. Poor Don. He was sunk, and she was blue, too. It seemed to her that if they could have told each other their troubles, talked them out, they would both have felt better.

Well, Don didn't want to talk. That was evident. Trudy glanced at the figure which, instead of being relaxed, leaned rigidly against the old log. Don's eyes stared upward at a tiny birdlike cloud which floated overhead, and not once had he looked in her direction.

Trudy's own eyes fixed themselves on the cloud. What a world. It was so beautiful, yet one could be so unhappy in it. She wondered if Miss Compton knew how perfectly miserable she had made her. Probably she wouldn't care if she did know. A twinge of self-pity made Trudy's eye fill with tears, and Don must have turned his head at just that moment, for he spoke.

"What is it, Trudy?"

"Oh, nothing," Trudy compelled herself to say, for clear in her mind was a picture of the day Meta had spoken critically about Miss Compton. The foursome had gone to Tony's for dinner and was lazily sipping coffee.

"Well, our dear assistant was certainly on the warpath this afternoon," Meta had said in her breezy way; then had stopped abruptly.

Trudy had looked up to see what had interrupted her, and knew at once that it was the expression on Donald Kerr's face. A moment before he had been laughing at one of Sam's jokes, his mouth curved, his eyes warm with appreciation. Now he looked cold, severe and disapproving.

Meta had hastily changed the subject, and later had told Trudy that Sam said Don thought it unethical for members of hospital departments to discuss each other.

"There's no maybe about it. He just doesn't like it," Meta had said, "and that's that. Far be it from me to bring that expression to his face again."

"Me, too." Trudy had resolved then and there that she would respect his feeling.

So, no confidences about Miss Compton, about the reprimand which, partly just, partly unjust, still smarted. Don would be sympathetic if he knew, she comforted herself and smiled away her tears.

After a moment Don spoke. "I know. You don't want to

talk," he said, misunderstanding the reason for her silence, while at the same time his eyes darkened with his own trouble.

The tide slipped down the sand, the little cloud overhead grew rose-colored with the approach of sunset. Suddenly Don took Trudy's hand. He held it tight; then as suddenly released it. "Come on." He got abruptly to his feet. "Let's find Meta and Sam and have dinner. I'm ravenous."

The tranquil hour on the beach, and the touch of Don's hand which told her he understood, had relaxed Trudy. She hoped it had lightened his spirits, too, but it had not. During the rest of the evening he looked grave and abstracted, and his conversation hardly went beyond yes and no.

"Don was sunk, wasn't he, and no wonder," Meta said after the foursome separated. Trudy was to stay all night in her apartment and the two girls were on their way up to it in the self-service elevator. "You remember his arthritic case, the girl in Three C who was doing so well? Sam told me that for no known reason, she began to run a terrific temperature yesterday. She died at two o'clock this afternoon."

"Oh, poor Don," Trudy said. "No wonder he was blue. I suspected it was something like that."

"Yes, and poor us," Meta went on. "Do you know what else Sam told me?"

"No." Trudy, full of sympathy for Don, of sadness for the young girl to whom the gates of life had so suddenly closed, paid little attention at first.

"Sam said Miss Swift has told the hospital board that because of poor health she must go on a long vacation."

"Oh, no!" Trudy couldn't believe her ears. Miss Swift, their comfort, their buffer, their wise head who stood between them and Miss Compton's severity, she couldn't leave. They couldn't let her. Still, Miss Swift mustn't get sick. They'd have to let her go.

"You're sure?" Trudy asked Meta.

"Oh, yes. It's all settled." Meta's voice revealed as deep a regret and concern as Trudy's.

The two girls were silent as the elevator clicked past several floors. Then as it slowed to a stop, Trudy said, "I don't see how we're going to get along without her."

CHAPTER XII

"WE CERTAINLY have grandstand seats." It was the Fourth of July, and Trudy and her family, including Duzenbury, had climbed Pike's Peak in the early twilight. As soon as it was a little darker they were going to set off their fireworks and watch the displays in the neighboring towns.

Susan was impatient. "Come on, Daddy, let's do ours. Other people are doing 'em." She waved her hand toward the rose-colored afterglow against which rockets and balloons were beginning to rise. "Have we any real big pieces with lots of bangs like they had in the park last year?" she asked as her father began to open the package.

"No, we haven't," Trudy answered regretfully. Considering the state of the family budget, she had felt they couldn't afford any fireworks at all, yet had bought a few for Susan's sake. A little girl couldn't be asked to go without everything.

The small assortment of Roman candles, pinwheels and sparklers was soon exhausted. Then Trudy and her mother and father were content to watch the display which grew increasingly brilliant as the light faded, but Duzenbury

167

wandered off on one of his woodchuck hunts and Susan
followed him. Presently they saw her poised on a little ledge
below them.

"I wouldn't jump. You know your back hurts sometimes,"
Mrs. Westcott called, but she was too late.

There was a joyous, "Here I go!" from Susan; then a cry
of pain, for Susan had not only jumped but had fallen as
she landed. She did not get up, and Trudy could never
remember afterward how she and her father got down to
the little huddle of gingham dress which was Susan.

"My back. I've hurt my back," she moaned, and Mr.
Wescott would have picked her up, but Trudy cautioned
him not to.

"Wait until she gets her breath," she said, not wishing
to alarm him.

After a minute Susan stopped moaning and straightened
to a more comfortable position of her own accord. "I'll be
all right;" she said stoutly. "Don't you come down, Mummy,"
she called to Mrs. Wescott who was trying to negotiate the
steep slope. "You might fall, too."

Trudy had long felt apprehensive about Susan's back. To
her its continued aching seemed to indicate some injury
which had not cleared up. However, additional X-rays had
shown nothing and Dr. Billings had concluded that the ache
was due to a sprain and would gradually disappear. Now,
as she stooped above her small sister, Trudy's fears became
acute. Was Susan headed for more trouble and, most pressing at the moment, how were they to get her out of this
difficult spot without injuring her still further? She was on

the point of suggesting to her father that he go back to the house and bring a shutter or plank which they might use as a stretcher, when Susan sat up.

"I'm all right, now," she said and proceeded to get to her feet.

"Better let Daddy carry you," Trudy said with a sigh of at least temporary relief, and while Susan protested that it was nonsense, she allowed her father to do so.

The trio reached the top of the hill where Mrs. Wescott stood looking a little pale. "Are you all right, darling?"

"Oh, yes." Susan was quite herself now. "We don't have to go down yet, do we?" she protested as the grownups of the party, having completely forgotten the fireworks, turned toward the path.

"Well, not if you're all right," Mrs. Wescott agreed reluctantly, and the quartette sat down again.

Trudy did not know how her mother and father felt, but she herself could hardly watch the brilliant show the countryside presented. Her thoughts raced ahead. She was supposed to go back to Hillhaven next morning, but she wasn't going, not a step, if Susan wasn't all right. Suppose she was correct in fearing the child had aggravated some spinal disturbance by her fall? Suppose Susan had to have an operation? Suppose the family was put to more expense?

I'm a regular sob sister, Trudy rebuked herself. She realized that the little accident had unnerved her, probably a great deal more than it should, and turned her attention resolutely to the lights which spangled the darkening sky.

Next morning Susan did not seem to be much the worse for her fall. "Just stiff," she said as she came to breakfast with a funny, halting little gait. "I shook myself up something awful."

"Shook myself awfully." Trudy felt sufficiently relieved of anxiety to correct her. There seemed to be no symptoms that indicated she ought to stay at home, so she turned to her father. "All right, Dad, I'll catch the early bus if you'll take me to town."

"If Susan keeps on being lame, take her to the doctor, won't you?" she said later at the terminal. Again she did not want to alarm him. "Since her back wasn't quite right before she fell it may bother her now."

"We will," Mr. Wescott promised, and Trudy rattled away toward the city, feeling for the first time in her life that a holiday at home had failed to be happy.

And what awaited her at the hospital? Another not too happy time, she judged, for a second incident involving Emily had led Miss Compton again to accuse Trudy of giving her too much attention. This time Trudy was entirely innocent. Ward B had sent word that it was having unexpected rounds and that Old Nick would not come to the shop that morning.

Fine, Trudy had thought and at once planned to give the time to Emily who was at a difficult point in her weaving. She and Emily had their heads together trying to locate a mistake Emily had made in the pattern, when Trudy felt rather than heard Miss Compton behind her.

"Miss Wescott, your next patient is waiting."

Trudy turned to meet Old Nick's glare. He had come after all. Ward B must have changed its plan.

"Oh, Ward B—" she began, but it was the same old story, a sharp sarcastic reprimand, no chance to explain, and almost unendurable surveillance afterward.

Miss Swift as usual poured the balm of her smile and tact on the troubled waters, but Trudy and Meta often wondered what they would do while the director was on her long vacation.

As the July days succeeded one another Trudy worked with the endless stream of in-patients and out-patients which flowed through the shop. Her specials, with the exception of Nick, who was the same unrepentant sinner, were doing nicely. Robin not only handled the rings of the game with more skill, but added the extra motion of lifting them toward his mouth as if he were going to eat them. This was a bit of training toward teaching him to feed himself. Trudy thought it an ingenious device and wished she had invented it. Emily Lansing was stronger, was weaving diligently and turning out a very beautiful piece of work.

Emily ought not to have been so distrait, Trudy thought, yet she was, and increasingly so, even in the face of the fact that Rehabilitation had braces made for her and, in conjunction with crutches, was teaching her to walk again. This method of walking might not prove to be functional— Trudy used the O.T.'s term for it, meaning that the patient's progress would be so slow and labored that the wheel chair would always be the quicker and better way of getting about—but as a rule just the act of standing on his feet encouraged the patient, gave him a sense of independence. Emily was the opposite. She seemed to be discouraged and, at times, to be sunk in depression.

Emily had said nothing, but Trudy thought she knew why. Perhaps her husband was planning a summer vacation, was writing about coming home, and Emily was in dispair at the thought of facing him with her disabilities. Trudy was doubly sympathetic because she was unhappy and anxious herself. She would not have blamed Miss Compton if she had accused her of a divided attention, for the letters from home were not encouraging and Trudy could not keep from thinking about Susan.

"Still limping," her mother wrote one week; in the next, "Still lame." On the third week she stated, "I can't see that she's any better," and on the fourth, "She seems to drag one foot."

This statement, with its hint of a paralytic condition, stirred Trudy to action. "I'm going home this week end," she said to Donald Kerr when she met him for a late swim at the beach.

"Yes, I think you should." Don had long since become himself again. "What's your doctor out there say?" he asked.

"I can't quite tell from Mother's letters," Trudy answered. "Maybe she's holding out on me, just as I myself have been holding out on her and Dad. I mean I've never mentioned a possible spinal injury. I've just talked about a sprain, a temporary stiffness, something like that."

"It's more than any of those things," Donald said gravely, confirming Trudy's fears.

"Would you risk a guess as to what it might be?" Trudy asked. It seemed as if her anxiety was more than she could bear. Her knowledge of anatomy had led her to several possible diagnoses of her own. Would he corroborate them?

He did. "Well, it might be a hemorrhage into the spinal cord, or it might be a dislocation of a disc between two vertebrae." Don considered the matter. "I'd say the latter's most likely, fits with all the symptoms and circumstances. Don't feel so low." He put his hand over Trudy's for a moment. "It's operable."

Yes, praise be that it was operable, Trudy thought, over and over again, on the bus trip home that Saturday afternoon. But, oh, how she dreaded an operation for Susan, the suffering inevitably entailed, the confinement of a cast. These things which Trudy had taken as routine in the hospital now assumed an entirely new aspect. It's different when it's your own, she thought. Her concern for Susan threw every thought of the expense involved in this new complication into the background. Never mind it. Just let Susan live, let her be well again.

Trudy's father met her at the bus terminal, and from the look in his eyes she knew that he, too, considered Susan's condition serious. Perhaps he had been told some things which she had not, she surmised.

It seemed as if they would never reach the little white house under the hill. While her father put the truck in its shed, Trudy hurried into the house. Susan's bed was again in the dining room.

"Oh, Trudy!" She held out her arms when she saw her. Great tears brimmed in her lovely dark eyes. "Oh, Trudy, my legs won't mind me! I can't walk."

"The second leg is involved now," Dr. Billings said when he came an hour later. He and Trudy sat on the porch beyond Susan's earshot. "It's a paralysis, of course, caused by a pressure of some sort on the spinal cord."

Trudy looked about her with eyes which saw, yet did not see. Oh, the mockery of this lovely summer day, of Susan's little flower bed in full bloom. Susan was in trouble, such trouble. Suppose an operation shouldn't be successful.

"I would say," Dr. Billings corroborated Donald Kerr's opinion, "that a loosened disc in the spine is indicated. That would not show in the X-rays, and would be a logical injury, since the principal stress of the blow from the car fell on the pelvic region. A loosened disc might stay in place for months, even for years, causing a little casual aching and unnatural fatigue; then be displaced by some sudden movement like Susan's fall. And then, of course, with the pressure on the spinal cord, a paralysis of some part of the body would follow. It all fits Susan's case, and that's what I believe it is. But I'd like another opinion on it."

Another opinion. At the words Trudy's mind flashed instantly to Donald Kerr. It wasn't just that she liked him so well, and she realized suddenly that she did like him immensely. There really was no doctor whose judgment she would value more than his. She would want him to operate, too. She would trust him. This, also, was not entirely a matter of her personal confidence, but that he ranked high among the younger orthopedic surgeons at her hospital.

Could it be arranged? It seemed as if Dr. Billings followed her thoughts, for he said, "We want someone who can do the operating, as well. I don't do orthopedic surgery."

"Yes." Trudy, sure herself of whom she wanted, felt she ought not to take a step in such an important matter without consulting her family. "There's a good man at our hospital," she said, "but I think I ought to talk to Mother and Dad before I suggest him."

"Right." Dr. Billings collected his hat and bag and rose. "Susan should be operated on as soon as possible, so settle it as quickly as you can and let me know."

Susan demanded considerable attention and it was not until an hour later when she dozed off in a nap that Trudy managed to talk with her mother and father alone. They agreed at once that if Dr. Billings approved, Donald Kerr should be the consultant and surgeon.

"He will want Susan to come to Hillhaven," Trudy stated.

"That will mean we can't see her so much," Mrs. Wescott said wistfully, but Mr. Wescott put in:

"Yes, but Trudy can. And she'll know better what to do for her than we would. She'll need exercises, won't she, once her back is healed?"

"Yes, but P.T. will work with her first. Oh, of course, O.T. will follow." Trudy could not allow her beloved profession to be slighted. "I can help with that."

"That's another reason for her going to Hillhaven," Mrs. Wescott said resignedly. "Susan wouldn't get O.T. here at Knolton."

"Of course all this depends on Dr. Billings' diagnosis being correct." Trudy turned to the practical angle. "The thing now is to consult Donald Kerr."

"Yes." Mr. Wescott would have got out the truck at once to take her to a telephone, but Trudy checked him.

"Don will be on duty this afternoon and evening. It will be better to 'phone him at nine when he finishes. He's always in his office for a few minutes then."

It was a long wait. Trudy was actually glad that Chet, who had heard of their trouble, dropped in after supper. No blarneying, no teasing this time, he was all sympathy.

"Poor kid, poor kid," he kept saying as Trudy laid the situation before him.

Trudy was too absorbed in anxiety to realize how often she mentioned Donald Kerr.

"Of course you would want someone you know and trust," Chet said when she had finished, "and I gather you think this Don Kerr is tops." Apparently he forgot himself for a moment, for his voice grew suddenly loud. "Is he your boy friend?"

"Oh, Chet!" Trudy looked at him reproachfully. To joke and tease when she was in such trouble!

"I'm sorry." Chet changed the subject. "I wish I could find that hit-run driver. All this is his fault; more agony for Susan, more expense for you and your family, and I can't locate him and make him come up to the mark."

"You've done all anybody could, Chet," Trudy said gratefully, and he laid his hand over hers for an instant.

"Thanks for those kind words."

As she had expected, Trudy succeeded in getting Don on the telephone at nine. Would he, could he, come out and see Susan?

"Of course." His voice was warm and reassuring. He would be off duty next day. He would come at whatever hour she arranged with Dr. Billings.

After that, although events moved fast as far as hours were concerned, it was all a slow motion picture to Trudy. Don came at noon Sunday, agreed with Dr. Billings on the diagnosis, and on Monday Trudy and her mother accompanied Susan in an ambulance to Hillhaven. There the diagnosis was verified by further examination and by an intraspinal injection of an opaque liquid which made the injury visible in X-rays and on the fluoroscopic screen. Tuesday morning was set for the operation.

It was a long day for Trudy and her mother. Trudy did not know how Mrs. Wescott endured it, sitting in the waiting room with nothing to occupy her. As for herself, her work kept her moving and busy. Half her mind seemed to be somewhere else, however. She found herself reviewing endlessly a spinal operation which she had once observed. It had been intensely interesting at the time. Now she shuddered to remember it. If I could only think of something else, she moaned, and watched the hands of the clock. They seemed to stand still.

At last, however, Donald Kerr stood in the doorway of the shop. How good of him to come himself to tell her about the outcome of the operation.

"May I go for a moment?" Trudy asked, and Miss Compton with genuine kindness in her voice, said:

"Of course."

"Susan's all right," Don stated reassuringly. "No complications. The operation, in itself, was successful."

By that Trudy knew he meant that the disc had been successfully removed. The ultimate outcome of the operation, the matter of whether Susan would walk again, still hung in the balance. It depended on many things; whether the spinal cord had been permanently injured by the pressure of the disc, whether the operation had been in time, how well the operative area healed, how well the vertebrae fused.

Trudy was glad her mother did not know of all these uncertainties.

"Now she's going to be all right," Mrs. Wescott said an hour later as they looked down at Susan in the few minutes the nurse allowed.

Susan, coming out of her anesthetic, was beginning to fret a little in the cast which now encased her.

"Walk." She murmured the word ceaselessly, and there were tears in both Trudy's and Mrs. Wescott's eyes as they turned away.

Susan was very ill for a few days. It was not until Donald Kerr announced Susan definitely better that Trudy, who had thought of no one but her sister, really grasped the fact that Miss Swift had gone on her long vacation.

CHAPTER XIII

MISS SWIFT had been gone two weeks, and to Trudy's astonishment the shop had fairly radiated calm. She had known the place would run like clockwork, efficiency being Miss Compton's middle name, but she had not dreamed that the assistant director could be so pleasant and magnanimous. Miss Compton was patient with the inexperienced student who had arrived just before Miss Swift left. She was also understanding of Trudy's situation.

Susan, in the wards, was making a good recovery but, childlike, could not see why Trudy should not be with her more, and was subject now and then to a drop in morale. Either Mr. or Mrs. Wescott came once a week to see her, but that was not enough. She demanded constantly that her sister be with her, and it was hard for Trudy to tear herself away from those pleading hands and eyes. Miss Compton arranged Trudy's schedule so that she never missed spending one of the ward's visiting hours with Susan, and in return Trudy did everything she could to make up for the time she was away from the shop. Consequently, for the time being at least, a pleasanter relationship than she could have believed possible existed between her and the assistant director.

"She's so different," Trudy commented as she and Meta went down to the record room together—they were both to have new patients and were on their way to look up case histories and charts. "Why, a thing happened this morning that would have made Miss Compton explode a few weeks ago. I had Mrs. Willis—that arthritic, you know—working on a piece of needlepoint, with the light right where it should be. One of the attendants must have swung her wheel chair around, for suddenly I noticed the light was wrong. I swung her back, but of course Miss Compton had noticed it at the same moment. I thought she would think it was my carelessness and be furious. But no. She was as nice as anything, let me explain, and said, 'Those things will happen.' I could hardly believe my ears."

"New broom sweeps clean, of course," Meta said, then added, "but it isn't all that. Miss Compton knows her way around better now; and I think she has steadied under responsibility. She loves it. She loves Miss Swift, too, and wants to turn out a good job for her."

"She's certainly showing a different side of herself." Trudy lowered her voice as they entered the record room. Her thoughts returned to her job. "I only hope I'm not in for another Old Nick in this hemiplegia patient."

Hemi—half, plegia—a stroke of paralysis. Half her patient's body was paralyzed, Trudy reflected as she ran through the files until she came to his name. "Ralph Upton, 40," she read. "Married. Three children. Upholsterer. Cause of

illness, overwork. Contributing cause, cardiac disturbance."

Poor fellow, he was up against it, she thought as she read
further. It was his right side which was affected, and that
made it all the worse for him unless he was left handed. He
had already been treated by P.T. for a year and had only
a fair amount of muscular power in his right leg and his right
hand and arm. Opposition had just begun to return. Trudy
read on to find that Ralph had come to Sayre City recently
and had been referred to the department by Social Service.
He had, of course, along with P.T., been doing O.T. work.
His history showed that he had improved considerably.

It was a tragedy in any case to have a paralytic stroke at
forty, Trudy thought, and sensed the possibility of an additional tragedy in Ralph's having come through Social Service. This could mean that he had no financial reserves to support his family, and might mean as well that he could not pay
for the treatment he would receive at the hospital. Hillhaven
made no distinction between charity and paying patients so
she might never know. Social Service would shoulder the
expense, and what a fine organization it was, helping hun-
dreds of people who, through no fault of their own, found
themselves in financial straits.

Trudy and Meta made their notes and turned toward the
shop. As they walked along the corridor Meta grinned at
Trudy. "Isn't friend Chet coming to the city this afternoon?
Any regrets that you're not his fiancée?"

"Not a regret," Trudy said firmly; then added, "but it
really was hard to turn down a perfectly good dinner and

theater invitation. Chet wanted to take me, and he always gives me a grand time. I thought it wasn't fair to either of us to accept, so I said, 'Thanks a lot, but no.'"

The girls were passing the door to Susan's ward and Trudy lifted her hand in case she should be looking.

Susan, flat in her cast, didn't see her, but there was a fresh bouquet of flowers on her bedside table, and Trudy turned to Meta with an exclamation. "More flowers! And did I tell you that last week a perfectly wonderful coloring outfit came from that big toy shop on the avenue? No card enclosed, as usual. That hit-run driver—if it is he or she who is sending things—certainly is on the job.

"That's what Chet is coming about," she added as she and Meta waited for the elevator. "He's going to the florist's and some of the shops to see if he can find out anything about the sender. He'll talk with the telephone people, too, and see if the calls can be traced."

"I hope he finds something," Meta said sincerely. Then with the astuteness which was typical of her, she added, "I imagine that to collect some damages in the form of good hard cash would be welcome, considering the expense your family's under."

"It would," Trudy said fervently, for she and her parents were now confronted with a second series of expenses. Donald Kerr had presented no bill as yet, of course, and would undoubtedly make it moderate since Susan was a ward patient. However, the hospital bills, along with incidentals, were considerable; and too, Susan had been so ill that she had needed a special nurse for the first few days.

Trudy did not know what Chet did that evening—probably took some other girl out—but she did know that he spent the next morning scouting about the city for clues to Susan's mysterious sender of gifts. He met Trudy at the hospital at the beginning of the ward's visiting hours. Miss Compton had again kindly consented to Trudy's being away from the shop, and she guided Chet at once to Susan's bedside.

"Hello, Chet!" Susan, lying on her face in her cast, located him in the little hand mirror which she, like Tommy and many of the other patients, used to look about the ward.

"Hello." Chet's voice, usually so assured, held a faint note of shock and uncertainty. "Is she all right?" he asked Trudy in a low tone.

"Yes, of course." Trudy knew just how Chet felt. She herself had had the same feeling when she first saw the great casts in her days of clinical training. There was something almost sadistic about them, as if the patients were being tormented rather than cured. "Susan's all right, and she's going to get well fast," Trudy said. "Aren't you, Suze?"

"Yup," Susan answered inelegantly. She turned her head toward Chet as much as she could. "Did you get a line on that man who hit me? He—or maybe it's a woman 'cause I heard a woman scream—is still sending me things. Look at this." She felt under her pillow and drew out a pretty red autograph album. "I'm going to get everybody in the ward to write her name in it. But I won't let you, Chet"—she smiled roguishly at him in the mirror—"not until you catch that fellow for me."

Pert. Her illness had made her worse than ever, Trudy thought, but she was amused rather than annoyed. That was what came of loving her so much. Trudy did go through the motion of a disapproving headshake, but Chet spoiled her effect by laughing.

"You're as fresh as ever, Suze. They can't get you down, can they? No, I didn't get a line on your fellow." His face sobered. "I'll try again this afternoon, and maybe Trudy will have better news for you tomorrow. I'm going to see her just before I leave town—we'll have a snack, won't we?" He turned to Trudy. "I'll have to leave by six o'clock, for I'm due to preside at a Rotary Club meeting tonight."

"I wish I could leave at six o'clock. I wish I could go home," Susan's voice had a hint of tears in it.

"Never mind." Trudy tried to cheer her. "Someday you'll be coming in at home"—Trudy avoided the word walking because it would be a long time still before they would know anything about the degree of Susan's recovery—"you'll come in saying, "Hello, Mummy! Hello Dad! Hello Duzenbury! Where's my black kitten? Oh, is that him all grown up?'" Trudy forgot her grammar in trying to stage her little act, but it was no matter, for Susan did brighten.

"That's just what I will say, and I hope there'll be a new calf in the barn for me to name, too."

"I'm sure there will be." Trudy touched Chet's arm and indicated that it would be a good idea to go while Susan was in a cheerful frame of mind.

"Well, bye-bye, Susan." Chet put a kiss on his fingers and

touched Susan's forehead. "I'll send you the news by Trudy. Wish me luck, and keep right on the way you're going."

Trudy, too, kissed Susan. As she and Chet moved away she saw that Susan followed them as far as she could in her mirror.

"Poor kid," Chet said, but Trudy, although the lump in her throat made any speech hard, compelled herself to say:

"No. Lucky kid, that she had the type of injury from which she has a good chance to recover. I could show you some around here who would break your heart."

Again that afternoon Chet scouted Sayre City. He met Trudy at five, and as he had only the hour, suggested they have a snack in the corner drugstore.

"Oh, I don't know," Trudy demurred. So far Chet had been businesslike, and she didn't want to give him opportunity to be otherwise.

"Aw, come on. Don't be so noble!" Chet took her arm and fairly forced her into the shop.

"I wish I had something to report, but I haven't," he said as they sat down in one of the booths. He looked as downcast as a person of his assurance could. "Break the news to Susan as gently as you can, but I didn't find a clue. The florists couldn't remember—it had been a different shop each time, and they keep no record of purchasers who pay cash. The toy shop was the same, the telephone company, too. The operators at the hospital simply held up their hands when I asked them. With all the traffic they have to handle? No."

"Oh, dear. I had hoped—" Trudy felt her voice trail to nothing.

"I had, too," Chet said. "Well, it's always darkest before dawn, and it's been my experience that just when you're ready to give up is the moment when something breaks." He looked at his watch and got to his feet. "I must go."

"Yes." Trudy had not finished her malted, but she rose, too. As they left the booth she thought of all the trouble Chet was taking for the Wescott family. "I haven't half thanked you for making this trip," she said and looked up at him in genuine gratitude.

"You don't need to." Chet's reaction was instantaneous. He put his arm around her. "If you'd just care for me a little," he was saying when Trudy saw Donald Kerr coming through the door.

"Hello." Even if he had wanted to, it was impossible for Don to avoid Trudy and Chet. They were too near.

"Hello." Trudy spoke with what composure she could. Chet's arm had tightened and it was a moment before she could free herself from it. She realized that his encircling arm might easily imply a relationship which did not exist, and realized further with a sudden force that was like a blow that of all the people in this world she wanted no misunderstanding with Donald Kerr. Why? Why? Her whirling senses asked. She had no time to answer herself but heard her own voice saying clumsily, "Don, I want you to meet our friend from Knolton. Chet Fielding, Dr. Kerr."

The two men shook hands.

"Chet came to town to see if he could get a line on the person who's sending Susan all those presents," Trudy managed to explain.

"And to see my best girl," Chet said boldly.

"Fine."

"It sure is." Chet put his hand possessively under her arm and Trudy realized that he was deliberately creating the impression there was some understanding between them.

Indignation filled her to the point of making it almost impossible for her to act. What could she do to set things straight? She floundered helplessly, and then said, with what she knew was a touch of malice, "Chet didn't succeed about the clues." Then her wits returned enough for her to end the situation.

"You've got to run, Chet, or you'll miss your bus."

"So I will. Good-bye, Trudy." For one dreadful moment Trudy thought he was going to complete the scene by kissing her, but he did not. "Good-bye, Kerr. Glad to have met you." He hurried through the door.

"Sit down and finish your malted."

"I don't want any more of it, thanks." Trudy's one idea was to get away. "Excuse me, will you?" She could not make herself meet Don's eyes and hurried awkwardly through the door.

Once she reached her room, Trudy threw herself half sobbing on her couch. What a horrid thing to happen. How mean of Chet. Why did she care so much? And she did care terribly. The scene kept flashing before her eyes as if a movie film had stuck at a certain point and repeated itself endlessly. Chet's arm about her, Don's approach, and the instant advantage Chet had taken of it. How well Don had behaved—dignified, reserved toward Chet, kind to her by ignoring the situation. She heard his voice again, "Sit down and finish your malted."

Involuntarily Trudy pictured Don, his reserved face with its kind eyes, its charming smile, the crisp hair above it, and suddenly every feature was clear. If it had been Don who had asked her to marry him, would she have said no as she had to Chet? Would she have been annoyed with him if he had persisted as Chet had? Was she falling in love with Don? At the thought Trudy buried her face in her pillow.

After a time she could think more clearly. So this was why she minded so much what had happened in the drugstore! This tenderness toward Don must have been coming on for some time and she hadn't known it.

And Don, did he care for her? Would he care after the scene in the store? They had been the best of friends, yes, but the only sign of affection he had ever shown her had been in taking her hand on the beach that day they were both so blue. He had held it so briefly, had withdrawn his own so quickly, that Trudy felt it meant nothing but sympathy. She wished she could think it meant more. She also wished she had been able to meet his eyes before she left him in the drugstore. They might have told her whether he was hurt because she seemed to belong to Chet, or was unconcerned and only amused at Chet's buffoonery.

Had Chet ruined everything? Trudy sobbed into her pillow. Please not! Oh, please not! Hours later when exhaustion compelled her to fall asleep, the words wove themselves into unhappy dreams.

Trudy had an engagement with Don the following evening. That will tell how he feels, she thought and blushed, realizing that she herself cared so deeply. She sighed, too. It was no fun to find yourself so fond of a person—it seemed to be something you could not control—and not know how he felt about you.

Their meeting revealed nothing, however. When Trudy met Don at the agreed place he said casually, "We'll have to wait a minute. Sam wants to see this picture, too, and he's bringing Meta. I knew you wouldn't mind."

"Surely not." Trudy speculated as to whether Sam had really wanted to see the picture, or whether Don had arranged the foursome to avoid being alone with her. There was no way of telling, for the foursome often changed overnight into a twosome, or vice versa, as unexpected duties came up for the young surgeons.

Nor could Trudy tell from Don's behavior how he felt. All evening she studied him as much as she dared. Always self-contained, he acted as usual, laughed at the others' sallies, made none himself. Toward her he was courteous, gave her the usual attention. "Want your wrap?" "Have another cup of coffee?" "Watch it, there's a step here." Trudy returned to her room in the same suspense in which she had left it.

In the following days she was glad that her new patient took much of her attention. Ralph Upton was far from being an Old Nick. Round gray eyes, an unruly crop of hair, and a chin as deeply dimpled as a character actor's, made him look younger than his forty years. A few hours' work with him, and Trudy knew that he burned with a tremendous determination to get well.

"I want to get back on a job of some sort just as soon as I can," he said, and added with an impulsiveness that had considerable boyishness about it, "I have three of the sweetest little girls you ever saw to take care of."

"You have! What are their names?" Trudy asked as she examined his hand and arm.

"Diane, Patricia and Esme. My wife says they're too fancy, but I wanted 'em so she finally gave in. I've got a picture of 'em." Ralph dove into his pocket with his normal hand and pulled out a snapshot of the three little girls.

They were like stair steps, Trudy thought. Ralph pointed out which was which; then his mouth straightened into a line of determination.

"Yes, sir. I must get back on the job."

Trudy was glad she could honestly encourage him. "I believe there's a great deal you can do to help yourself," she said. She had noted as he came into the shop that, although he limped, his leg was not crippled to any extent. Lower extremities always responded to treatment more readily than arms and hands, so probably the limp could be at least partially eliminated. The flaccid muscles on the paralyzed side of his face gave it an expressionless look, but that would make no difference about his getting a job, and her examination of his arm and hand had shown Trudy that they were not too bad.

"You are an upholsterer by trade, aren't you?" she asked, and he nodded. "Well, perhaps in a few months we can get you where you can run a power sewing machine again." She did not add what was in her mind, that she doubted if he could ever take a full-time job at upholstering, but said, "The thing is to get back as much strength in your weak hand as we can, and educate your left hand to do the things your right hand used to do. We'll start out with something that will help your game leg at the same time. Suppose you begin on the bicycle saw."

"Whatever you say." Ralph, so unlike Old Nick, looked about for the saw and Trudy led him to it.

"I think, until you're stronger, we'll have to strap your foot in place so it won't slip off," she said. She attached a wooden sandal to his foot, then to the pedal. "Now, suppose you saw a toy out of this plywood."

"All right." Ralph was very clumsy with his left hand, but there was no doubt as to his will. He did not waste a minute. Nick's hour in the shop overlapped his, and Trudy hoped the old curmudgeon, as she called him to herself, would notice how well Ralph worked.

Perhaps Old Nick noticed. Perhaps he didn't. But Trudy was sure that Ralph, with the effort he was willing to put into the work, would make good progress. Eventually he would be able to go to Shelter Shops, Incorporated, and take a part-time job, unless, of course, some further illness prevented.

A wonderful institution, Shelter Shops, planned for just

such people as Ralph, men, and women, too, who were handicapped yet wanted to help themselves as much as possible. The work was graded to their strength and they were paid in proportion to their ability. The money would delight Ralph, who yearned to support his three little graces.

"What remarkable progress that patient has made," Emily Lansing commented to Trudy a month later. "You've been very successful with him. Congratulations."

"The patient's been successful with himself, rather." Trudy laughed. "It's the will that counts," she said.

"Yes, it's the will, up to a certain point." Emily's eyes grew shadowed, and Trudy knew she was thinking that with all the will in the world she would never walk successfully again. Rehabilitation had sent word to the shop that the experiment with braces and crutches had not come out well.

Pityingly Trudy looked at her lovely patient. Emily had grown thin and her face was drawn. It was not the heat. Some inner anxiety gnawed at her.

Like me, Trudy thought, remembering the ache of uncertainty that was always with her, her unhappy suspense as to how Donald Kerr felt about her these days. No, that wasn't fair, to compare her anxiety to Emily's. Emily's was pure tragedy. Her own was—well, not comedy. It wasn't easy constantly to wonder with a throb that was almost pain, if someone you cared about, cared about you.

Trudy would have liked to ask Meta if she thought Don had changed, or was it her imagination that he was formal and constrained? She could not bring herself to speak of it, however; for although she told Meta about the scene Chet had staged in the drugstore, she had not told her everything.

Meta thought, as Trudy did, that Chet had been unpardonable and had put Trudy in an awkward position. "Especially awkward if Don had been your best young man. Or is he?" Meta had asked with an astute glance. But although Trudy had blushed, she had not been able to confide in Meta. No, it was something she had to keep in her heart.

There had been several little happenings since that day in the drugstore which might have strengthened Don's belief that Trudy was interested in Chet. Chet had visited the city again, on business of his own, and had dropped in at the hospital. Trudy had been cool and had declined his invitation to lunch, but had felt compelled to accompany him to the ward to visit Susan. Don had seen them there. Then when Trudy had gone home for Labor Day, feeling that she must because her parents seemed depressed, a feeling which she shared, Sam, his brother, Meta and Don had dropped in at the farm. Chet had been there to ask the total of Susan's expenses so far. He had not staged another act—the blaze of indignation which Trudy knew was in her eyes had probably checked him—but he had very cleverly in his conversation implied that he was intimate with the family.

Oh, dear, Trudy thought as she waited for Meta in a little ice-cream bar on the river's edge which the two girls had haunted since the hot weather, oh, dear, what a mix-up it is! I always thought it would be wonderful to—to love somebody. Instead it's just wretched.

Tears were in her eyes when, instead of Meta, she saw Donald Kerr approaching. She dabbed them swiftly and, as he came near, made herself smile. "Hello, there!"

"Hello." Don's face was grave and noncommittal even after he saw her.

Trudy thought he was going to pass her by. Instead, however, he put his hand on the back of the chair opposite her. "Waiting for somebody?"

"Only Meta," Trudy said involuntarily.

"O.K. Then I'll join you." He ordered sodas for them both and sipped his slowly. "Glad to see you for a moment," he said, and Trudy felt breathlessly happy until he went on. "I wanted to speak to you about that theater date we four have for next week. Sam won't be able to go."

"Oh, that's too bad." Trudy, her feelings reversed, wondered what Don was going to say.

"Yes, it is too bad." Don nodded and stirred his drink; then without looking up, he added, "What do you say we take a rain check on it? After all, half the fun is in hearing Sam laugh." Don himself laughed, but Trudy thought it was not her imagination that he sounded dry and forced.

"Why, that's all right with me," she compelled herself to say, and was thankful that she saw Meta coming. Her spirits, which had risen as if they had wings, dropped to earth now. Don had definitely side-stepped a twosome with her. He wouldn't have done that a few months ago, even a few weeks ago, she thought. She was right. He had changed.

So everything was over. Chet's meanness had done its

work. Don didn't care for her any more, or thought she was Chet's fiancée. Either way, he didn't want to take her on a twosome, and either way—Trudy looked after his retreating figure—it broke her heart.

CHAPTER XIV

"WELL, I CAUGHT it yesterday afternoon while you were in the record room," Meta said to Trudy one blistering morning in mid-September. "Mrs. Atkins wanted to paint her handkerchief box blue and I forgot and got down the green paint. That was enough to set Miss Compton off. She said, 'Miss Tripp, your patient will not have much confidence in you if you don't keep your mind on your work.' Just like that."

"And how well are you succeeding in being philosophical about it?" Trudy teased, for Meta's face was a little more flushed than even the hot weather warranted.

"Oh, I'll admit it got under my skin," Meta granted. "It's a lot easier to tell you to keep calm than it is to do it myself."

"Especially when it's so hot," Trudy said as she dabbed yellow enamel on her market basket. She and Meta were getting ready for ward work on the fifteenth.

"Yes, it's scorching weather." Meta nodded as vigorously as the languid air would allow. "I suppose there's a sunspot; or one of those masses of cool air the weather bureau is always talking about has preferred to stay in the Arctic. I should think it would." Meta started to mop her face with the paint rag, recollected herself just in time, and substituted her handkerchief. "I pity the patients in casts these days," she said, "I'll bet the scratchers are working overtime."

Trudy knew that by a scratcher Meta meant a loose strip of gauze slipped between the patient's body and his cast. It protruded at top and bottom of the mass of plaster, and by pulling it back and forth the patient could scratch unreachable areas of his skin.

"The patients hate the heat so, and I don't blame them. Of course the surgeons try to begin the long-term cases in the fall, but they can't always arrange it."

"No." Trudy thought of Susan. Susan was having a hard time and was growing restless and irritable.

Well, weren't they all, Trudy reflected, looking about her at the flushed worn faces of both staff and patients. No one slept well, no one ate well, and it was so hard to work. Tempers were thin. Old Nick was like a surly bear, sweet little Robin was petulant, Emily Lansing looked thinner than ever, and even Ralph Upton had lost some of his determination.

Of the staff, only Miss Blaine with her ice-green eyes seemed to be impervious to the heat. The students were wilted. Meta, with her long upper lip dewed with perspiration, looked rather comically hot, just about to boil, as she stated. Miss Compton was waspish, and as Trudy, worn not only by the heat but by her unhappiness about Don, felt the same, she feared there were breakers ahead.

It was a good thing she was going back to the wards in a

day or two and would see less of Miss Compton. On the other hand the weather might turn cool any moment now, Trudy thought, even as she reached for a fresh handkerchief.

The weather did not turn cool, however. It remained hot and sultry, and Trudy and Meta found the wards like ovens.

"Any work today? Like to make a change purse? Like to make a belt?" The two O.T.'s did not dare so much as mention articles made from wool.

"No." The patients waved them languidly away or snapped refusals. A few hardy souls, especially those who were coming to the end of their hospital stays and consequently had new enthusiasm, worked on with hands that stuck to their materials.

Trudy's heart went out to Susan. The child looked pale instead of flushed in the heat. She had grown thinner in the confinement of the cast and her dark eyes seemed enormous. As the first week of ward work progressed, Trudy found herself involved in a daily struggle with her. Susan, accustomed to seeing her only during the leisure of visiting hours, could not understand why Trudy could not now stay in the mornings.

"I'm on duty, Susan," Trudy explained. "I have to see every little girl in this ward, the boys in the next ward, and the grownups in the others."

"Let 'em go. Let Meta see 'em," Susan said with a momentary return of her old spirit.

"No, I can't. It's my job." Trudy gently disengaged herself from the clinging hands. "I can only stay long enough to ask you if you wouldn't like to make a new hat for your doll, out of ribbon, you know," she said beguilingly. "Or maybe color a new book?"

"No, I wouldn't like to," Susan declared promptly, and to divert her, Trudy said:

"I see you have fresh flowers this morning."

"Yes, and I don't want them, either." Susan was openly in a bad humor now. "That nasty old person, whoever it is that's sending them, needn't bother. He got me into this place and I don't want anything to do with him."

"And with that, I think I'd better leave," Trudy said to Miss Ericson who came along just then. " 'Bye now, Susan."

This procedure, with minor variations, went on day after day. Sometimes Meta had left the ward before Trudy could get away, and once or twice as she hurried after her she saw Miss Blaine in the corridor. Miss Blaine, radiating coolness in the midst of the heat, smiled sweetly. "Hard to leave your little sister?"

If the weather would only moderate! Trudy did not know how many times she and other members of the staff repeated those words. Miss Compton was definitely irascible now. She was curt with her workers, especially curt with Trudy for some reason she could not fathom.

Never mind, she consoled herself, Miss Swift will be back soon. Six weeks' vacation, the director was to have had. Trudy counted on her fingers. The time was nearly gone.

At last a morning came when both radio and newspaper predicted cooler weather, but the day itself was harder than ever to bear. The accumulated heat and sultriness of the hot spell seemed to hang over the city like an invisible cloud. The older patients, especially the cardiac cases, suffered from short breath. Ralph Upton had an area of white about his mouth, while down in the wards, Susan, too exhausted to be cross or persistent, lay whimpering in her cast.

Trudy and Meta moved about their work like automatons. "The radio said thunder showers this afternoon. I wish they'd come," Trudy sighed. At last a shadow fell across the sunlight. At four, when the girls had practically finished their rounds, the air was growing dark. Black clouds piled up in the west, and the atmosphere seemed to tighten before the storm. Now the patients, especially the children, were restless. They tossed in their beds, demanded endless attention, and a few who had especial fear of storms began to cry.

Trudy had never known Susan to be afraid of a storm, but as she passed Three C on her way back to the shop, Miss Blanchard who was on duty there beckoned to her. "Your sister seems about to go off the deep end," she said. "See if you can quiet her. It's bad for the ward."

Trudy hurried to Susan's bed. Where the children who were actually afraid of the storm had huddled under their covers, Susan had flung hers back, and Trudy saw at first glance that it was not fear, but exhaustion and accumulation of nervous tension which had caused Susan to go to pieces. It was the same old plea which met Trudy's ears above the rumbling of the shower.

"I want to get out of this cast. I want to go home!"

"Susan!" Trudy knew that sympathy only increased Susan's pity for herself. She made her voice firm. "Susan. Pull yourself together. You're making it so hard for the other girls. For your nurse."

The plea fell on deaf ears. "I want to go home." Susan's voice took on a hysterical tone.

"You can go home soon. You just have to wait a little while." Trudy tried another tack; then seeing that the sobs were increasing tried to smother them against her own face.

"Susan, Susan." It was fortunate that the storm broke just then, and the crashings of the thunder drowned Susan's voice, for she and Trudy went through a bad time together. Trudy was at her wit's end as to how to cope with the situation. She was not doing Susan any good, was having no success in helping her back to self-control. Yet to whom could she turn? Miss Blanchard had really used poor judgment in calling her; the nurses could so often do more with a child than her own people could.

Even in her distress for Susan, Trudy realized it was growing late and she ought to be back at the shop. It was out of the question to leave the little girl. What should she do? She lifted her head to see if the nurse was near and instead, with the thrill which she could not help even if he didn't care for her, saw Donald Kerr coming through the door.

Don came directly yet unhurriedly to Susan's bed. No word was needed to explain the situation to him. He motioned to Trudy to go, and as she picked up her basket, she heard his voice, gentle yet authoritative, "Susan," and had not the least doubt that Susan would respond.

The clock in the corridor told Trudy that it was almost five and she hurried as fast as she could to the elevator. As she stepped off at the eighth floor she almost collided with Miss Blaine who was ready to leave.

"You were delayed?" Miss Blaine smiled too sweetly. "Isn't it wonderful that the storm has cooled the air? I think the heat wave's broken."

In her preoccupation Trudy had not noticed it. She entered the shop to find only Miss Compton there. "I'm late, and I'm sorry. Susan—" she began, but Miss Compton held up her hand.

"I know you were with Susan, Miss Wescott. I sent Miss Blaine to see. It's the same old thing." Miss Compton's mouth drew to a paper-thin line. "Your emotions always run away with you. First it was Mrs. Lansing. Now it's your sister. I felt sorry for you when she was so ill, and I allowed you considerable leeway in seeing her. Instead of gratitude, you have taken advantage of me. Oh, I know what has been going on in the wards, Miss Wescott, those extra minutes with your sister every morning. Now this afternoon"—Miss Compton motioned toward the clock—"it is an hour."

"But Miss Compton—" Trudy tried to speak. Again the assistant director cut her short.

"An O.T. cannot do as you have done. You have a job here."

Trudy felt like a creature under the lash. Which way to turn? How to get away? Already somewhat unnerved by the scene with Susan she found herself trembling. How was she to endure this injustice? Was there no ray of comfort anywhere?

Yes. Miss Swift would be back soon. Trudy did not know

that she had spoken aloud until Miss Compton answered her.

"Miss Swift is not coming back. She is resigning. Do not let this happen again," she ended. "You may go."

Trudy dragged herself to her rooming house, and later went listlessly with Meta to dinner and a movie. Meta called the movie tops, but to Trudy it was dull as ditch water.

"Another unpleasantness with Miss Compton? She's been rough on you lately," Meta said as, after the program, she and Trudy ordered sundaes in the ice-cream bar.

"Yes." Trudy looked at the light-spangled river before she told about this latest reprimand. "I can't even try to be philosophical this time," she said with an unsuccessful attempt at a smile. "I don't see how I'm going to go on, now that Miss Swift isn't coming back. I've been hanging on to that like—"

"Like a drowning man to a spar," Meta finished for Trudy. "We all have. In your case," she continued, her voice sympathetic yet full of common sense, "you've got to go on, haven't you?"

"Oh, yes. With Susan's expenses I can't afford to be out of work, to change jobs now."

"Then there's only one thing to be done," Meta said firmly. "You'll have to come to a better understanding with Miss Compton."

Trudy caught her breath, and Meta went on. "It's important because I imagine she'll be the new director. She's— you know General Sherman's definition of war—on her staff, but she gets the work done, gets results, and that's what counts with the hospital board."

Trudy hardly heard Meta's last words. Her mind had stuck on "You'll have to come to a better understanding with Miss Compton."

"How can I?" she asked incredulously.

"Beard the lioness in her den. Tell her just that. You want to straighten things out with her. Oh, I know it won't be easy," Meta said as Trudy raised a protesting hand, "but you'll know what to say when the time comes. You know how to handle yourself better than you did when you came to the hospital."

"I know I do with patients."

"Certainly. Well, now, just take that same confidence in your hand and walk up to Miss Compton. And do it soon," Meta counseled as she and Trudy separated at the street corner.

It was after midnight before Trudy slept soundly, yet it was a fine night for slumber. Cool and smelling of autumn leaves, the west wind swept in from the country. It billowed Trudy's curtains and touched her face with sweet fingers, yet she turned her head on her pillow, thinking, Meta's right, but how can I do it? What shall I say? What will Miss Compton say? Well, her own common sense told her at last, when things get so you can't bear them, you have to do something. I can try. With that thought Trudy drifted into sleep and did not wake up until the sun, angling between buildings, touched her window.

The morning was beautiful. Under a crystal-clear sky the city seemed part of a world made new. Trudy herself felt new, with a new confidence filling her. The time to see Miss

Compton is first thing this morning before either she or I is tired. She's always a minute early. I'll hustle right over as soon as I have my breakfast.

Like the city, Hillhaven seemed to be made new this morning. Both patients and nurses looked refreshed, and when she entered the shop Miss Compton was smiling. No one else was there and with only a moment of qualm Trudy approached her.

"Miss Compton, may I speak to you a minute?"

"Surely. Come into my office." She led the way and, sitting down at her desk, motioned Trudy to the guest chair.

Trudy took it, and as the realization struck her that the time was now, her hands grew cold. However, she found that she could speak directly. "Miss Compton, I'd like to come to a better understanding with you. I try to be a good therapist, even if it doesn't seem so to you sometimes. I've felt that things were worse instead of better lately, and I wish we might straighten them out."

Trudy realized that her voice had taken on a deeper timbre, a timbre of assurance and sincerity. The assistant director responded to it.

"Miss Wescott," she said, "I'm glad you've come to me. I think we have misunderstood each other at times, and I'll be delighted to talk things over with you. I may tell you in confidence—it won't be made known for a few days yet—that I am to take Miss Swift's place. I learned it last evening. So, it's all the more important that I should be on a good clear footing with my staff."

No wonder Miss Compton was in such an approachable mood. Trudy was not the person to begrudge a deserved success, and Miss Compton did deserve it. The department was doing excellent work.

"Congratulations," she said warmly.

"Thank you." Miss Compton's eyes showed that a deep ambition had been fulfilled. "Now, tell me what troubles you and we'll see what we can do about it."

The criticism of the day before came to Trudy's mind before anything else. "About Susan, Miss Compton," she said. "I wish you'd believe I've done my very best not to give her too much time. She's just a little girl and she can't understand why I can't stay with her. She clings to me so that sometimes I have to loosen her fingers to get away. Yesterday afternoon she had a sort of nervous collapse. Miss Blanchard asked me to stay with her."

"I see." Miss Compton very evidently weighed Trudy's words carefully before she spoke. "I was given the impression," she began; then hesitated, and in that instant Trudy thought, Miss Blaine. Is that why Miss Compton's been so hard on me of late?

Miss Compton did not finish her sentence. Instead she said judicially, "Yes, I can understand if that is Susan's attitude you would find it hard to get away, and I didn't know about the collapse yesterday afternoon. I think you were justified in staying."

"It was the same about Emily," Trudy went on, but Miss Compton raised her hand and her old sharpness reappeared.

"No, it was not the same. You cannot say that, Miss Wescott. You transgressed, even after I had warned you, in her case."

"I did transgress once," Trudy found herself using Miss Compton's stiff, almost biblical, word. "It was the time we were in the roof garden. I admit I forgot all about my schedule. The second time truly wasn't my fault. I could have—" Suddenly Trudy saw the abyss ahead of her. Could she accuse her superior of not having allowed her to explain?

Apparently Miss Compton saw the abyss, too, and was adroit enough to side-step it. "What would your explanation have been?" she asked.

Gratefully Trudy told about the message from Ward B, the change in plan, and Old Nick's unexpected coming.

Miss Compton nodded. "That clears you. And now, is there anything else?" She glanced through the door and Trudy's eyes following hers, saw that the staff had arrived and the shop was filling with patients.

"Oh, just one thing more," she said impulsively. "I'm glad to have criticism, but could you criticize me all by myself? And if there's any doubt about things, let me explain? That's the way my mother did at home." Trudy felt for a moment like a little girl. "That's what I'm used to."

"It's a very good way," Miss Compton said. "And now, on my part, I'm going to ask you to be less emotional, less sensitive to criticism. I—er—" She checked herself—"that is, an executive sometimes finds those qualities annoying."

Wasn't that Miss Compton, forever and ever? Tact would never be her outstanding virtue. However, Trudy granted the fairness of her request and said, "I'll try hard, Miss Compton."

A patient approached the office door and the new director rose. She held out her hand to Trudy. "Let me say again that I'm glad you came. It shows genuine growth on your part. Now we must get to work."

That noon Trudy and Meta resumed their habit of going to the little park. Shut in between buildings, it had been an inferno during the heat wave. Now it was a pleasant place once more. Its drying city leaves fluttered cheerfully in the west wind, while across the river their country cousins blazed in lovely color.

Except for a handwave from Trudy to say that everything was all right the two girls had had no opportunity to discuss Trudy's interview with Miss Compton. Now they plunged into it at once.

"It worked, Meta. I feel so much better." Trudy leaned back on her bench. "In fact I feel like a different person."

"So do I, but I'm just reacting to the weather." Meta let the breeze ruffle her curls. "What'd she say?" she asked inelegantly.

Trudy outlined the conversation. "She didn't put it as well as she might, of course, but she was really very nice."

"Is Miss Compton going to be the new director? Oh, you needn't answer," Meta added. "Your eyes gave it away."

Trudy laughed, "Did they? Well, anyhow, I think things are going to be better."

Meta nodded. "Yes, just as they were when Miss Swift first went away. The responsibility will steady Miss Compton. And she'll be happy at being promoted, too." Meta's eyes twinkled. "Happiness always makes us human beings act nicer."

"Oh, Meta, you're so funny." Trudy's thoughts ran ahead. "Who do you think will be the new assistant?"

"Well, my dear fellow O.T., I believe that lies between us three graces, you, Miss Blaine and me. As you know there was an epidemic of marriages in our department just before we came. We all arrived at so nearly the same time afterward there's little question of seniority between us. We stand purely on our virtues."

"I'm out," Trudy said sincerely. "I know I'm not ready for such a job, and even with our better understanding I don't think Miss Compton would choose me."

"The Hospital Board decides it," Meta said, "although what Miss Compton says carries weight, no doubt about that. Blaine would like to have the job," Meta went on. "That gal's out for advancement. She's been playing up to both Miss Compton and Miss Swift all along, hoping something would come of it. If she doesn't get this promotion I wouldn't be surprised if she leaves. She'll know there's nothing for her here and try somewhere else. See if she doesn't.

"Well"—Meta's face took on its philosophical look—"she may go far. She knows her O.T. stuff. The only thing about her is that nobody who works under her will be able to trust her. She will always twist things to her own advantage."

"I'm sure she made trouble for me." Trudy thought back to the talk with Miss Compton. It must have been Miss Blaine who had given her the idea that she was spending too much time with Susan, and she had probably put in a word about other things, too.

Oh, well, let it go. Trudy's mind shifted suddenly to the fact that Meta had made no mention of her own chances, her own aspirations. "How about you?" she asked.

Meta straightened on her bench. Her eyes shone. She leaned forward. "I'd love it! Not for the same reason that Blaine would, that it gave me promotion, but because I'd feel I was succeeding, had the makings of a good O.T."

"That's how I'd feel," Trudy said, and added wistfully, "if I ever had a department of my own."

"You will have," Meta said without hesitation. "I can see it coming. You've developed a lot in the last few months. For instance you're beginning to have definite ideas on how a department should be run. Of late when Miss Compton has reprimanded you, along with your righteous indignation"— Meta smiled as she said those two words—"you've been thinking, 'She shouldn't have done it that way. She should have done thus and so.'"

Yes, that was true.

"You and I, my dear gal, have vision. We know what it's all about," Meta added complacently, and somehow it didn't seem conceited when Meta said so.

In spite of her happier mood Trudy did feel some misgivings as she approached Susan's ward that afternoon. How would she find her after her breakdown of the day before?

Trudy need not have worried. Susan, along with everyone else in the hospital had responded to the change in the weather, also to her talk with Donald Kerr.

Lying on her stomach in her cast, her face was reflected in her round hand mirror with an expression as benign and serene as any little angel's. Trudy wondered that wings were not sprouting from her back.

"Hello, Trudy, I'm good today," Susan said calmly, "and I'm going to be good. Donald Kerr—"

"Dr. Kerr," Trudy put in, horrified.

"Dr. Kerr said that if I kept on having hysterics and flouncing around in this cast, I wouldn't get well so fast. So I'm going to be gentle as a lamb and quiet as a mouse." Susan put the matter in good country terms.

"Fine. Stick to it," Trudy said, and Miss Blanchard, who also seemed to be in fine fettle, actually laughed.

"I believe she will. Dr. Kerr certainly laid her out straighter than any cast could yesterday afternoon."

Susan did stick to it. "Aren't I good?" she asked day after day, and Trudy could agree that she was.

The following week Miss Swift returned to wind up her affairs and hand over the reins to Miss Compton. Now and then, in spite of the new understanding, Trudy lost confidence and wondered how, in the long run, she would get along with the new director. How different it would be to step through the office door and be greeted by Miss Compton's sharply shining glasses instead of Miss Swift's smile. Well, time would tell, as it did about so many things. Her thoughts branched off to Donald Kerr. Time would settle that matter for her, too.

Miss Swift left on a Saturday morning. "I hate to go. I simply hate to!" she said, smiling impartially on everyone.

"You've been so good to me, so cooperative! I'll be back to see you often when I'm better, and then of course I'll find my niche in some less exacting line of the work. Good-bye." She shook hands warmly with each of the staff. When she came to Trudy, Trudy did not think she imagined that she lingered a moment.

"You have made great progress, my dear. You're going to be a good therapist."

Trudy walked on clouds for the rest of that morning. How nice this would be to tell her parents, for she was going home. Susan, still in angelic mood, had said she did not mind. Dr. Billings had brought a patient to the hospital and would take Trudy back with him. That would save bus fare.

Dr. Billings left Trudy at the little farm in mid-afternoon. After the greetings and in spite of the pleasure of being at home she felt restless. The house was empty without Susan. There seemed to be nothing to do. Perhaps she missed, not Chet, but his attentions, and there was no happiness in idling and thinking about Donald Kerr. How pass the time until supper?

Some months before, Mr. Wescott had taught Trudy how to drive the truck, saying she might need it in an emergency. Now she got it from the shed. "Come on, Mumsy. Let's go for a spin."

"I wouldn't think you'd want to after driving from the city this afternoon." Mrs. Wescott laughed. "And it won't be much of a spin in that old rattletrap."

"Well, then, let's go for a rattle." Trudy turned the truck toward the open country.

She and her mother rolled along between trees that were like great bouquets of color: red, amber, yellow, russet. The only blues were in the sky, the lakes and streams. It was really an especially beautiful autumn, Trudy was thinking idly, when her mother said:

"There's that old wood road where we found the De Soto."

"So it is." Trudy's interest roused. "Let's drive in."

"Think you can get the truck out again if you get it in there?"

"Oh, sure." Trudy maneuvered turns and thank-you-mams until they came to the old log where the picnic had been spread.

"Better stop," Mrs. Wescott cautioned. "There's space to turn here."

"O. K. I think I'll get out and look around."

"I won't. For once I feel lazy. I'll just sit still and enjoy the woods." Mrs. Wescott made herself comfortable and looked about.

When Trudy first stepped to the springy earth she thought she would walk down to the bend where they had found the De Soto, but suddenly she lost her ambition. The past summer's growth would have filled the space where the car had stood and there really would be nothing to see.

Well, she wouldn't disturb her mother for a while. Goodness knew she got little enough rest. Trudy sat down on the log. Picking up a stick she brushed aside the leaves at her feet and began to scratch doodles on the ground. Lazily she played games of ticktacktoe with herself, beat herself twice and was about to drop the stick when it caught on something hard at the edge of the log. A stone, she thought, but a second thrust told her the object was square, and where the stick had scratched away the dirt bright metal showed. Her curiosity aroused, Trudy dug furiously and soon unearthed it.

She picked the object up and, brushing off the dirt, turned it in her hand. A small square box, a compact probably, gold finished and with a design in enamel on its lid, somehow it seemed familiar. She scrutinized the design, a girl's head with a wreath of flowers around it, very nice work. Now, where had she seen it before? Had someone at the hospital brought it in? As she speculated, her mother's voice came from the truck.

"What are you looking at?"

"I don't know." Even as she spoke, Trudy's memory cleared. "Why, yes, I do. It isn't a compact, it's Elsie Hayes' pillbox," she said, and her thoughts gave a sudden leap.

Elsie had been here, perhaps in the De Soto. If she had, she knew who was driving it. And 'f the De Soto was, as they all thought it might be, the car that hit Susan?

"Oh, Mother, come on! Quick!" she cried.

CHAPTER XV

"WHAT'S THE RUSH, all of a sudden? And who is Elsie Hayes?" Trudy saw that her mother could not understand her excitement.

"I must get Chet. He'll know what to do." Trudy gave her mother a rapid if not too coherent explanation. "Elsie's an old classmate of mine, lives at Garville. I met her on the bus last Thanksgiving time and she had this pillbox. She faints easily."

"All Greek to me," Mrs. Wescott said calmly, "but if you want Chet, get him."

Trudy had not seen Chet since the day he had stopped at the farm when Sam, Meta and Don were there, and he had, for a second time, she felt, definitely tried to alienate Don from her. He had written several times, but she had not answered his letters.

Now, however, she left her mother at the house and drove directly to his office. She felt there was no time to get her father. He was at the very back of the farm repairing the fences, and she was on fire to follow what seemed to her a definite clue.

Chet was evidently delighted to see her. "Hi, sweetheart."

"Skip all that," she said coldly, and before he could speak again, burst into her story about finding the pillbox.

"What do you think the box has to do with the case?" Chet was so calm that Trudy's spirits fell.

"Well," she said a little lamely, "I just thought that if Elsie's pillbox was there where the car was found, she was there. If she was, she'd know who was driving it."

"Elsie might not have been in the stolen car." Chet was purely professional now. "She might have been there at some other time."

"Yes, but Susan heard a woman scream," Trudy argued. "You'd think from that, a woman was involved in the case."

"Hmm." Point by point, Chet constructed a hypothetical case. "Well, now, grant some big ifs. Grant first, that Elsie was in Marston's car, the stolen car. She might have been with the driver, or been the driver. Know if she drives?" he interrupted himself to ask.

"No, I don't."

"Then, say she's with the driver. Now, who is he, or she? Since Susan said she heard a woman scream, a woman may have been the driver. Of course children aren't too dependable on these details, you know. Now. What's the situation? They hit Susan, drive away. Turn in that old wood road, probably to conceal the car. Elsie faints. Out comes the pillbox. She drops it, leaves it behind."

"Yes." Trudy felt very impatient as Chet set up his case. Her certainty that they were on the verge of finding the hit-run driver had returned. "The thing to do is to go and see Elsie," she said and Chet agreed.

Trudy parked the truck and they took Chet's car. It was only five miles to Garville, yet although Chet drove at top legal speed it seemed to Trudy as if they would never get there. Trudy did not know Elsie's address, so they had to stop at the factory office. Chet as the lawyer in the case secured it, and five minutes later they drew up before a plain little house on a side street.

"If she's only home!" Trudy breathed as she and Chet went up the steps.

"If she's only involved," Chet growled. He still held to his skepticism. "Don't get your hopes too high."

Elsie's father came to the door. Trudy remembered him faintly from Knolton days, a tremendous man with not too kindly a face. He had his hat on as if he were going out.

"Yes?" he asked brusquely.

Even in her eagerness to see Elsie, Trudy thought of what this man's wrath could be and felt an impulse to shield Elsie from it. After all she might be entirely innocent, might not have known the car was stolen, or, as Chet pointed out, might have been at the spot at some other time.

"Hello, Mr. Hayes," Trudy said as casually as she could. "Is Elsie home? I'm an old classmate of hers from Knolton."

"Yes, she's home." Mr. Hayes was more friendly now. He motioned them through a narrow hall into the living room; then turned to the foot of the stairs. "Elsie? Friends to see you."

"She's always primping," he explained with rough cordiality. "Sit down." Then to Trudy's great relief he left the room.

"Let me do most of the talking," Chet said while they waited.

"Yes." Trudy lowered her voice. "But let's not get her father and mother into it, not unless we have to."

Chet nodded, and they waited for several long minutes; then from where they sat they glimpsed Elsie's feet as she came lightly down the stairs. "Greetings!" She stepped through the door from the hall; then turned as white as chalk when she saw who it was. Her hand sought a chair back to steady herself and Trudy thought she was going to faint.

"Oh, it's you," she said in a barely audible voice.

"Yes," Trudy couldn't think of another word to say, but Chet held out the little pillbox. His voice was as Trudy had never heard it before, sudden and sharp. That's how he is in court, she thought.

"Do you recognize this?"

Elsie swayed where she stood.

"Yes," she whispered.

She looked so ghastly that Trudy hurried to her and helped her into a chair. "Hadn't you better take one of your pills, Elsie?"

"In a minute." Elsie leaned her head back. "Dad and Mom are going marketing. Ought to get a little water. The back door'll slam."

Trudy thought that the older people might well expect

some sounds of conversation from the living room, so she began to talk as easily as she could. "It's about a year since I saw you, isn't it, Elsie? Well, a lot's happened since then." She ran on, hardly knowing what she said until, as Elsie had predicted, a door at the rear of the house banged sharply.

Trudy waited a moment, then rose. "Is there a glass in the bathroom, Elsie?"

"Yes. The pills are in my handbag in the hall." Elsie turned to Chet as well as Trudy. "I'll tell you everything, everything." Two great tears formed in her eyes. "I've wanted to for a long while."

So Elsie did know. Trudy hurried to get the water and medicine. It was hard to wait until the latter had time to take effect, but at last Elsie's color began to return. What would she tell them?

Chet's tone had changed when he began his questioning. There was no need to be harsh now. "Start at the beginning and tell us what happened," he directed.

"Well, John Marston and I were out driving—"

"What!" Chet jumped as if he had been stung. "Marston was driving the car himself?"

"Yes." Elsie nodded. "He and I were driving along on that highway that goes past Trudy's house. We were laughing and fooling. John was trying to poke a candy into my mouth. He wasn't watching the road, and he was driving fast. He always does—did," Elsie corrected herself. "Just as we got to a side road that has a hedge along it, Susan came out on her bike. John tried to swerve, but it was too late. We hit her."

Elsie paused and put her hand to her eyes. "I'll never forget it, the crash, the glass and the bike. And then, Susan. I screamed, and John, instead of stopping drove right on. When I realized what he was doing I begged him, 'John, we've hit a little girl! Stop! Stop! And then I fainted.'"

Trudy felt as if her head were whirling. John Marston was driving the car himself? It hadn't been stolen? Then how—she would have asked these questions, but Chet motioned to her to be silent. He himself said quietly, "Yes. What happened next?" and Elsie went on:

"When I came to, the car was at that place where you found the pillbox. John had gone down to the brook and got some water. He put some on my face and I took one of my pills, and when I felt better I got out and sat down on a log. I thought I put the pillbox in my pocket, but I must have dropped it. I missed it afterward, but I didn't dare go back and get it."

"What did you do after that?" Chet asked.

Elsie shuddered. "John said we'd leave the car right there in the woods. He was wild, said his business wouldn't stand any publicity. That was why he'd left Susan, and was why he didn't dare drive the car with its broken headlight and dented mudguard. The police might spot it and catch him. He ran the car on farther and jammed it into the bushes; then he brought me back to the highway and told me to take the bus to Garville. He told me not to tell about the accident or he'd—well, it sounded as if he'd kill me."

"You went alone on the bus to Garville?" Chet asked.

"Yes. John beat it back into the woods as soon as he got me to the highway."

"Did he tell you what he was going to do?"

"Yes. He said he'd go back to Knolton on another road." Elsie was talking more easily now. "He told me later that he went into the drugstore, to establish an alibi by being seen there; then he reported to the police that his car had been stolen."

"He certainly got away with it," Chet said bitterly. His former harshness returned. "Why didn't you notify the police?" he fairly shot the words at Elsie.

"Oh, I wanted to. I didn't sleep that night." Elsie twisted her hands. "You see I was on a spot My father—"

Trudy thought of the burly high-tempered man.

"My father had said he'd break my neck if I went out with John any more. I was afraid—" Elsie's voice trailed away to nothing. After a moment she began to speak again, slowly as if she were very tired. "Toward morning I made up my mind that if Susan—I didn't know who she was then, of course,—if Susan was badly hurt, or dead—

It was Trudy's turn to shudder.

"I thought if Susan was in bad shape, I'd tell, no matter what happened to me. I'd face it. But when I read in the morning paper that she was resting comfortably I thought I needn't tell. So I just telephoned the hospital as often as I thought I could without giving myself away and sent some presents."

"Mr. and Mrs. Mystery," Trudy put in, and Elsie turned to her.

"Why, yes. Is that what you called the dolls?"

"Susan did," Trudy said tersely. The thought of Susan's suffering, of the family's anxiety, of the financial strain she and her parents had been under, struck her like a succession of blows. All because this silly feather-headed girl wouldn't tell, and her sympathy for Elsie suddenly turned to bitterness.

"I suppose you never thought of the expense we were put to," she said, "of what all this hospitalization, of what an operation, cost. And is still costing," she added. "It was our right to collect damages and you kept us from it."

"Did you never think of that angle of the case?" Chet's voice was edged.

"Well, yes and no." Elsie moved uncomfortably. "I knew it must cost a lot, but I thought Trudy's folks had that nice little farm and she and her father both worked. I thought they'd manage all right. You can collect damages now that you know who the driver was, can't you?" she asked.

"There's considerable doubt about that," Chet said sternly. "So much time having elapsed since the accident complicates the situation."

Trudy's heart sank at his words. She realized that ever since Elsie had said she would tell who the hit-run driver was she had been filled with hope. Perhaps we are at the end of our difficulties, she had thought. Chet will make the man pay. When Elsie had revealed that the car was not stolen, but that John Marston was driving it himself, and that the "King's enemies" no longer figured in the situation, her hope had grown even brighter. Now Chet said there were still complications.

"How long is it since you've seen Marston?" He shot another question at Elsie.

"Oh, not in a long while." Again Elsie's eyes filled with tears. "And I don't know where he is. Even though I didn't tell, that accident spoiled everything. He seemed to be afraid to see me, and at last I could tell he didn't want to see me. There wasn't anything I could do. I even went to his office once in a while. Finally I went one day and he was gone. The office was vacant. I never did know what company he worked for, or what his business was," Elsie ended miserably. "I only know he said it couldn't stand any publicity."

"John Marston's gone?" Trudy's heart fell still further.

"That doesn't matter too much." Chet brushed aside this fear. "I doubt if he left because he was afraid. He undoubtedly felt safe when almost a year had gone by without discovery. We can find him when we want him. Marston carried accident insurance," he added as if to himself.

"Oh, yes," Elsie said eagerly. "He told me he did. He said he wouldn't drive a foot without it. Won't that help?"

"It may and it may not." Chet's tone was dry. "I suppose since Amos Black issued the theft insurance he probably issued the accident insurance, too. I'll see him right away."

While they had been talking the October afternoon had slipped into dusk. A second slamming of the back door told that Elsie's parents had returned. Chet asked a last question.

"Will you come with us and make a sworn statement to what you've told us?"

"Yes," Elsie said. Her voice was sad. "It doesn't matter

now. I wanted to tell you long ago," she spoke to Trudy, "and I nearly did once. It was a Saturday afternoon and I'd just come out of the factory. I was standing on the steps. You were in a car that slowed down and I beckoned to you. I thought, 'If she sees me and stops, I'll spill the whole thing.' "

As near as that? Trudy remembered the time. It had been the day before Easter when the foursome drove out to her house. Perhaps then, six months earlier, they might have had a better chance to collect damages. Bitterness filled her again.

It was plain that Elsie sensed it. "I'll do all I can to make things right," she said. "Maybe I can help a little with Susan's expenses. I did send the presents and they cost a lot. I made John pay for them at first, but after"—her voice faltered—"after he was gone, I paid for them myself. I went without things to do it."

Trudy felt a moment's pity for Elsie, and thought that probably Chet with his tender heart did, too. He gave no sign of it, however. "Let's go," he said.

"Yes." Elsie got her coat and hat, said a brief word to her parents, and she, Chet and Trudy crowded themselves into the coupé. Chet turned toward Knolton and his office, to draw up the statement for Elsie to sign. It might take quite a little time, Trudy thought.

"I'll get the truck and go on home," she said, for she felt that her parents ought to know of this new development at once.

"Sure." Chet came to a stop in front of his office. "I'll come out to the farm and tell you what I've found after I've seen Amos and taken Elsie home."

"Oh, I'll go on the bus," Elsie said humbly. "I'm used to them now. And I'm awfully sorry for what I've done." She turned to Trudy. "I've been wicked."

Trudy sensed that the girl was ready to cry. "I suppose you didn't realize," was all she could make herself say. "Good-bye, Elsie. See you later, Chet."

It did not take Trudy long to give her parents an outline of what she and Chet had found, Elsie's confession, the fact that the car had not been stolen, but that John Marston had been driving it himself.

"If only there wasn't this complication about the insurance," Trudy sighed.

"Well, Chet's smart," Mr. Wescott said. "He may work that out."

"And somehow it's a relief to know what actually happened," Mrs. Wescott commented.

That was true, Trudy realized. At least she need not torment herself with speculations any more.

"Yes, and in any case, even if we can't collect damages, we're not a whit worse off than we were before," Mr. Wescott said stoutly. "Susan's better. We've managed the bills so far and, if we have to, we'll keep right on managing them until she's well."

Chet did not come to the farm until evening. Then he dashed in, banging the door behind him. His eyes were keen with excitement.

Before he could speak, Trudy said, "You found out something!"

"You bet I have, something I didn't dream of before. It's this. John Marston didn't own that De Soto."

"He didn't! Whose was it?"

"His father's. And it was insured in his father's name."

"Does that make a difference?" Trudy asked.

"All the difference in the world!" Chet said emphatically. "This is the point. The insurance policy states that the person insured agrees to report any accident promptly. If he doesn't the policy can be voided. Now. John Marston certainly didn't tell his father, nor any one else for that matter, that he'd had an accident. So, how could his father notify the insurance company? He couldn't, and consequently he is guilty of no delay. That fact may pull our chestnuts out of the fire."

"What will you do?" Trudy could feel her spirits rising like bubbles in a spring.

"Notify John Marston's father, get him into action," Chet said. "I'll tell him I'll have to sue him if the company doesn't make a settlement."

"Will John Marston be brought to justice as a hit-run driver?" Mrs. Wescott asked. The question had been in Trudy's mind as well.

"Yes, if you press charges against him," Chet answered.

"I don't think we want to do that," Mrs. Westcott said.

"We don't want to, but I think we ought to." To Trudy's

astonishment, it was her father, always gentle and humane, who said these words. "How are our country's laws to be enforced if we don't uphold them?"

"Right," Chet said. "I'll set the legal machinery in motion. And don't count one hundred per cent yet on collecting from that insurance company. There's still a battle ahead."

Chet got his hat; then turned to Trudy. "You wouldn't want to go dancing?" he asked, and it seemed to her that his voice was wistful. Perhaps at long last he was beginning to believe she really didn't care for him, never would.

"No." Gratitude for all he was doing for her family made Trudy add, "But thanks just the same, Chet."

"O.K." Trudy was sure there was something final in Chet's voice, as if in accepting her refusal to dance he accepted the larger refusal which lay behind it. "O.K.," he said again. He made a dispirited little gesture with his hat. "Good night, folks."

Despite Chet's warning Trudy returned to the city quite agog that Monday morning. "We solved the mystery," she said as she entered the shop.

The entire staff turned toward her. "What happened?" They stopped their work while she told about finding the enameled pillbox and the subsequent chain of events. It took considerable time, and she was suddenly aware of a change of expression on Miss Compton's face.

"I'm sure we are all interested, Miss Wescott," she said stiffly; then checked herself, and Trudy knew that she had remembered their agreement.

"Yes, Miss Compton, I'll get right to work." Trudy nodded and Miss Compton smiled.

How much nicer this was than the old days, she thought as she took her basket and turned toward the wards. And how excited Susan would be over the news. She must manage to give her the gist of it as she stopped to inspect her work.

"Hold everything, Susan," she said when she came to her bed in the course of touring the ward.

Susan had, of course, seen her coming, and had jerked the horse reins she was making from her table drawer. Trudy examined them cursorily. "Too loose. Draw your strands tighter and don't let them snarl." She stooped over Susan's wide eyes. "Don't squeal, not loud anyhow," she said, "or Miss Blanchard will get after you. We've found out about the hit-run driver!"

"You have!" Susan's voice turned every head in the ward. "Who is he?"

"A man by the name of John Marston, Elsie Hayes' boy friend."

"Was she with him?"

"Yes."

"How do you know?"

"I found her pillbox." As she told Susan what had happened, Trudy worked conscientiously at untangling the strands of Susan's reins.

"There, that's all I have time for now. I'll come back when I'm off duty and we'll talk it all over." Trudy laughed, for she judged that Miss Blanchard was going to have an interesting day. As she left the ward Susan's voice followed her, rising excitedly above the others.

"Hey, kids! They've found my hit-run driver! Listen, and I'll tell you all about it!"

By the time the day was ended Trudy was hoarse with talking. She had repeated the story more times than she could count; to her specials, Emily Lansing, Ralph Upton, even Old Nick; then to various people about the hospital, nurses who knew Susan and were interested, nice Miss Ericson, Miss Duncan in the nursery, Mr. Bell at his cashier's window, even Sam Bradford whom she met on the street. She wished it had been Don instead. Of course Sam would tell him, but she would have liked to tell him herself, see his eyes brighten with interest, his smile come and go, even if it did bring a little choke to her throat. Well, it was no use.

"I think everybody knows now," Trudy said to Meta as they sipped their favorite hot chocolates in the drugstore at five thirty.

"If they don't they soon will," Meta said. "Good news travels fast. By the way, I have some myself." Her eyes were bright. "Don't I look as if I'd eaten the canary?"

"What in the world are you talking about?" Trudy realized suddenly that Meta did seem to be in some sort of seventh heaven, her eyes shining, her mobile mouth curved in a smile.

"What is it?" Trudy asked.

"Well, my dear fellow O.T.," Meta's smile grew even wider, "Miss Compton told me just as I left the shop that I'm to be the new assistant director."

"Oh, Meta!" Trudy jumped up and ran around the table to kiss her. "That's the nicest news I ever heard. You'll make a wonderful assistant. All the luck in the world, and"—she paused in astonishment—"why, Meta, you'll be my boss!"

CHAPTER XVI

A YEAR AGO today I came to Hillhaven, Trudy said
to herself one November morning as she packed her
basket to go to the wards. I feel so different now.

She recalled with what qualms she had gone on ward work
in those days. Now she had none at all. The hospital and its
staff were as well known to her as an old shoe.

No, Trudy was entirely sure of herself as she took the
elevator to the wards. She was also happy for Susan, because
on the previous day the little girl's original cast had been
changed to a lighter one. With the exception of a few minor
lapses, Susan had been a very good girl during the weeks
since Donald Kerr had had that serious talk with her. She
was progressing nicely now. Tests and observations showed
that her operation was healing well and the P.T.'s reports
were excellent. It was still impossible to predict the degree of
Susan's recovery, but her future looked bright.

Trudy would have liked to go directly to Susan, but the
regular routine had to be followed, so she toured the wards
as usual, stopping at bed after bed to leave materials, inspect
work, or help a patient to plan a new project; a bit of whittling

for a man who, like Old Nick, had only scorn for "women's work," clay for a young woman whom she thought of as having fairy fingers. In fact while Trudy made the rounds of the other patients the young woman deftly shaped a little Christmas angel, its hands cupped to hold the socket for a candle. What a lovely talent, Trudy thought. It seemed a shame to say so soon, "I'm sorry, but I must go on," then after a thorough search to make sure no particles had fallen among the bed clothes, take the clay from the patient. "You'll have to come up to the shop as soon as you can. Then you can work for hours," she said to the young woman who smiled wistfully.

"It will be a while. I haven't had my operation yet."

"Well, I'll be back tomorrow." Trudy went on to the next patient, a girl who was doing functional rather than diversional work, which was an exception in the wards. Tendon transplants on both hands had been necessary because of injury from burns, Trudy recalled as she fastened a frame for cross-stitching to a bar over the bed. The hands had been operated on successively, the first hand being given time to heal before the second one was done. This first hand had responded nicely to O.T. and P.T., and to prevent its getting stiff and losing ground while the patient was in bed after the second operation, both departments were keeping up their work.

"There we are." Trudy finished adjusting the frame while the girl watched, smiling. "Now, what's it to be?"

"A guest towel." The girl motioned toward a small package on her bedside stand. "My mother brought it yesterday.

I want to cross-stitch my initials on it. I'm going to be married as soon as my hands are well," she added shyly.

"Oh, lovely!" Trudy's heart felt both warm and sad; warm for the girl to whom it seemed so just that, after all her suffering, happiness should come; sad for herself because, with a flicker of self-pity which she could not check, Trudy thought such happiness might never be hers.

Feeling rather subdued, she came to Susan's ward, but her mood changed when she saw the little girl. Susan did not look different, since the new cast followed the same lines as the old. But her eyes were like stars.

"I'm better! I'm ever so much better! Don—" she corrected herself hastily—"Dr. Kerr says I can wiggle a little, soon. What'll he do to me next?" she asked, and Trudy laughed.

"Oh, put you in lighter and lighter casts, and finally in a strait jacket."

"A strait jacket!" Susan was horrified. "Like Dad says they put crazy folks in?"

"Not a real one, goose. A canvas support that's something like a strait jacket. Then you can move around a bit, come up to the shop to work."

"Oh, goody." Susan started to give a flounce, thought better of it and clapped her hands instead.

"And now as to the matter about which I really called, Miss Susan." Trudy smiled down at her. "How would you like to celebrate your improvement by starting a new project? Anything in mind you'd like to make?"

"Yes. I've been thinking about it a great deal." Susan grew amusingly serious. "You know, Duzenbury must have missed me an awful lot since I've been gone. He hasn't had anybody to play with but the kittens. I'd like to make something to take home to him."

"Grand idea." Trudy wanted to laugh, but managed to keep her face straight. "What will it be?" she asked to give herself time to conjure up some idea of her own.

"A collar," Susan said firmly. "A collar like that belt I made."

"Out of felt?" Trudy asked incredulously. "It wouldn't be strong enough." She visualized Duzenbury in a felt collar, and the outcome if he caught sight of a rabbit. "He'd go through it as if it was butter."

"Well, could I make it out of something else?" Susan was downcast and a little resentful. She copied the speech of the older girls on the ward. "I thought it was a marvelous idea."

"It was, is," Trudy corrected herself. "All but making the collar out of felt."

She reflected that Susan's hands were not strong enough to work on heavy leather. "I suppose a strip of good tight knotted work would hold Duzenbury," she said. "Even if it wouldn't do for week-days, he could wear it Sundays and Christmas."

"Now you're teasing," Susan pouted, but she really didn't care. "What color could I have?"

"Whatever you think would be becoming to Duzenbury." Trudy kept a grave face.

"Let's see. He's sort of gold colored."

"Trimmed with white."

"I should think green would be nice."

"Perfect." Trudy made a note in her book. "I'll bring the strips and frame tomorrow. All right?"

"Yes." Susan nodded, then changed the subject. "Has Chet got my damages yet?"

"No. There's no hurry." Trudy side-stepped the question, partly because the matter was not settled, although Chet had told her father the outlook was encouraging. The insurance company had agreed to what he called "handle" the case. Her main reason for avoiding a direct answer was she did not wish to say to Susan that the sum they might collect depended on the degree of her recovery. That was still unpredictable, and Chet had said he would not make any settlement until Donald Kerr gave the word that Susan's recovery was as complete as it ever would be and there was no likelihood of further trouble.

"Well, I'll have to go, Suze." Trudy took up her basket and moved on around the ward.

It was almost noon when she finished her circuit. She was in a relatively happy mood as she went toward the shop. Things were pretty good, Susan better, Meta successful as assistant director, Miss Compton serene in her own promotion. Yes, everything was fine—except Donald Kerr.

At that very moment she met him in the corridor.

"Good morning, Miss Wescott." His eyes were withdrawn.

"Good morning, Dr. Kerr."

Trudy, hurrying by, found it hard to hold back tears. She rarely saw Don now, except in hospital routine. Seldom a foursome, never a twosome, and if he happened to come into the drugstore when she was there, he avoided her if he could.

"What's come over our Donald?" Meta had said one day. "He's as cold as an iceberg; and Sam says he's as cross as two bears."

Trudy was glad Meta did not insist on an answer to her question but answered it herself.

"You know, he's sort of old-fashioned and quixotic, Trude. I wonder if he thinks you're engaged to that Chet-bird. If he did, with his reserve, he wouldn't say anything but just drop out of the picture. Yes, sir"—Meta spoke with conviction—"that's the way he'd act."

"If he cared," Trudy said involuntarily, and Meta gave her an astute glance.

"I don't mean to pry, but—you care, don't you, Trudy?"

Do I care? Trudy thought. I can't sleep nights. I keep thinking about him. I see his face everywhere. I'm never really happy. There's an ache—She tried to conceal her feeling, but knew she did not succeed.

"Oh, sure," She pitched her voice casually, yet it took a husky turn. "He was such a grand friend and he isn't even that any more."

"Never mind." Trudy felt Meta's arm around her. "I'll tell Sam to tip Don off, tell him you aren't engaged, never did care about that no-'count Chet. That ought to straighten things out."

It should, but would it? Sam was not adroit but rather bludgeoned his ideas into people. Might he put this matter so crudely that Don would think she, through Meta, had asked Sam to tell him, or that she had discussed her emotions with Meta so freely that he felt her heart hung on her sleeve for him to pluck?

With his reserve, she knew that he would never forgive that, wouldn't want her even if he knew he could have her.

As she thought it over later, Trudy was sorry rather than glad that she had tacitly agreed Sam should speak to Don. At first it had seemed a possible way to accomplish something which, because of her depth of feeling and her own reserve, she had so far been unable to do.

Several times there had been opportunities, little lulls when by chance she and Don had been alone, but she had not been able to shape the words. One opportunity had been especially good, but it had come to nothing.

The foursome had met accidentally in the drugstore, and Meta who was in high spirits that day had had a wonderful time arguing the constancy of girls as against the constancy of men.

"Sailors have a girl in every port," she had declared.

"And girls have a sailor on every corner." Sam had risen to go to the cigarette counter, and Meta had gone with him.

Trudy had drawn a quick breath. Here was her chance, the stage, the mood all set, if she could speak. "Chet Fielding has a million girls," she said, but Don had turned to watch Sam and Meta, and if he heard her he gave no sign.

Trudy hadn't been able to get the words out a second time, and had given up miserably. Now, if Sam tried to hammer the idea into Don's head, mightn't he do more harm than good?

In the next few days Trudy again found herself watching Don whenever she saw him. Always the little choke in her throat, had Sam told him yet? How had he reacted?

Of course, in the hospital where etiquette was so rigorous, only Don's eyes could have indicated any change. But on the street, in the old meeting places? No. With a sinking heart Trudy realized there was no change. Cool, aloof, Don passed her as if she were the most casual of his acquaintances.

Somehow the situation made Trudy think of the title of an old book at home, *Ships That Pass in the Night*. Yes, it was like that. What might she and Don have meant to each other if this darkness had not come between them?

If I could only stop caring, Trudy said to herself as she approached the shop one noon. The staff, with the exception of Meta who stood in the office door, and all the patients but one, had gone to their midday meal. Meta motioned toward the patient and Trudy saw that it was Emily Lansing. Apparently her attendant was late in coming for her, and Emily, whose hand was very good now, and who, in fact, was practically ready to leave the hospital, had swung her chair so that it faced the window and the view.

Emily's appearance was very smart these days, Trudy thought as she approached her. In preparation for her return to the outside world she was being fully dressed each morning. In gray slacks and rose-colored sweater she looked charming and, Trudy coined a word, very un-invalidish. Her new wheel chair was as smart as could be, too. Made of chromium, and styled like modern furniture, it had as little of the sickroom about it as possible.

Trudy had thought that Emily was enjoying the view, but as she reached her side she saw that Emily's seashell color was gone, that her eyes were drained of their blue. Tears hung on her dark lashes and several had fallen on a letter in her lap. Her receiving the letter in the shop was understandable. The South American postmark had made it seem important, so someone in the office had delivered it.

But should she approach Emily? Trudy, her heart made tender by her own trouble, debated. For Emily Lansing was not enjoying the view. Instead she was crying softly. Trudy decided to slip away, but Emily heard her. She held out her hand. "Oh, Trudy," she forgot all hospital formality, and Trudy forgot it too.

"Oh, Emily," she said and put her arm around her.

It was fortunate that it was Meta and not Miss Compton who stood in the office door for the next few minutes. Miss Compton would not have liked such a show of emotion on the part of either patient or therapist. Emily's tears fell thick and fast, and Trudy, drying them tenderly, used all her ingenuity to be of comfort to her.

"Robert's coming." Emily's breath caught like a child's. "His job is ended. There's no way around it now. I've got to face him." Her affected hand was still weak. It began to tremble, but her limbs and feet remained as always, motionless as those of a statue.

Never to walk again. The tragedy made Trudy's own trouble seem small. How could she comfort Emily? First of all, reassure her that she was still lovely, even if she couldn't walk.

"Emily," she said aloud, "you're still you, just as you were before. If Robert loved you then, he will now. He couldn't help it."

"He did love me when he went away. We were the whole world to each other." Emily's voice faltered for a second. "I had only him. He had only me."

"You'll be the same again." Trudy had faith in what she said. Who could help but adore this lovely creature whose soul, she was sure, had grown more beautiful with her trial?

"Robert says we will be. He's written from the very beginning that my handicap wouldn't make a bit of difference. He's full of plans."

"And why shouldn't he be?" Trudy said firmly. "It takes a little longer in a wheel chair, but you can go practically anywhere you did before, to concerts, to the theater, on trips in your car. Evenings, when you don't feel like going out, you and Robert can listen to the radio, watch television, read books together. Oh, there's no end to the companionship you can have."

Trudy was aware that Emily was listening with all her heart. "While Robert's at his job, during the day," she went on, "you can entertain yourself with sewing, knitting, weaving." She swung her hand toward the loom. "You can even be useful, do a bit of housework, dust, make your bed, wash your lingerie. As soon as you have full muscle power in your hand and arm again, the Rehabilitation people will teach you how to slide in and out of your wheel chair. You can even slide into your bathtub and take your own bath. How much more do you ask, for goodness' sake?" Trudy laughed, and after a moment Emily laughed with her.

"I know," she said, touching her handkerchief to her eyes. "And you ought not to have to tell me all this. It seems very ungrateful of me not to remember it myself. You O.T.'s and P.T.'s along with Rehabilitation have not only restored my muscles, you've taught me how to occupy my time, how to handle myself and get about. You've really re-educated me so I can lead a fairly active life.

"I *am* grateful." Emily took both Trudy's hands, "and I'll be a good girl after this. It's just when something like this letter"—she touched the square in her lap and her eyes grew clouded but merely for an instant—"it's only when something like this comes along that I slip."

Emily's attendant came for her then, and Trudy turned to Meta who was waiting for her. "I really think Emily ought to have a full happy life," she said. "She can do all the things I mentioned. She'll be O.K. if her husband's the right sort."

"After all, that's a big if." Meta motioned Trudy out of the shop and locked the door. "We're late for luncheon," she commented.

Trudy refused to have her thoughts turned aside. "I know it could be a big if, but somehow I think Robert's all right. Emily couldn't have loved him so much if he weren't. Why!" A new thought struck Trudy and despite Meta's urging she came to a halt in the middle of the corridor. "Why, Emily might even have a child."

"There have been cases like Emily's who did," Meta agreed; then as no one was about she suddenly gave Trudy a hug. "Trude, you darling, sometimes you're so wise you seem a hundred years old. Another time you're so naive you don't seem grown up. But I like you." Meta's eyes were warm. "I like you just as you are. Now, come on and ring that elevator bell before we starve."

Trudy did not go home for Thanksgiving. Instead her mother and father came to the city, and Susan, for the first time, was bolstered up on pillows for the occasion.

"Look at me!" She gave herself a resounding thump on her plaster-covered chest. "Soon I'll be in that strait jacket Trudy's always talking about—"

"Good place for you," Mr. Wescott joked, but Susan ignored him.

"And soon I'll be home."

"Better hurry up with that collar for Duzenbury," Trudy said and meant it, for Susan was improving fast and the physical therapist reported that she could detect considerable evidence of returning muscle power in her legs.

"It's wonderful, and we have you to thank for it," Mrs. Wescott said to Donald Kerr when the trio met him on the hospital steps as they were going out to dinner. "We're so grateful to you."

"No, don't be," Don said, and Trudy knew that his modesty was genuine. "I only did what any orthopedic surgeon would do. It wasn't a complicated operation and the degree of recovery still can't be predicted."

His eyes met Trudy's for a moment, and she read his

thought, that in spite of all his skill, while Susan would walk, she might never run and skip like other little girls.

"Susan's excellent physical background and the cooperation you all have given," Don said, "have helped a lot."

How gentle he was, how kind, Trudy thought as she watched him smiling down at her mother, and adding warmly, "You'll have to take the credit for that."

"Oh, but that's the least of it," Mrs. Wescott said. Then she added impulsively, "Won't you come out to dinner with us? I know it's sudden. I wish we'd thought to ask you before."

"Thank you very much, but I'm on duty."

Don's voice made Trudy wonder if he really was. Well, of course, someone had to be. Her heart sank just the same. She felt that in any case he would have avoided her.

"Then won't you come to the farm next Sunday? Trudy's coming, and we're going to have our real Thanksgiving dinner. We don't feel that this city dinner"—Mrs. Wescott's gesture indicated her scorn of restaurant cooking—"is going to amount to much."

Oh, if he'd say yes, and he would have in the old days, Trudy thought, they'd have such a good time. She pictured the hours at the farm; one of her mother's delicious dinners, a lazy siesta by the fire; then a walk perhaps, to Pike's Peak, to the never-freezing spring in the lower pasture, to the beech trees beyond it which, at this time of year, stood like a group of gray ladies, on a golden carpet of their own leaves.

Perhaps in such a lovely place and in such a companionable mood, she might be able to tell Don again, "Chet has a million girls. He's nothing to me."

Trudy almost sighed as Don declined her mother's second invitation. "Believe it or not, Mrs. Wescott," he said, "I'm on duty then, too." He turned to Trudy as if he felt some explanation were due her. "I'm a long way from home, can't get there in any case; but Sam Bradford and some of the fellows nearer could get home if they had a chance, so I told them I'd do double duty."

"We'd have liked to have you," Trudy said in a low voice, and her mother added:

"You must come some other time."

"Thank you very much." Don bowed formally, and with the familiar choke in her throat Trudy watched him disappear through the hospital door.

CHAPTER XVII

"I THINK," said Miss Compton, bustling about with her preparations for the Christmas sale, "I think we'd better put the doll house on a table of its own. Then it won't interfere with the carpenter's bench or any of our regular work."

"Grand idea." Meta brought a stout folding table from the storeroom and set it up while the ambulatories and even the patients in wheel chairs, crowded around it.

The main structure of the house, the usual four-room affair, was finished, but the painting was still to be done, the furniture and accessories to be constructed. Trudy, back on shopwork, thought she had never witnessed a pleasanter sight in an O.T. shop than the patients working wholeheartedly together on this single project. For the time being they had forgotten their handicaps, forgotten even their neuroses, and that was a major achievement.

"I'll make a brass knocker and a mailbox for the door," said a man who had been one of Miss Blaine's patients. Miss Blaine, as Meta had predicted, was gone now. And good riddance, Trudy interpolated to herself.

"I'll embroider the little bedspreads. I think I can get them done—before I leave," said Trudy's own Emily, and only Trudy caught the note of courage in her voice.

"I'll paint the bathroom fixtures," said an arthritic. The fixtures, whittled from blocks of wood, were to be coated with white enamel.

"What can I make?" piped Susan's voice, for Susan was coming to the shop now. Donald Kerr was greatly pleased with her progress and had put her in the strait-jacket cast which Trudy had predicted. An attendant brought Susan to the shop in a wheel chair, but Susan could stand on her feet for short intervals and could also take a few steps in the walker.

"Perhaps you can weave a rug for the doll house," said Miss Devine, the young O.T. who had taken Miss Blaine's place. To both Trudy's and Susan's disappointment, although Trudy knew it was probably better, Miss Compton had assigned Susan to the new therapist. Susan had argued at first, but was soon reconciled, and Trudy had to admit to herself that her interest in Susan might have run away with her and caused her to give the child too much time. For I'm still a human being, Trudy thought with a little laugh, and I always will have faults. There was the point, too, that Susan would undoubtedly give more explicit obedience to a stranger. On obeying instructions one hundred per cent and executing movements in just the right way, as Trudy well knew, depended much of the success of O.T. work.

Trudy had watched a little wistfully as Miss Devine set Susan at a foot loom, showed her how to place her feet on its pedals and helped her to press them down while her hands slipped the shuttles through the warp. Susan was quick to learn, but it would be some time before her weakened limbs would be strong enough to do the pedaling alone. Trudy saw that Miss Devine was both patient and conscientious, very careful not to let Susan exceed her fatigue level, which was low at first, and with that she had to be content.

"Is there anything I could make for the doll house on the power machine?" Ralph Upton's voice brought Trudy back to the moment. He had just come to the shop and was looking at the house with shining eyes. "Wouldn't Diane and Patricia and Esme be crazy about it?" He said the little girls' names lovingly and touched the doll-house chimney with a gentle finger.

Trudy wished the little girls might have the doll house, but knew it was far beyond Ralph's means. However, Ralph was happy anyhow, and why wouldn't he be? He had made excellent progress in the three months that Trudy had been on the wards, and his physician, after a consultation with Miss Compton and the physical therapist who had worked with him, had decided he might be discharged from the hospital. His right hand had shown the maximum improvement to be expected, his left had been taught to take its place, and he was to go to Shelter Shops, to work as a power-machine operator.

It was all arranged. At first Ralph would not be strong enough to work a full day, so his hours had been planned to fit his level of fatigue. Also, since he still limped and was slow in getting about, they had been set so that he would not have to travel during the rush hours on the city's transportation lines.

Ralph would never be as quick as an unhandicapped power-machine operator, would never be able to take a job in a commercial factory. "But I'll be making real money," he had said delightedly when he told Miss Compton that his doctor thought he might "graduate" from Hillhaven. "I'll at least be helping to support my three little girls."

Again this morning he was overflowing with gratitude. "I don't know how to thank you and the other O.T.'s," he said to Trudy. "And the P.T.'s too. You've made my world over for me."

"You've made it over for yourself, Ralph," Trudy said with considerable feeling. "It's your strong will and hard work that have done it. It's been a pleasure to have you in the shop. We're all proud of you."

Trudy noticed even while she spoke that Old Nick was waiting for her beside the carpenter bench. Nick worried Trudy. She felt she had failed with him. Of course he was a hard nut to crack, but somehow she should have touched him. In a way it was her fault he had not made more progress.

She saw now that, as usual, he was not so much as lifting a finger to take up his work by himself, but was listening to her conversation with Ralph Upton. The contrast between him and Ralph struck her so forcefully that her voice was cool and sarcastic when she came to him.

"Well, Nick, what are you going to make for the doll house?"

The moment she had spoken Trudy expected the roof to lift. Nick, the he-man, the hater of women's work, contribute something to a doll house! There would be roars to make every head in the shop turn! Instead his voice came to her meekly.

"Anything you say, Miss Wescott."

Trudy stared at him, and it dawned on her there was a look in his eyes which she had never seen there before. Their fire was gone, and instead their faded blue had taken on a tractability of which she had not dreamed they were capable.

"Mebbe I could make some of the furniture. I've done so much sawin' and sandin' that I'm pretty good at it," Nick suggested.

Trudy stared again. He was offering, volunteering, to make furniture for the doll house. Suddenly she realized that Old Nick, the pest of both ward and shop, was capitulating. The months of patient effort, of pitting her will against his and cajoling him into working, had made an impression on him after all.

It seemed sudden, but it might have been coming on for some time. Trudy was sure she understood how it had happened. Nick had seen Ralph's progress, envied it, longed for it for himself, and at last had seen there was only one way to get it. This morning he had heard the warmth in her voice when she spoke to Ralph, the praise she had given him. Suddenly Old Nick had wanted that, too—to be liked, to be praised. Her blunt little question had shown him that she felt far differently toward him. He had flung aside his prickly shell, had capitulated.

That was the way to handle Old Nick, was it? And if she could handle him, couldn't she handle almost any patient? Trudy felt triumphant. A brand-new world of self-confidence opened before her. Hurrah! I'm going to be a good O.T., she shouted to herself; then with joy in her voice turned to Nick.

"Why, yes, Ol—er—Nick, it would be grand if you'd make the furniture."

"Trudy had a major victory today," Meta told the foursome that evening. For the first time in several weeks the young people were together. Meta had arranged the date, and Trudy felt Don had come because he could not well refuse her.

Was he enjoying himself? She scrutinized him as closely as she dared, and doubted it. His eyes seldom met hers, and two rather hard little lines accentuated the corners of his mouth. She herself was frankly miserable. Like Don, she would not have come if Meta had not forced her to.

"Don't be a silly," Meta had said. "This is all going to straighten out some day, just like a tangle in a ball of yarn."

Trudy wished she could think so. Meta and Sam hadn't been able to straighten it out anyhow. Trudy had finally learned that Sam reported Don wouldn't let him even mention Trudy. When Sam had persisted, had, in fact, yelled at the top of his lungs so that Don could not help hearing:

"Meta says Trudy isn't engaged!"

And very subtle, that, Trudy had thought.

Don had yelled in return, "Oh, gals! They tell you anything they want you to think!" Then he had gone banging out of the room, nearly taking the door off its hinges.

That, at least, was a good sign, Meta had insisted, but while Trudy knew the incident had its humorous side—the two young surgeons yelling at each other—it did not lighten her spirits. She was far away in her thoughts when she realized that her companions were laughing at her.

"Here we rack our brains for suitable words in which to congratulate you on squashing Old Nick," Sam said, "and all you do is droop as if you had a secret sorrow."

"Perhaps she has," Meta said daringly, and Trudy was terrified for fear she would say more. Of course she wouldn't, but Trudy lived in apprehension these days. Suppose some-one, an unscrupulous someone like Miss Blaine, for instance, spotted her feeling toward Donald Kerr. How the hospital grapevine would hum! Then, too, Trudy was never entirely sure of Susan. She had promised, cross my heart and hope to die, that she would never tell about Chet's proposal, and in so far as Trudy knew she never had. Now, however, with the intuition that some children have, she seemed to sense Trudy's feeling about Don. At least she linked the two men together, for one day, mercifully in the relative privacy of the hospital's sunroom she had burst out with, "I'm awfully glad you turned Chet Fielding down. I like Donald Kerr ever so much better."

Suppose she had said that to someone else! Trudy had known her face was crimson. Involuntarily she put her hand over Susan's mouth with so much force that it hurt.

"Hush!" She looked about to see if anyone had heard; then whispered, "Donald Kerr isn't in it at all. Understand? And you must never say such a thing again."

"O.K." Susan had rubbed her lips. "But I like Don best, just the same."

"Does Christmas always sneak up behind you and grab you? It does me," Miss Devine said to Trudy at closing time one dark December afternoon.

"Yes, it does." Trudy looked out for a moment to where the river, a black ribbon banded with gold, reflected the lights on its shores. Christmas should be such a happy time, but this year it wasn't.

"I think I have everything under control," Miss Devine went on, "then I find I can't get half my presents done."

"That's the way it goes." Trudy thought of the new outfits she was trying to finish for Mr. and Mrs. Mystery. She had started in plenty of time, but—she felt a touch on her shoulder and found Miss Compton beside her.

"Will you come to my office a moment?"

"Surely." Trudy rose at once. She felt a little trepidation, for although things were infinitely better since her talk with Miss Compton, a few minor incidents had shown her that the new director would never be entirely easy to work with. A leopard couldn't be expected to change all its spots, Trudy realized, and it would always be a matter of her controlling her own reaction. So keep calm, she counseled herself even as she wondered if she had made some mistake or forgotten some direction. She judged not, for Miss Compton's manner was entirely pleasant as she preceded Trudy through the door.

"Have you had your mail today?" she asked.

"No, none's come up from the office, and I haven't been to my room since morning," Trudy said.

"Then you haven't heard from Miss Swift. I had a letter from her this afternoon and she said she'd written you. I'd like to talk with you about it."

Trudy felt puzzled as, at her invitation, she sat down in Miss Compton's guest chair. Why was Miss Swift writing to her, Trudy Wescott? Just out of friendliness, probably. But no. If that were all, Miss Compton would hardly know about it, and certainly would not call her into her office to discuss it.

Full of speculation, Trudy had to wait while Miss Compton got the letter from her desk drawer, reread it, leaned back and thought a moment, touched the paper weight, the very same papier-maché pear which Miss Swift had fingered on that first day of Trudy's work at Hillhaven, and finally spoke.

"Miss Swift has written me that she's improving nicely and that she's—But perhaps you'd rather read all this in your own letter at home," Miss Compton interrupted herself. "If you would, we can talk it over tomorrow."

"Oh, no!" Trudy's curiosity would allow her no other answer. "Do go on, please."

"Very well." Miss Compton nodded. "Miss Swift writes

that the directorship at Farview, a special convalescent home that's under construction on the outskirts of the city, had been offered to her. She thinks that by the time the buildings are completed she will be entirely recovered, and as the work, although fully as interesting, will be less strenuous than here, she has accepted the position."

"How nice," Trudy said, happy for Miss Swift, but still wondering where she came into the situation.

"It will be six months, possibly more, before the buildings are finished," Miss Compton went on, "and in the interim Miss Swift wishes to assemble her staff."

A faint glimmer of understanding broke on Trudy. Could it be? Dare she hope? She heard Miss Compton's next words rather confusedly.

"Miss Swift feels that you have the personality she would like in her assistant; the friendliness which brings out the best in patients, the idealistic viewpoint which makes for high standards."

"Oh, does she?" Trudy knew her face was radiant.

"Yes." Miss Compton nodded; then went on, "She thinks, and I do, too, that with another six months' experience here, you will have matured sufficiently to handle the assistant directorship. In a smaller institution it won't involve as much responsibility as it would at Hillhaven. She will recommend you, and so will I, if you care to consider it."

Would she consider it? Work with Miss Swift again? Help her to build a new department of O.T.? Be an assistant director? Trudy could hardly keep from shouting, **Yes!**

"If you decide to accept the position, I shall be sorry to see you go, Miss Wescott. I wouldn't have said that a few months ago," Miss Compton continued with a touch of her old devastating candor, but Trudy, aware that she meant only kindness didn't care. "Now, however, I can say I'll be sorry to have you go. You will make a good assistant."

"Thank you, Miss Compton." Trudy rose. In fact she could sit still no longer. She must get out of the hospital to where she could be alone and think about this miracle which had happened to her.

It was five o'clock when Trudy stepped from Miss Compton's office. She was glad that the rest of the staff were gone, even Meta, for it seemed to her that for the time being she couldn't speak coherently. She hurried to her rooming house, glad that the early December dusk concealed her from both acquaintances and friends.

Once in her room she sat down at the window and stared at the street lights and at the shop or two which already showed the red and green of Christmas decorations. She would leave this familiar view, this room, and have to get acquainted with a new one when she went to Farview. As her exuberance about the new job steadied to where she could think, she discovered that she felt very solemn. It was a serious thing, this new position, her first step up the O.T. ladder, a turning point in her life. The increase in salary, for there would be an increase, of course, would be most acceptable. It wouldn't matter quite so much as it would have earlier, because it looked now as if Susan's damages would be collected without difficulty. Mrs. Wescott had written that Chet had stopped at the farm to say the insurance company had made a fair offer of settlement, but he had told the company, "Nothing doing until we see what recovery this child makes."

That was fine, meant the end of their financial worries, also that they could pay Chet in full and without delay. Bitterness always mingled with gratitude when Trudy thought of Chet these days. She was quite certain now that he had given up trying to win her affection. He had not written her, nor been more than casual since that evening when she had felt the tone of finality in his voice. If only he had believed her the first time, had not given that wrong impression and ruined her friendship, or what might have been more than friendship as far as she was concerned, with Donald Kerr. Tears blurred the Christmas lights as suddenly she thought of what had not occurred to her before, that in leaving Hillhaven she would be leaving Don as well

Not see him every day, pass him in the corridors, consult him about patients, run into him on the street, in the drugstore? In spite of Miss Swift's presence, it would be a lonely world at Farview with no Don. Still, of late, there had been more pain than joy in these brief cool contacts with him. Trudy had felt sometimes it was like turning a knife in a wound, to see his aloof eyes, his tightened mouth, to listen to his formal words.

Oh, Don, everything's all wrong now, and if I go away you'll forget me. I won't forget you—Trudy almost spoke aloud—I can't. Her imagination ran crazily ahead to picture years when she, lonely, unloved, would hear of Donald Kerr, the prominent surgeon.

"He married so and so."

"Yes," she would murmur, "I used to know him."

It was fortunate for Trudy that a tap on the door broke into her unhappy thoughts. Meta stood there glowing.

"Hi! I've heard the news. Miss Compton told me on the quiet. It's grand." Meta kissed Trudy. "Now you and I'll be equals again, both of us assistant directors. But I haven't looked down my nose at you, have I?" Meta noticed how quiet Trudy was. "You are happy, aren't you?"

"Oh, yes, I'm happy," Trudy said softly. "It's just—"

"Don," Meta finished for her. "I keep telling you that will straighten out. Maybe your leaving Hillhaven will jolt him back into his senses. Come on!" Meta was too excited to dwell on the subject. "We've got to celebrate."

The two girls bought a steak and trimmings and, in honor of the occasion, cooked themselves a wonderful dinner in Meta's apartment.

"Ice cream, too." Meta brought a tray from the refrigerator. "And demitasse." She lifted down fragile cups from the top shelf of the closet, cups so seldom used that they were thick with city dust and had to be washed before Meta could fill them.

Over the coffee, she and Trudy discussed various ramifications of the new job, how large the staff at Farview was likely to be, who might take Trudy's place at Hillhaven. As the conversation progressed, the new position took on reality and substance, and Trudy's distress about Don slipped to the background. She was happy as she started for her rooming house.

Oh, I need cold cream, she thought as she passed the drugstore. She turned from the street and for a moment was dazzled by the store's brilliant lights.

"Hi!" a voice hailed her, and as her vision adjusted itself she saw Sam and Don sitting in one of the booths. "Come join us," Sam said, and both men rose, Don with the little stiffness that was always in his manner nowadays.

Trudy hesitated; then realized that Sam's presence would make it easy for her to let Don know about the new job. She could speak casually, keep from revealing any emotion, with Sam there.

"I can't eat or drink a thing." She laughed as she sat down. "Fact is, Meta and I have been celebrating."

"Celebrating what, the approaching holidays?" Sam waved a hand toward the drugstore's synthetic wreaths and holly.

"No, no, something nicer than that. Well, maybe not." Trudy laughed. "I suppose nothing is ever nicer than Christmas. But this is very nice. I have the offer of a new job, an assistant directorship."

"Good for you!" Both men leaned across the table and shook hands with her.

"That's your first step up the ladder." Don's face lit up with his charming smile. His voice was warm. "You're so interested in your profession. I know what it means to you."

This was like old times, Trudy thought. Oh, if he'd stay this way.

"Where is the job?" "Who's to be director?" Both men asked questions and supplied additional information about Farview. Don knew people on the board of directors. Sam knew a surgeon who was to be on the staff.

Suddenly Sam looked at the clock. "Cripes! I'm on duty in ten minutes. You see Trudy home, Don." He grabbed his hat and dashed through the door.

"I don't need to be seen home," Trudy protested as Don rose with her. Nevertheless her heart beat like a little trip hammer as he accompanied her through the door. It was nice to feel his firm hand under her arm at the crossings, to catch a glimpse of his face each time they passed through the light from a store window. Perhaps as they walked along he would give her some inkling as to how he felt about her going to Farview. Meta was right. For the time being anyhow, the news had jolted him back into his old self.

"How soon do you go?" Don asked, and Trudy told him:

"Not for six months anyhow."

"That's fine."

Trudy glowed; then felt correspondingly cold when Don added, "I've a case coming in that I hoped would be detailed to you."

He spoke at length of the case, a broken hip which had resulted in a deformity, patient definitely neurotic. "I thought you might do a great deal for him, you're so friendly and en-thusiastic, and were so successful with Emily."

"Well, perhaps I'll still be at Hillhaven when he comes." Trudy looked up at Don as they stood under the light of her doorway. Her spirits fell. Here she was, no nearer to knowing his real feeling than she had been when they left the drugstore.

"Good night. Thanks for the convoy." She forced herself to be gay.

"Good night." Suddenly Don pressed her hand. "I'll miss you, Trudy." His voice was vibrant.

CHAPTER XVIII

"WELL, THE DIE is cast," Trudy said to Meta one January morning as the two girls made ready for the day's work. "I've had a letter from the Board of Directors at Farview confirming my appointment as assistant director of their O.T. staff."

"Grand news, partner!" Meta said over her shoulder as she pulled out strands of cane to be used in repairing the seat of a chair. "I knew you'd get it, what with Miss Swift wanting you and Miss Compton rooting for you. You must be up in the clouds."

"I am, with reservations," Trudy said. "I'm going to miss you awfully."

"Oh, I won't be so far away, only across the city. We'll get together lots, even have foursomes."

Yes, if all the members of the foursome want to, Trudy thought. Still, Don had said he would miss her, and his voice had been so warm, she felt that even if he didn't care as she did, he felt friendly.

"My next step, I suppose," she said aloud, "is to notify the Hillhaven board that I'm resigning, although I don't know

just when it will be. Three or four months, I'd say, from the
way the Farview buildings looked when Miss Swift and I
were there last Sunday. The walls are up and the roofs on,
but no window sashes or plaster or anything. Oh, Met"—
Trudy thought with unalloyed pleasure of that Sunday ex-
cursion—"Miss Swift is such a darling, and Farview's lovely.
It's on a bluff like our hospital here, but with fields and
woods instead of houses all around. You can't see the river.
Instead you look off the opposite way across the hills toward
Knolton. I felt as if, if I'd had field glasses, I might have
seen our farm. Maybe I did see Pike's Peak. When Susan
gets home I ought to have her go up there and flash a mirror
in the sun, say at ten some morning. Then I could watch for
it."

"And you think you'd see it, all those miles away?" Meta
laughed. "You're an optimist!"

Trudy was forced to laugh herself. "Well, anyhow, Farview's a grand place."

"It must be. When are you going to tell the general
public?"

"Why, I should think it would be all right to as soon as
I've notified the Board."

It did not take Trudy long to file her resignation. The
Board accepted it "with regret," which pleased her greatly.
Then, during the next few days she told her special patients
about her new job and that she was leaving Hillhaven.

Ralph Upton had already gone to Shelter Shops, but Old
Nick, who was doing a bit of weaving, not because it was one
of the best exercises for him but because he wanted to please

her, Trudy knew, took the news with averted eyes and hands that trembled. In a voice suddenly husky, he murmured that the place wouldn't be the same without her.

Robin, who was improving slowly but steadily, and had progressed to a set of plastic dishes along with knife and fork, puckered his charming face. "I just won't practice my eating off those old plates for anybody else!" he declared, and Emily Lansing, despite her new courage, was in a panic for a moment. Emily was an out-patient now, living in her sister's home and coming to Hillhaven twice a week for treatment.

"Oh," she said, when Trudy told her, "I'd hoped you'd be here when—" her voice broke for a moment—"when Robert came. It won't be long now. He's sailed."

"But I will be here," Trudy said. "I'm not going for quite a while."

"I didn't understand that." Emily brightened. "Then we needn't even think about losing you yet. Sorry I went off the deep end," she added apologetically. "As I told you, it's just when anything hits me suddenly that I lose my grip. The best of everything to you, Trudy Wescott," she added with an affectionate glance. "You deserve your promotion. Some day you'll be a director. Then how much higher can you go?"

"Oh," Trudy laughed and waved her hand in an upward spiral, "head of all the O.T. departments in a big city's hospitals, dean of a school of O.T., tops in a national organization of O.T.'s. I'll be all those," she said jokingly.

"Unless you get married," Emily suggested.

"Oh, nowadays you can do all those things even if you do marry," Trudy declared, but the fun died out of her voice.

"How are you getting along at your sister's?" She changed the subject.

"Beautifully." Emily's smile was both radiant and amused. "I haven't tubbed myself yet, my arm's not strong enough for the slide from the wheel chair, but I've done all the other things you predicted. Why, I'm so independent that I believe Robert's going to be astonished. It's possible he'll actually be proud of me."

"Of course he will be!" Trudy nodded, and reflected that only she knew the courage it took to say those words. Valiant Emily, she thought as she turned to go on with her day's work.

Later in the day Miss Compton sent Trudy down to Three C with some wool which had just come in for a patient. As Trudy entered the ward she saw that Donald Kerr was there. Susan, a cane in her hand, was walking a little hesitantly across the floor while he watched her.

Susan's lovely eyes were shining. "Trudy." She came toward her as fast as she could, "Trudy," she repeated in a voice so loud that Miss Blanchard turned her head, "he says I can go home."

"Really?" Trudy turned to Don for corroboration.

"Yes." Trudy saw that his eyes were filled with pride, pride in his profession, justifiable pride in himself as a surgeon. She thrilled for him. This was his big moment, to see and know that as the result of his skill Susan could walk again.

"Yes, this little girl is about ready to leave us," he said. "Of course, this is provided your folks will take her to Knolton Hospital every week for her treatments, and will keep up her exercises at home."

"Oh, yes, indeed." Trudy thought of Susan's old bicycle rigged up in the woodshed, of the grindstone. And there were plenty of other projects she could plan for her mother tc carry out.

"I'll be good, Don—Dr. Kerr," Susan promised.

"You'd better be!" He tweaked one of her curls. "If you aren't I'll come out to Knolton and clap you in a cast so big you can't see out of it."

Susan giggled, and Don turned to Trudy, his hospital formality returning. "Susan doesn't need an ambulance for the trip. Could you or Dr. Billings arrange transportation for her?" His expression changed a little in spite of himself, Trudy thought, and his next words seemed forced. "Possibly Mr. Fielding will be coming to the city and could take her home."

"Oh, no!" Before Trudy could speak, Susan put in, "Trudy doesn't let Chet come to see her any more. She hasn't for ages and ages. She said it wasn't fair when she didn't care about him."

"Hush." Trudy came near putting her hand over Susan's mouth as she had in the sunroom. Never adept at turning a conversation she floundered for words. Don helped her out.

"That's no go, then. Well, no doubt something can be arranged. Good morning, Miss Wescott. 'Bye for today, Susan." He moved toward his next patient.

"Susan!" Trudy turned to her sister.

Susan's expression was a mixture of anxiety and remorse.

"Oh, Trudy, I didn't mean to. It just came out. Now I've broken my cross my heart and hope to die." Suddenly she wailed, "I won't really die, will I?"

"No, certainly not." Trudy consoled Susan as well as she could and nearly forgot to deliver the wool, for her thoughts were elsewhere. Don knew the truth now. What would his attitude be?

She felt tears in her eyes as she hurried back to the shop. It had been hard to wait, but she would surely know soon now.

Trudy tried to forget herself in telling Meta the good news about Susan, and of course Meta was as pleased as she was. She had an engagement with Sam Bradford that evening and announced next day that Sam had arranged with Don to set Susan's discharge for a Saturday. Then he would borrow his brother's car and the foursome would take Susan home.

"Oh, grand!" Trudy's heart beat a little tattoo. It seemed such a good sign that Don would go with them. "I'll write and tell Mother to get up a dinner for us."

"And will Sam enjoy that!" Meta laughed. "To tell you the truth, I think that's what he had in mind when he offered to take Susan home. I wish I was such a good cook," she added irrelevantly and it was Trudy's turn to laugh.

"Oh, it's that, is it?"

"Well, maybe, sometime."

Don agreed to Sam's suggestion and the date was set for a week from that Saturday. Trudy, like a child with a birthday, made an X on her calendar, and her mother wrote that of course the young people must stay for dinner. Should she have turkey, roast beef or lamb? Spiced peaches or crab-apple jelly? Mince or pumpkin pie? Dad would have to get the green vegetables in Knolton and would build a fire in the parlor fireplace on Friday and keep it going so that the room would be good and warm. On she went with all the homely details of entertaining in winter on a country farm. They made Trudy feel as if she and Susan were already there. And how would Don act? What would he say? Trudy was so filled with suspense that she made only mechanical note the first time Emily did not come to the shop. The second time Emily was absent, however, her attention focussed on it. "Where's Emily, I wonder," she said, and suddenly she knew. Robert had come.

Now Trudy found herself in still greater suspense. It had been all well and good to tell Emily to have faith, that everything would be all right. Emily's own apprehensions assailed her. Would Robert Lansing be able to bridge the gap which lay between his old life with Emily and the new? For despite Emily's improvement, her re-education, there was a gap, deep and wide.

If he were the right sort he would, Trudy repeated as she had so many times. Oh, let him be, she added, and the four words were a prayer.

During the next few days Emily was constantly in Trudy's mind. Each morning she hoped Emily would come for her treatment, but each evening she had not come. It was hard for Trudy to wait, hard not to know what Robert's return had brought to her favorite patient.

On the afternoon before Susan's discharge, Miss Compton sent Trudy out to do some shopping. Gray yarn for that elderly woman—what's her name? Some of the new plastic that's hard to get. Red leather. Trudy ran over her list as she went down the hospital steps.

Absently she noticed that a car had stopped at the patients' entrance. A man had got out of the driver's seat, taken out a folding wheel chair and, with a few quick movements, made it ready for use. He was powerfully built, and as Trudy reached the sidewalk he lifted the patient, a woman, from the rear seat as easily as if she were a child.

Something made Trudy, already a little distance away, glance back. That lovely fair hair—she felt her breath catch —it could only be, it was, Emily Lansing's. The man must be Robert, her husband.

Neither Emily nor Robert saw Trudy. Oblivious to everything about him, Robert paused with his wife held tightly in his arms. He looked down into her face and smiled, while Emily with a little gesture of love nestled against his shoulder.

It was all right. Everything was all right. Trudy tried to steal away before they should see her. She was not quick enough, and Emily's voice overtook her. "Trudy! Trudy Wescott!"

Trudy came back. Robert had seated Emily in her wheel chair. In her fur coat and toque, her dainty shoes, her well-styled dress, she looked very smart, but it was her face that drew Trudy.

Never had her color been lovelier, her eyes a deeper blue. "Trudy, I want you to know Robert. And Robert wants to know you."

"Yes." Robert held out his hand, and Trudy liked him at once.

Dark hair to contrast with Emily's; red-brown eyes which were, yes, she thought with a thrill, just as kind as Donald Kerr's; the sort of smile that betokened a sense of humor, a firm direct handshake, Robert was all right.

"Emily tells me you've done so much for her," he said.

"And she has." Suddenly two great tears brimmed over from Emily's eyes. She wiped them away. "Oh, I'm so glad we're out here where we can emote." She laughed.

"Yes, it's wonderful what you therapists have done," Robert went on. "Even after all her letters, I didn't realize that Emily had improved so much, or could do so much. Why, she buzzes around like a bee."

Trudy studied Robert surreptitiously as he spoke. She read in his look that he adored his wife, that he was only thankful she was alive, had survived her terrible illness, and that he and she had years ahead in which to love each other.

"It's our job." Trudy side-stepped the praise. "Emily was a fine patient." They were going to bog down in sentimentality if they went on, so she changed the subject. "You'll miss your P.T. appointment, Emily, if you don't run."

"We'll run." Robert swung the wheel chair toward the door. "See you often," he said.

"Yes, see you often," Emily called, and Trudy, turning to go on her errands, said a second little prayer. "Oh, Robert and Emily, live happily ever after!"

Trudy was at the hospital long before the workshop opened next morinng. She wanted to have Susan's possessions packed and ready so that there would be no delay when the foursome started just after lunch. The child's luggage had grown to be extensive in the six months she had been in the hospital, clothes, gifts Elsie and various people had sent her, Duzenbury's collar and a heterogeneous mass of objects which she herself had collected.

Trudy jammed everything into suitcases and a box or two, and was back at the shop when Miss Compton unlocked the door at five minutes to nine. The telephone began ringing as they stepped inside, and Miss Compton, who still had to change into her uniform, motioned to Trudy to answer it.

A voice so thick and croaking that it took Trudy a moment to recognize it as Meta's said, "Is id you, Trudy? I'b gedding subding, I don't know what, bud I won't be able to go wib you today."

"Oh, Meta, what a pity." For a moment Trudy thought rather wildly that the trip would be off. Susan would have to wait until they could make some other arrangement; then she realized that what Meta was trying to say was true, there was no reason why the rest of the party should not go."

"Yes, I suppose we can," she answered Meta. "I'd say we'd postpone it, only you know how disappointed Suze would be, and then the expense."

"Don't think of id. Tell Miss Compton I won't be in, will you? See you Monday, I hobe." Meta hung up before Trudy could say again that she was sorry.

Dear, dear. Meta would miss Mother's good dinner, and she herself would have to entertain the two men, Trudy thought as she took up the morning's work. It was with the hospital's school children and it seemed to her that they were unusually exuberant. She had to admit, however, that perhaps the trouble lay with herself. She was surely impatient to have the hours go, so that she, the doctors and Susan, could be on their way.

At last the hands of the clock stood at noon. Trudy almost shooed the children to the elevator; then changed into her street clothes and ran down to the dining room for a hasty lunch.

Across the room she saw Don and Sam at their usual table. They bowed formally to her and left the room before she did. Another few bites of salad and a pudding which was perfectly tasteless because she was so excited; then Trudy went to Three C to collect Susan and her baggage.

Susan was going solemnly from bed to bed making her farewells. Trudy tried to hurry her, but without success. " 'Bye, 'bye. Come see some time." She insisted on shaking hands with each patient while Miss Blanchard looked on with an air which said, How glad I am to be rid of that little pest!

Finally Susan completed her round. The attendant was waiting and Trudy bundled her into the wheel chair. Susan could have walked from the hospital, but Don had directed that she should not be fatigued before beginning the journey.

"Good-bye, everybody!"

"Good-bye! Happy landing, Susan," said a chorus of voices as Susan was wheeled into the corridor. Trudy felt a great lump in her throat. Oh, that their hospital experience might end as happily for all these children.

Down in the elevator, where a nurse or two recognized Susan and wished her good luck, across the foyer, through the wide doors, and there ahead was Sam's brother's car at the curb. Donald Kerr sat in the driver's seat. Sam was nowhere about.

"Where's Sam?" Trudy asked as soon as they reached the car.

Don didn't answer. Instead, he slid from behind the wheel, and directed rather professionally that Susan was to sit in the middle of the front seat with Trudy beside her. Then he got back behind the wheel again.

"But where is Sam?" Trudy asked again. It was not until the car was moving smoothly in traffic that Don answered.

"He couldn't come, either. Emergency case." Did Don look self-conscious, or did Trudy imagine it?

"Then it's just us three," Susan commented. "I think that's grand."

"Except that Mother will be disappointed." Trudy looked at Don across the top of Susan's head. "We'll have to eat an awful lot to make up for the other two."

Trudy could not help watching for Don's reaction. This was the first time she had seen him unprofessionally since Susan had blurted out the news about Chet. This then, was the moment for which she had waited so anxiously. She felt breathless.

Don's smile lines showed. His eyes met hers unreservedly.

"You think this threesome is O.K. then?" he asked, and with a thrill Trudy realized that he was his old self. She was so happy that she forgot to answer until Susan nudged her.

"Don"— no one reproved her for the use of his first name— "Don asked you a polite question and you haven't said a word."

"Oh, I'm sorry." Trudy felt herself blushing to think how very well indeed she liked the threesome. She had to content herself with, "I think it's fine. I suppose Sam didn't know until the last minute that he couldn't come," she said.

"No." It seemed to Trudy that a flush rose to Don's ears. No doubt Sam had teased him, said, "You old so and so, I bet you won't even miss me. Two's company. Right?"

Susan broke the silence as the car slid into the suburbs, and fields and woods began to show. "I wish I could get out. You know how easy grasshoppers lose their legs? Well, I feel as if I was a grasshopper and had new ones. I want to try 'em on the ground."

Trudy and Don laughed. "You can tomorrow," Don said. "The trip's enough for you today."

Susan chattered constantly, her head rising, like a mud turtle's from a pond, each time the road took a new turn. Don and Trudy found it hard to carry on any connected conversation, but they did manage to speak of Emily and Robert. Don had seen the young couple, too. They had called at his office and he verified Trudy's impression that all was well with them.

"It's just—oh, beautiful," Trudy said, her voice husky with feeling.

"Yes, it is."

Inadvertently Trudy's eyes met Don's above Susan's head and surprised a look of deep tenderness in them. Why, that was the way Robert had looked at Emily, she thought. Was the look for her? Did it mean—? She didn't dare to answer her own question.

Only five miles to Knolton now. There was the factory at Garville, the familiar turns in the road. As they passed Johnny's Place, Susan's head came up again.

"This is where Trudy used to go with Chet, years and years ago," she exaggerated, child fashion. "And there's his car!" she cried. "Stop, stop! I want to ask him about my damages."

"Very well, Commander." Don turned the car into the space in front of the roadhouse.

Trudy felt no embarrassment at meeting Chet. Don knew the truth now, and there would be no misunderstanding, especially as Chet had a wonderfully pretty girl in the car with him.

"Just a minute, sweetheart," Chet said loudly to the girl as he saw Trudy, Don and Susan.

Well, if there was any doubt left in Don's mind that ought to settle it. Trudy smiled in amusement.

"Hello, folks!" Chet, his old jaunty self, stepped toward them. "How's everything, and how's Suze?"

"Fine," Trudy said. "She's going home to stay."

"Is she really all right? Likely to have any further trouble?" Chet addressed Donald Kerr.

"No," Don said professionally. "I consider her recovery complete."

"Then I'll close the settlement. The company made a new offer this week, a cracking good one; enough to cover all the bills and a nice little nest egg left over. I guess I forgot to tell you it'll be kept in trust for Susan until she's twenty-one. That's the law."

"Will it be enough for my education?" Susan asked. "I'm going to be an O.T. like Trudy."

They all laughed, and Susan went on, "Where's that old hit-run driver?"

"He's out on bail, awaiting trial," Chet said. "There's no doubt Elsie's evidence will convict him. He'll get his just deserts."

"Well, tell 'em not to be too hard on him," Susan directed, "not since I'm getting well."

"O.K." Chet said, and added with a grin. "I've got to go. Can't keep my girl waiting any longer. Be seeing you." He turned toward his car, and as Don threw in the gear they heard his voice, "Was I too long, darling?"

The same old Chet, Trudy murmured to herself. She discovered that in her own happiness, her bitter feelings had slipped away. She forgave him his transgressions, hoped that he really cared for this new girl and would be happy.

Now the little farm was in sight. Susan fairly bounced.

"There it is! There's Duzenbury! There's the cats! There's Daddy watching in the window."

Out came Mother and Father, coats hastily flung about their shoulders. They were so full of joy they were radiant. Mr. Wescott lifted Susan tenderly from the car and carried her into the house.

"Where are the others?" Mrs. Wescott peered past Don and Trudy's shoulders.

"They couldn't come," Trudy explained.

For a moment her mother looked disappointed; then she laughed. "And I'd looked forward so to filling up that Dr. Bradford. Well, anyhow, there never was a happier homecoming than this one. Look." She motioned through the kitchen door to where Susan had squeezed herself into her rocker and, with a cat in her lap and Duzenbury prancing around her, stuck out first one leg, then the other, for her father to zip off her leggings.

"And she was helpless when she went away. Her legs are going to be all right?" Mrs. Wescott asked Don in an undertone.

"Yes, I'm sure now," he said as he had to Chet.

The dinner was like Thanksgiving and Christmas rolled into one, Don declared, and he did it justice. The Wescotts did, too, and as he finished with a sigh of repletion, Mr. Wescott smiled at his wife. "Mother, you outdid yourself this time."

When they rose from the table, Don said that Susan must rest, so Mrs. Wescott made her comfortable in her own little room. Then she and Mr. Wescott joined Trudy and Don for a while by the living-room fire. Mrs. Wescott had rearranged the furniture since Trudy had last been home, drawn the sofa up in front of the fireplace, modern fashion, and flanked it with two rocking chairs. Mrs. Wescott sat down on the sofa, Trudy joined her, and the two men took the rockers.

"Nothing like 'em." Mr. Wescott cast a teasing glance at Trudy as he tipped forward and back. "Trudy doesn't care for 'em, though; says they date from Adam."

"Oh no, Dad, not any more." Mrs. Wescott's voice was full of amusement. "They've come into style again, so she thinks they're worth a king's ransom."

Trudy had to laugh with the others. Mother and Dad liked Don. If they didn't they wouldn't joke this way in front of him. How nice since I—well, out with it, Trudy said to herself, since I love him.

As the twilight set in, the older people had to leave.

"Milking time," said Mr. Wescott.

"Time to feed my chickens and gather the eggs," said his wife.

When they were left alone, Don moved from his rocker to the old sofa. Trudy was so aware of his nearness that she felt her voice would tremble if she spoke. But Don spoke first.

"Trudy dear." He took her hands, and even in her breathlessness she was aware of the delicate strength of his fingers, a real surgeon's. His voice held the same deep tenderness that had been in his eyes that afternoon, and it was for her. She had no doubts now.

"Trudy," Don said again, "I didn't tell you the truth when we left the hospital. Sam could have come, but I wouldn't let him. I told him I had to have a talk with you. You see, I love you."

Before Trudy could more than return the pressure of his hands, he went on, "I've loved you ever since the day there were stars in your eyes when I told you about Janet King. You were so interested and sympathetic, I thought, Here's a real girl. Here's my girl! But then I thought there was such a long pull ahead, so many years before I could marry, I hadn't any right to say anything, or even show any feeling."

Don paused to laugh happily. "I nearly did spill it all once. You remember that day on Sand Beach? We were both so blue—"

His voice died away, but Trudy knew to what he referred. Yes, she remembered clearly, the old driftwood log, the rose-colored cloud, the clasp of Don's warm fingers.

"I had to drop your hand." Don laughed again. "I knew one word, one look from you, and I'd have you in my arms and be telling you what a darling you were, how much I loved you."

Trudy's heart beat fast at his words.

"After that day in the drugstore," Don went on, "I supposed you were in love with Chet Fielding, maybe engaged to him, so I felt I had even less right to speak than before. I must have seemed pretty stiff, holding myself in, and it wasn't all being chivalrous. I nearly died of jealousy. Sam tried to tell me, but I wouldn't let him. It wasn't until Susan blurted it all out that I got things straight. Could you love such a fool as me?" Don asked humbly.

"Oh, but I do."

Trudy found herself in Don's arms. He stroked her hair. "Then you'll marry me?"

Trudy could not trust her voice, so she nodded.

"I still ought not to ask you," Don went on, "We'll have to wait. We'll be poor for a while, and goodness knows a doctor's wife leads a dog's life."

"She doesn't!" Trudy protested indignantly. "It's the nicest life I can think of. I'd rather be—"

Don's kiss stopped her words. After a while he said, "You know there's no reason you shouldn't go on with your profession as long as you want to. It fits so well with mine. You'll always know what I'm talking about when I discuss my cases. I'll always understand about yours. We'll be so happy together." He kissed her again. "Tell me, Trude. When did you begin to love me?"

"The very same minute you began to love me, I think, only I didn't know it for a while." Trudy put up her hand and touched Don's crisp hair. "I was a fool, too, Don. Why couldn't I have come right out and told you I wasn't engaged to Chet? I did try once, but you didn't seem to listen, and I thought you'd feel I was—well, giving you the come-on. I was miserable."

"So was I. I'm sorry I put you over the jumps, Trude. Will you forgive me?"

"Of course." Trudy snuggled against him and he held her close. Just like Robert and Emily, she thought.

The fire crackled softly in the old fireplace. The twilight deepened. After a time Don turned his head to listen.

"Your father and mother are coming."

"Shall we tell them now?"

"Why not?" Don kissed Trudy tenderly before the door opened. "Why not?" he said. "Isn't it the finest news in the world?"